FROZEN

ALSO BY L.A. CASEY

FROZEN

L.A. CASEY

Montlake
Romance

Published by Montlake Romance Publishing, Seattle
www.apub.com

Amazon, the Amazon logo, and Montlake Romance Publishing are trademarks of Amazon.com, Inc., or its affiliates.

ISBN-13: 9781503933118
ISBN-10: 1503933113

Cover design by Ryan Young

Printed in the United States of America

Nanny,

I'll see you later <3

CHAPTER ONE

"Neala? Are you home?"

No.

"Neala?"

Be gone.

"Neala Hayden Clarke, you had better not be ignoring me!"

Would I dare?

"Neala!"

Argh!

"I'm coming, Ma! Keep your bloody knickers on," I called out in a raspy tone.

I rubbed my chest as I yawned and crawled from my warm haven, then shivered as the cool morning air surrounded me. I grabbed my housecoat, put it and my slippers on, and then folded my arms across my chest as I scurried out of my bedroom towards my front door. I peeked through the peephole out of pure habit. When I spotted the overly happy face of my mother, who was dressed from head to toe in bright red, I couldn't help but roll my eyes.

I reluctantly unlocked my door and opened it wide.

"Heya, Ma," I yawned.

She smiled as she glided past me, looking like a jolly bull's target.

"Heya, honey. Did I wake you?"

Was she really asking me that? She just had to *bang my door down* to get me out of bed.

"Nah, Ma. I've been up for hours," I deadpanned.

My mother clucked her tongue at me and gently swatted at my head with her red-gloved hand. I snickered and ducked away. I turned and walked down my narrow hallway and into my box-sized kitchen. I glanced over my shoulder at my mother's attire once more and sighed.

"What the hell are you wearing, Ma?" I asked as she followed me.

My mother gasped. "It's Christmas time!"

That, in her mind, justified the monstrosity of the outfit she was decked out in.

I rubbed my hands together, silently cursing myself for not having set the central heating to automatic before I went to bed. The apartment would have been nice and toasty had I done that, instead of chilled. With cold and shaking hands, I filled the kettle with water from the tap, and then flipped the switch on the base.

"It looks like Santa puked on you, Ma," I said, then squealed when she not-so-gently whacked my behind.

"You watch your mouth, and stop picking on me, you little shite. I'm your mother; I should be revered."

Yes, Your Highness.

"I'm only messing with you, Ma." I smiled teasingly.

I wasn't messing – she looked ridiculous.

"What's the emergency anyway? Why're you banging me door down so early in the morning?"

"I wanted to tell you that I can't do lunch with you because I have to go shopping for last-minute bits for Christmas for your father and so on."

I raised an eyebrow in question. "You couldn't have just phoned me to let me know?"

My mother clicked her tongue. "You know I don't like technology."

I knew she didn't know how to *work* technology.

"I forgot. Sorry."

"Good. Now make me a cuppa."

I saluted her. "Yes, ma'am."

I made us tea and headed into my living room, where we sat on the couch facing my plasma-screen TV. I smiled as my mother kicked off her shoes and tucked her legs under her bum. We both sat the same way, and that wasn't where the similarities ended between us. She was twenty-seven years older than me and the woman was hot.

Well, she was when she didn't dress like someone from *The Grinch*.

She was fifty-two years old and didn't look a day over thirty-five. She was mistaken for my older sister nine times out of ten, and we had a bond where we were not only mother and daughter, but she was also one of my best friends.

We both had frosty green eyes, long brown hair, pale porcelain skin and freckles sprinkled across our noses. My father jokingly called us twins from time to time.

"Tell me, how did your date on Friday night go with what's-his-name?"

I could have gone the rest of my life without her asking that question.

I sighed. "His name is Dan Jenkins and it went . . . okay."

If *okay* meant *horribly*, then yep, the date had gone A-okay.

My mother snickered. "That bad, huh?"

Understatement.

I nodded reluctantly. "It was awful. His idea of small talk was to ask me if I was planning on having children anytime soon since me eggs wouldn't be as reliable after I crossed over to the dark side and turned the dreaded three and zero. The man is a weirdo."

My mother burst out laughing and I found it both amusing and annoying.

"You *just* turned twenty-five; you have years yet to think of kids."

"*Exactly.* That's what I said, but this lad was having none of it. I bailed on him. I told him I had to go to the bathroom, and then I ran for the door the first chance I got. It sucks; he seemed so normal when I met him at the bookstore, but it turned out he's a nut job."

My mother was now snorting from laughing so hard.

"It's *not* funny. What if I bump into him? He lives in the city centre but has family here in the village. I would freeze up, because I'd have *no* clue what to say to him. I didn't say goodbye or give him a reason as to why I was leaving. I just ran out on him. He probably thinks I'm a massive bitch."

My mother wiped under her eyes and smiled. "You could tell him you got a sudden bad case of the runs."

"Ma!"

I shook my head while she cracked up at her sick suggestion.

"I'm sorry." She chuckled. "I couldn't help meself."

I rolled my eyes. "Yeah, yeah. Where is me da? How come he didn't come around to see me with you?"

My mother grunted. "He has his friends around for the match; it's an early kick-off."

That didn't surprise me in the slightest. My father had been a hard-core football fan for as long as I could remember; he lived and breathed football like it was essential to his continued existence. Weekends, and even some weekdays, were a time that my father cherished. It meant football time, and everyone in our household had to respect that or God only knows what would happen.

Men and their sports.

"It must be an important match for it to be on a Wednesday," I commented.

My mother shrugged. "He said something about it being the last game the club was playing before taking a break for the Christmas holidays or something like that. I wasn't really listening to him."

She never did; she hated football.

I smiled. "In *that* case, do you wanna go get breakfast instead of lunch? I have to go to Smyths in the afternoon, and I'd rather get there when it's relatively quiet. No doubt people will drop in on their lunch hour to buy last-minute presents."

Smyths was a huge toy shop.

My mother frowned. "What did you forget to buy?"

I cringed. "Why would you think I forgot to buy—"

"Neala."

I groaned at my mother's tell-me-now tone.

"A doll for Charli," I mumbled, and avoided eye contact.

Charli was my niece. She was five years old, and was both evil and adorable, but she was also cute enough to make you forget how evil she really was. She had told me a few weeks ago that she wanted a doll from me for Christmas, and I'd told her I'd make it happen. That was before I realised how hard it was going to be to find the particular doll she wanted.

My mother widened her eyes. "Christmas is in *six days!*"

Don't remind me.

I winced. "I know, but in me defence, I ordered the doll she wanted online, but bad weather halted the order till January, so I just cancelled it and got me money back. I tried other sites, but everywhere is either sold out or couldn't make any deliveries until *after* Christmas and into New Year's."

My mother lifted her hand to her face and pinched the bridge of her nose. I'd bet my life that she wished she had something stronger than a cup of tea to drink.

When I was growing up, she was *that* mother, the one who started her Christmas shopping in August and never left anything until the last minute. It grated on her nerves that I'd never developed that trait.

"Nothing is ever an easy ride with you," she muttered, and took a gulp of her tea.

I snorted, because it was true.

"Are you saying I'm difficult?" I devilishly grinned.

My mother cackled. "Honey, you've been difficult since the day you were born. It's a characteristic you share with Darcy."

The smile on my face vanished and my grip on my mug tightened at the mention of his name.

"Don't mention *his* name in this apartment," I said as politely as I could.

My mother sighed dramatically. "For goodness' sake, Neala, you're twenty-five, not five. Both you and Darcy need to get over this childish . . . *thing* you both have towards one another."

'Thing' translated into hate.

I growled in annoyance. "I hate him, and he hates me. Period. End of story."

My mother's shoulders slumped as she sighed. "But he is such a nice young man, Neala. Couldn't you just—"

"Ma! We have had this conversation a billion times before. I am *never* having any sort of relationship with Darcy Hart, and that is *it*."

I had to put my mug on the coffee table across from me, because I suddenly felt like hurling it against the wall. I sat back and folded my arms across my chest in anger. This sudden feeling of rage was exactly what Darcy, or any mention of him, did to me.

My mother watched me with a raised eyebrow and smiled at me.

I blinked. "What are you smiling for?"

She shrugged. "No reason, Neala. I'm going to top up me cuppa."

Through narrowed eyes, I watched her get up and leave the room. She was up to something, and that worried me. I reached out and lifted my mug to my mouth and took a large gulp of my tea to calm my unsettled stomach.

Darcy Hart.

I hissed at my thoughts.

I hated thinking about Darcy, talking about Darcy, looking at Darcy, and hearing about Darcy.

I simply hated Darcy.

They say 'hate' is a strong word and an even stronger emotion. I agree with that, because the passion with which I hated Darcy filled me completely. It wasn't one-sided – that man hated me just as much as I hated him, and that's how it was between us. It's how it had pretty much always been between us. We hated each other, and that was it.

The feud between us started fifteen years ago, when we were both ten years old. We were in school when everything changed. Up until that point in our friendship we were a duo. We were best friends, and were together so much you could classify each of us as a limb to the other.

Then a girl happened.

Darcy had a crush on a girl in our class, a girl I despised. She was an *awful* person and picked on me day in and day out for no reason other than the fact that I existed.

Laura Stoke.

She ruined everything and changed my entire life. It sounds dramatic, but Darcy was a part of my everyday routine; he was always there, until one day he wasn't.

One lunchtime the whole school was out in the yard, playing and having as much fun as possible before we had to return to the evil that was learning.

I leaned my head back on my sofa as I thought back to *that* day when everything changed.

∽

Fifteen years ago . . .

"Neala?"

I'd looked over my shoulder when Shannon Burke, a girl I sat next to in math class, called out my name. I smiled when I saw she held two ropes in her hands.

Single skipping ropes!

"*How* did you get those?" I questioned as I rushed over to her side.

It was next to impossible to get single skipping ropes; the girls in sixth class always claimed them first. All the junior girls usually had to play with the rope that was large enough for a group of people to play with.

Never the single ropes.

"This is brilliant," I squealed in delight.

We put a metre or two of distance between us and began skipping with our ropes. We sang songs and laughed when the other got the words mixed up or missed a skip, and almost fell over when the ropes got tangled up in our legs.

We had had the ropes for only a few minutes when Shannon suddenly stopped singing, stopped smiling, and stopped skipping. With a frown, I halted my jumping and looked at her.

"What's wrong?" I asked, concerned.

She was looking over my shoulder, but glanced down at her feet when I spoke.

"Shannon, are you—"

"Are you two done with those ropes yet?"

I felt a chilling cold spread out over my skin when I heard Laura Stoke's voice ring in my ear. I held tightly on to my skipping rope and turned to face her.

I was surprised to find her so close to me, so I took a step backwards until I could see her. *All* of her.

I cleared my throat. "We just got them, Laura."

I tried to keep the venom out of my voice, but I couldn't help but lace a hint of it into my words. I hated Laura, and I had done for as long as I could remember. She was horrible to me and always went out of her way to make me miserable for no reason.

None.

Laura folded her arms across her chest and stared me down. "You've both had them for ages."

I blinked. "That's a lie."

"Are you calling me a liar?" she asked, her eyes narrowing.

I raised a brow. "Since you're lying, yes, I am."

Her left eyebrow twitched. "Give me the ropes."

I looked her up and down, shocked that she'd just given me an order like I was her little slave.

"No, we're playing with them. We'll give them to you in a few more minutes—"

"No," Laura cut me off. "I want them *now.*"

Over my dead body.

"I don't know who you think you are, but you aren't getting them."

I didn't realise what happened for a few moments, but one second I was on my feet, and the next I was on my arse. I blinked

9

my eyes and winced as throbbing filled the back of my thighs and behind.

She pushed me.

This wasn't the first time Laura had gotten physical with me, but it was the first time she had done it in the yard in front of other people. She usually kept her shoulder bumps and shoves for when I passed her by in the hallways.

She was the worst kind of bully.

I glanced to my left and right and saw that a small crowd of students had begun to form around us. I looked up at Laura, who had a skipping rope in her hand – my rope – and was in the middle of snatching Shannon's rope away from her.

Shannon didn't make a move to stop her; she practically dropped the rope as if it were on fire when Laura grabbed hold of it. She then retreated into the crowd and left me alone to face Laura.

I angrily pushed myself to my feet, grabbed hold of the two ropes in Laura's hand, and tugged, jolting her forward.

"Give them back!" I snapped.

"No!" she shouted, and tried to pull the ropes free of my grip. When she found I wasn't letting go, she lifted her hand and swung it in my direction.

I ducked my head just in time. Her hand sailed through the air where my head had been just moments before with a great big *whoosh*!

And she was going to hit me . . . *again*!

"What's going on?" I heard Darcy's voice shout over the students, who were now chanting "Fight!" over and over.

Without thinking, and with the pain in my behind and legs urging me on, I balled my right hand into a fist, pulled it back, and let it fly directly towards Laura's face.

With a scream she let go of the ropes and lifted both of her hands to her face as she fell backwards onto the ground, where she landed with a thud that could be heard over the chanting.

Ouch.

"Neala! What the hell?"

I looked up from Laura to find Darcy standing above her with anger in his eyes as he stared at . . . me?

What?

"Why're you looking at me like that?" I asked as pain suddenly spread throughout my hand.

Damn, punching someone *really* hurt!

I cradled my hand to my chest and stared at Darcy, who was shaking his head in disgust at me. I gasped when he bent down to a now crying Laura and placed his hand on her face.

"Let me see," I heard him tell her.

Rage shot through me.

"Darcy!" I shouted. "What are you *doing*?"

Seriously, what the heck was he doing?

He didn't look at me or give me an answer; he completely ignored me and focused on Laura. I couldn't believe it; he was caring for the girl who hurt me.

It hurt me even more that he was clearly siding with her.

"Darcy, she—"

"What happened here?" A deep voice suddenly cut through the loud murmurs of the crowd of students.

A teacher.

Crap.

"Um, well, you see—"

"Neala punched me in me face!" Laura all but wailed.

I don't know why, but I gasped when Laura ratted me out, as if I were completely innocent of the act, even though I knew good and well that I did hit her.

"Is that true, Neala?"

I noticed the teacher was Mr. Halford and instantly I became scared. He was known to be very tough on students when he was angry.

I was silent for a long moment, and before Mr. Halford could repeat his question, Darcy said, "It's true, sir. Neala punched Laura."

The ground might as well have opened up and swallowed me whole.

I felt my jaw drop open, my eyes widen, and my stomach churn. Darcy refused to look at me after he put me on the chopping block; he stayed focused on Laura.

Stupid. Laura.

"Neala, you'll have to come with me." Mr. Halford sighed, and then looked down at Darcy. "Bring Laura to the nurse to get checked over."

Darcy nodded mutely and helped Laura to her feet. I wanted to cry, but I refused to do so in front of so many people. I wanted to scream that none of this was my fault, but I couldn't get the words out.

It was like I was frozen.

On shaking legs I followed the teacher, while Darcy went off in the direction of the nurse's office with Laura. I was glad of the separation, because I needed time to think.

I had to plan everything I was going to say to Darcy very carefully, because I wanted him to be really sorry for what he had just done to me.

The next thirty minutes were filled with tears, pleading, and a distressed phone call from the receptionist to my mother when I wouldn't stop crying.

I was suspended from school; of course I couldn't stop crying. I was in a lot of trouble, and nobody believed that what I had done was in self-defence.

I don't really know if it *was* self-defence, because I was angry when I hit Laura, but she had knocked me over and hurt me. The teachers didn't believe that, on its own, that deserved suspension-whereas my punching her certainly did.

I was a wreck.

I was sad, angry, and feeling sick with worry about what my parents would do when they eventually arrived at the school to pick me up, but mostly I was gutted about Darcy.

I was really mad at him for not seeing to me. I mean, *I* was his best friend. Not Laura. She was just some stupid girl he thought was pretty. He shouldn't have picked a girl over his best friend . . . He just shouldn't have done that.

It wasn't right.

He hadn't even given me a chance to explain, hadn't bothered to hear me out, which was so unlike him. Everything he had done was very out of character for him. I just didn't understand any of it.

"Neala?"

I looked up and blinked when I saw Darcy standing in the doorway of the reception.

Speak of the Devil.

I sniffled and looked back down to my lap.

"Are you okay?" he asked me.

I nodded even though my hand hurt like hell.

"Laura isn't," Darcy replied casually. "Her cheek and eye are bruising because of what you did."

I jerked my gaze up to his. "She started it! I wouldn't have touched her if she hadn't pushed me onto the ground!"

Darcy frowned. "She said you wouldn't give her the skipping ropes—"

"So that makes it okay for her to push me down?" I cut him off, my sadness turning to blind rage.

"What? No, of course—"

"Why do you even care about her?" I snapped. "*I'm* your best friend, and you didn't even see if I was okay. You just ran to her and ratted me out to the teacher! Some best friend you are."

Darcy paled. "Now just wait a minute—"

"No, *you* wait a minute, Darcy Hart," I bellowed as my tears started flowing again. "I would never have chosen someone else over you, ever . . . So why did you choose her over me?"

Darcy blinked. "You hurt her, Neala."

"She hurt me too! Why don't you care about *that*?"

Darcy frowned. "I do care about you, Neala Girl; you know I do."

Tears flowed from my eyes.

"No," I cried. "You don't. You wouldn't have done any of this if you did. You like her and that matters more to you. *She* matters more to you than I do."

Darcy blushed, but didn't deny the charges.

"Get out!" I shouted. "I *never* want to see you again."

Darcy stayed rooted to the spot. "Neala, stop being a baby and just listen—"

"Now I'm a baby? Why don't you just throw a rock at me head? It'd hurt less."

He shook his head and looked at me like I was something he'd scraped off the bottom of his shoe.

"Neala," he began, sighing. "We'll speak later when you aren't so . . . We'll just speak later."

"Don't bother. Stay with Laura. I'm sure she'd love that."

He stared at me, his eyes dark. "You know what? Fine. I will."

"Don't come around me house anymore either, because I don't want to see you, talk to you, or be friends with you anymore."

Darcy raised both eyebrows. "You don't mean that; you're just angry and upset—"

"I do mean it. I *hate* you."

He stumbled back like I had struck him. "*Neala.*"

I heard the hurt in his voice, but instead of getting upset, I reminded myself that he had chosen Laura over me, and a fresh surge of rage flowed through my veins with the knowledge.

"Take it back, Neala."

I shook my head.

"Neala," he whispered. "Take it back."

"We aren't friends anymore, Darcy. You made your decision today. We'll never be friends again."

Darcy's expression was unreadable as he said, "Just like that?"

I nodded. "Just like that."

Without a word, he turned and stormed out of the room, and out of my life . . . so to speak.

~

I sighed as I came back to the present.

As much as I hated to admit it, Darcy had broken my heart that day, and after that I was done. We had been best friends since we could walk; then, in the blink of an eye, we weren't. I was a very emotional child, so I fought Darcy's betrayal and anger with my own. After that I didn't cry in front of him, and I never would. Instead, I became a devilish menace whenever I was in his company, and that turned out to be very often.

You see, Darcy and I were best friends by default. Our mothers were best friends, our older brothers were best friends, our dads were best friends, and even our grandparents, God rest them, were best friends. There was no escaping Darcy or his family after our falling-out, so we both learned to tolerate one another as best as we could . . . which was usually by fighting or pranking one another.

Our hate grew as we got older – he always blamed me for our falling-out, and even dated Laura into our secondary school days, which was like rubbing salt in my wound – while our tolerance for one another's company lessened. Our families didn't seem to understand our mutual loathing, because they always tried to force us together so we could learn to 'get on.' They still did. Never mind that we were now both twenty-five, and any chance of mending our joke of a friendship was long gone.

Our mothers, God help them, had this silly fantasy that we would get together, fall madly in love, and give them grand-babies, but I could tell you that was *never* happening. There wasn't a snow-ball's chance in Hell. You had a better chance of fusing oil and water together to form a single liquid than you did of Darcy and me being civil to each other.

We were a lost cause, and as far as I was concerned that wasn't a bad thing.

"What's that look for?"

I blinked and shook my head clear of my thoughts, then looked to my mother, who had retaken her seat next to me on the couch. I wasn't telling her I was thinking about Darcy and our past, because she would take it as a stupid sign that it meant he was my future or some bullshit like that.

I cleared my throat. "Nothing. This is just how I look when I zone out. It's me *duh* face."

My mother grinned and quietly sipped her tea, and it grated on my nerves. I hated when she looked smug after pissing me off about Darcy. I needed to change the topic of discussion to something mundane.

I blew a breath out through my nostrils and asked, "So, breakfast?"

My mother smiled to herself as she stood up and winked. "Yep, let's go get some brekky. You can tell me how you plan on getting

16

me grandchild that doll for Christmas along the way. I can tell it's going to be interesting."

I snorted. "Doubtful."

"I wouldn't speak too soon on that, lovely." My mother winked. "When you're involved, things are *always* interesting."

CHAPTER TWO

My mother and I went to a café in the village and had breakfast. Afterwards, she dropped me off at Smyths on her way to the shopping district. She had some errands to run – a trip to Smyths was included in that – but she didn't want to come into the shop with me.

I was an in-and-out kind of shopper, and she was . . . not.

I got there forty minutes before most businesses had their lunch hour. I was glad my mother had decided not to come in with me, because I knew I had a limited amount of time left in my mission, so I had to get to it.

My mother wished me good luck in finding a doll for Charli, and I foolishly told her that I didn't need it. It turned out I needed more than luck – I needed a bloody leprechaun with his pot of gold to appear and accompany me into the shop, because I was royally screwed.

"This can't be happening," I whispered in dismay as I scanned the doll aisle in the shop for the tenth time in twenty minutes, looking for a Fire Princess doll from a popular children's film called *Blaze*.

The film was huge; it had been months since it came out, and all the kids were still bloody crazy about it. That was *exactly* why I needed this doll. I'd told Charli that I would get it for her for Christmas, and I had already told my brother, Sean, Charli's father, that I had the damn thing, so I could *not* go home empty-handed.

If I did, it meant I would have nothing to give her on Christmas morning. She had only asked me to get her the doll, nothing else. I swallowed down bile as images of my crying niece and her disappointed father flooded my mind.

I *had* to get this doll; there was no room for error.

I knew that if I failed, it would be considered another disappointment in the eyes of those I loved, and it would be added to the list of mistakes I had made over the years.

My family didn't make the list; I did. It was a form of personal torture. I made a mental note of every time I let someone down. The truth was, in the eyes of my loved ones I wasn't the most reliable person, and it was no one's fault but my own.

I always fell short on delivering gifts on time, attending parties on the correct dates, showing up to babysit on time – or even remembering to show up at all – and a bunch of other things that made me suck as a person. I focused too much of my attention on work, instead of on my loved ones.

When I made the promise to my niece that I would get her the doll she wanted, I saw the doubt in my brother's eyes. I knew, in his mind, he was thinking of an excuse for me in case I fell through on my promise. He would cover for me on Christmas morning if I didn't come through with the doll – he covered for me a lot and had saved my arse on more than one occasion – but it was a cycle I was putting a stop to.

I made a vow that I would keep my promise to Charli, and myself, and I would get her this doll.

I couldn't fail.

I *wouldn't*.

I shook my head and the negative thoughts away.

"Why do they only have the princess's stupid sidekick?" I muttered aloud as I pushed aside box after box of the poor boy – who was really a prince in the film.

"Excuse me." I waved to a young man who was stacking boxes down the far end of the aisle.

He straightened up as I approached him. I smiled as he cleared his throat and said, "Can I help you with something, Miss?"

I nodded. "Yeah, you can actually. I need the redheaded Fire Princess doll from that children's film *Blaze*. You know, the one where the princess can make fire—"

"Sorry, mate, you couldn't tell me where the dolls from that popular *Blaze* film are, could you? I need the red-haired Fire Princess one."

My mouth lost all hint of a smile, and my stomach churned with the sight of him. My wide eyes narrowed and my hands balled into fists. This was cruel; as if having to put up with a conversation about him earlier wasn't suffering enough, now God was going to make me face him as well? All in the same day?

Not cool. Not bloody cool at all.

I narrowed my eyes to slits because he was merely feet away from me.

Darcy Hart.

My betrayer.

"Excuse me, are you blind? I'm standing right here, and I was talking to this fella *before* you were," I sneered.

Darcy leaned to the left and looked around the lad to see who was speaking to him, and when his eyes landed on mine they instantly narrowed.

"Neala Clarke."

He always spat out my name like it left a bad taste in his mouth.

I smirked at him. "The one and only."

Darcy gave me a bored once-over before he dismissed me with a glare and turned his attention back to the male worker. "Do you know where the dolls from the Fire Princess film are? I need the red-haired doll."

He just blanked me.

"You can wait your turn for help, Darcy. I was here first."

Darcy regarded me with an expression that suggested I was beneath him.

"What the hell is *that* look supposed to mean?" I asked, ready to curse him out if he said something mean.

The shop lad stepped back from between us. Now we had perfect views of each other. I kept the look of sincere disgust on my face as I stared at Darcy, but my stomach fluttered even though I willed it to stop.

I hated how good-looking the bastard was – he had always had a handsome face, but unlike in our school days, he wasn't a skinny boy anymore. He was filled out and *all* man, and from what I heard around the village, he was also now quite the slut . . . or ladies' man. Whatever.

Back in our school days, Darcy had been the nerdy, lanky pretty boy. He had a baby face that was accompanied by a killer smile, but that was all he had going for him. He had been a pain in my arse the last fifteen years, and I honestly could never see a day where that would ever change.

I blinked my eyes as Darcy's voice knocked me out of my trance and got my attention.

"It means you have a stick up your arse about waiting a few minutes for something."

Oh, hell, no.

"That's not bloody true and you know it, Darcy!" I stated, then flung my hair over my shoulder and quipped, "And for your information, I don't have anything up me arse."

He smiled.

I imagined Satan had a similar, if not identical, smile.

"You *sure* about that?"

I growled. "Me arse is *not* the topic of discussion here."

"Why not? You know I love to talk about your perfectly crafted arse, Neala."

"You disgust me."

Darcy winked. "Likewise, sweetheart."

A shiver ran up my spine, causing prickling tingles to spread throughout my body. I knew it was because I was appalled by his choice of words, not because I liked them.

I gave Darcy a dirty look, then turned my attention from him to the young worker, only to find him nowhere in sight. I looked up and down the aisle, but he was gone. He'd vanished into thin air.

I turned my head in Darcy's direction and hissed, "Look what you did."

I walked down the aisle, trying to put as much distance as possible between Darcy and myself. He apparently didn't feel the same way, because he quickly caught up with me until we were walking side by side.

"How is this *my* fault?" he asked me, keeping his voice low as we passed a couple who were scanning the shelves.

"Are you thick?" I seethed, lowering my voice also. "You scared him off with all your vulgar talk about—"

"Your arse?" he cut me off, grinning. "Yeah, you have a point. Your arse *would* scare any red-blooded male away. The lad was apparently no exception."

Dickhead.

"Listen to me, you tit. I'll have you know no male has ever referred to me arse as scary."

Darcy gleefully smiled. "Maybe not to your face."

I was going to kill him.

"I swear to God I will—"

"You'll what?" he asked as he jumped in front of me, halting my movements.

"Kill you!" I growled, and shoved at his chest with my hands, which he found hilarious.

"Your hands are so tiny," he cooed in a voice one would use when speaking to an infant.

I wanted to punch him in his smug face.

"They are *not*."

Okay, my hands *were* a bit on the small side, but I wouldn't have Darcy Hart saying they were. It was beyond childish, I knew that, but I didn't care.

Darcy chortled. "You'd disagree with me no matter what I say."

"No, I wouldn't."

He laughed.

"You hate me, don't you, sweetheart?"

"You bet your arse I do," I countered.

"Good. I'm doing something right."

With that said, he turned away and strolled down the aisle.

"Bloody gobshite," I muttered to myself.

I was about to turn and exit the shop to get away from the black hole of despair that was Darcy Hart, when I noticed the male worker from before walking towards Darcy with a box in his hand and a smile on his face. It got my undivided attention. Darcy's frame straightened up as he extended his arm towards the lad.

I squinted to get a better look at the box, and when the blazing red hair of the doll I wanted came into focus, I broke into a sudden sprint. I pushed my legs to move as fast as they could, and like a machine I zoomed down the aisle. Seconds later I collided with

Darcy's back and took him to the ground just before he could take the box from the worker's hand.

That was *my* goddamn doll, and I was *not* letting Darcy Hart take it away from me.

CHAPTER THREE

For the love of God!" Darcy's roar was all that sounded when we fell . . . Well, that and the loud thud of his body smacking against the tiled floor.

He sounded like he was in pain, but I was perfectly fine, which was all that mattered, because his hard, chiselled body broke my fall.

Wait.

Chiselled?

Darcy was chiselled?

Bleh.

I pushed myself upright, ignoring the tempting muscles of Darcy's back under my palms, then jumped to my feet and hopped into the empty spot in front of the now terrified-looking young male worker.

"Thanks." I beamed at the lad.

He swallowed. "It's the last one in stock. I'm sorry."

I paused to read his name tag. "Mark. No worries; this is *exactly* the doll I was look—"

"Oh, no, you don't."

I yelped as I was suddenly lifted up from behind and swung around to face the empty doll aisle where I'd stood alone a few minutes ago. Darcy set me down on the floor and I stumbled forward, off balance.

"Thanks . . . Mark, was it?" Darcy asked as he took the doll box into his hands. "Nice one, man."

Death.

That was what he just asked for.

"Drop. The. Doll," I demanded.

Darcy turned to face me. "Ne—"

I shot forward and snatched the container from his large hands.

My victory was short-lived, though, because Darcy quickly gripped onto my arm as I ran by him. He spun me around as if we were ballroom dancing, and the sudden movement caused the box to fall from my hands.

Darcy let go of me, and I quickly regained my footing and scooped up the doll box, turned, and sprinted up the aisle away from a wide-eyed Mark – who was on his phone, undoubtedly to security – and a fast recovering and fuming mad Darcy.

"Neala!" he shouted.

I did a stupid thing: I looked over my shoulder to see how far away Darcy was from me, and when I saw he was hot on my heels I panicked. I tripped over my feet and screamed as I fell to the floor.

Pain.

That was all I felt radiate throughout my body. Hot burning pain. My knees were on fire, my shoulder hurt, and my cheek stung slightly. I was hurting, but apart from my sudden scream I didn't whimper or make any sound of pain; Darcy would have enjoyed that too much.

I heard him sigh as he stood over me. "Are you okay, clumsy arse?"

No.

"I'm grand," I rasped.

Painfully, I pushed myself up. I was a little wobbly on my feet, but I was standing, and that was the main thing.

"Give me the doll, Neala."

I held the now slightly damaged box to my chest. "No way. This is Charli's doll."

Darcy glared at me. "No, it's Dustin's. Now give it here."

Dustin was Darcy's six-year-old nephew. He was a sweet kid, but right now he was my enemy too.

"Dustin?" I questioned. "Dustin is a *boy*, Darcy."

"Thank you for pointing that out, sweetheart. We would have never known otherwise."

Eejit.

"Cut the smartarse replies, Darcy," I growled.

He grinned. "I can't seem to help it around you. You bring it out in me."

Fantastic.

"Whatever. This doll is going to Charli. Go get an action figure or something for Dustin."

I took a few steps away from Darcy, but he quickly closed the space by advancing.

"No. Dustin specifically asked for the Fire Princess doll, so that is *exactly* what I'm getting him."

I furrowed my brows. "Your nephew wants a *princess* doll . . . really?"

Darcy glared at me. "He's a *kid*, Neala – it's princess toys this week and next week it could be man-eating dinosaurs. I don't expect judgmental people like you to understand that children like to play with all kinds of toys."

The nerve of him.

"I'm *not* judgmental! I just don't think Dustin would really have any fun with this doll, or any doll for that matter. I mean, the kid cut the head off all of Charli's Barbies last week for his own sick and twisted amusement. He is a serial doll killer, Darcy."

He guffawed. "Charli threw all of his dinosaurs in the bin earlier that day; it was payback. Besides, they spent the evening getting the dinosaurs back out of the bin and using the doll heads to play a new game. They're always messing with one another; you know that. It's how they've been since they could walk and talk."

I folded my arms across my chest and stared at him when I couldn't think of a snippy reply. Darcy looked at me with both pain and amusement.

"If I didn't know each member of your family like they were me own, I would think you were reared by a bunch of crazies."

He wouldn't be lying if he did say my family was crazy, because they were.

"I don't appreciate you insinuating that I'm—"

"I'm not insinuating anything; I'm flat-out saying you're a nut job."

I felt my eye twitch in annoyance. "I can't stand you."

Darcy smiled wide, revealing his perfectly white straight teeth. "I know."

Why did he seem so pleased by that?

"Don't you have somewhere else you'd rather be?" I asked, feigning boredom. "Like mattress dancing with some poor unfortunate soul?"

Darcy smirked. "Last night's adventures will keep me sedated for a while . . . trust me."

Ew.

I curled my lip up in disdain. "You're disgusting."

I tried to turn and walk away, but Darcy reached for the box in my arms. With lioness-like reflexes I sprang back away from him.

I gasped as, once again, I lost my footing and fell back into what felt like a mountain of pillows. Okay, so maybe I was a clumsy lioness, but I was still a lioness, and it meant I was dangerous.

Very dangerous, so Darcy should *never* underestimate me.

My embarrassment, as Darcy's laughter rang in my ears, quickly turned to seething anger when I opened my eyes and found I was buried under a bunch of smiling snowmen instead of plain old pillows.

"You know, you could give Charli one of these snowmen for Christmas instead. She might be just as happy."

"Shut up," I growled.

Darcy continued to laugh as he dug me out of the snowman mountain. I tensed as he took my hand in his and carefully helped me to my feet. I was very aware of how close he was standing to me. I could smell his aftershave, and the scent was so good it caused me to lean into him for just a moment. I licked my lips.

I looked up at him and found he was staring down at me, his expression thoughtful. I pulled my hand from his when his thumb rubbed over my fingers, the callused tip causing goosebumps to break out over my skin.

I made a show of brushing myself off with both of my hands when I was free of him, then glanced down and gasped.

Where the hell was the doll?

I spun around in a complete circle searching for it.

"Looking for this, Neala Girl?"

I growled and turned to face him.

It was a nickname he'd called me fifteen years ago, back when we were still friends. I had loved it when I was little, but now I couldn't stand the name. It hurt my chest.

"*Don't* call me Neala Girl."

Darcy raised an eyebrow. "That's your name."

No, it isn't.

"Give me the doll. Now!"

Darcy had the doll box against his chest with both hands on it. His fingers tapped against the sides. He glanced at the snowmen gathered around my feet and teased, "You've got to watch your step, sweetheart."

I blew out a frustrated breath. "I swear, if you don't give me that bloody doll I'll—"

"You'll what?" Darcy cut me off, his smug look in place on his handsome face.

Damn him.

"I'll shove me foot so far up your arse you'll need a surgeon to remove it."

Darcy's eyebrows rose. "You're a foot shorter than me and at least fifty pounds lighter. You're an itty bitty thing, Neala Girl. I'm not scared of you. You can't hurt me."

Wrong.

He was *so* wrong.

"I can hurt you, and I will unless you give me the doll."

Darcy thought on it for a moment and said, "How about . . . no."

Bastard!

I curled my lip into a sadistic grin. "Okay, you asked for it."

Darcy shook his head at me and moved forward so he could brush by me. "I don't have time for – What the hell?"

When he was close enough I manoeuvred my body behind his, hooked my arms around his chest and searched with my hands. When I found what I was looking for, I grabbed them between my index fingers and thumbs and pinched.

"Me nipples! Let go of me nipples!" Darcy roared.

I growled and tweaked a little harder. "Let go of the doll, and I'll let go of your nipples."

There was a sentence I never thought I'd hear myself say.

"Neala!" he yelped.

I heard the doll box hit the floor, and as I was a woman of my word, I let go of Darcy's nipples. I didn't linger long enough for him to recover. Instead, I moved around his body, grabbed the doll box off the floor and took off running up the aisle like a bat out of Hell.

"NEALA!"

I squealed and continued to run until I was clear of the aisle. I turned left and almost tripped again but got my footing and stayed upright. I stopped running when I noticed every single person in the shop was staring at me.

Mortification filled me.

I lowered my head and briskly walked over to the nearest checkout till. The young girl at the till was wary of me as she took the doll box from me and scanned it through.

"That'll be forty-five Euros and ninety-nine cents when you're ready, please."

For a stupid doll?

"Bloody expensive," I muttered as I pulled my debit card from my pocket.

I placed my card in the girl's hand at the same time that someone else did the same thing. I froze. Slowly, I glanced to my left, then looked up.

Darcy's furious face was glaring down at me, and I couldn't help but smile merrily and say, "Too late, Darcy. I'm buying it."

I looked to the girl and took his debit card from her hand, then handed it back to Darcy, who continued to glare. I turned my head and nodded to the girl. She scanned my card, printed out a receipt, bagged the doll, and handed everything back to me.

"Thanks." I smiled to her and began walking toward the exit.

I could feel him walking behind me, so I picked up my pace.

"Leave me alone, Darcy!" I hissed when I made it out to the car park.

"Not a chance, Satan," he snarled, as he rubbed his recently abused nipples. "Give me the damn doll."

Oh, that was rich; this eejit was calling *me* the Devil.

"This doll is *my* property. I paid for it, so feck off."

Darcy huffed with frustration. "If you think you're leaving here with that doll—"

"Oi, you two."

Darcy and I halted and turned our heads to the right. I was momentarily confused when I spotted two male Garda walking toward us, and neither of them looked happy.

"Are you talking to us?" Darcy asked the officers.

"Do you see anyone else out here?" one of the men replied snarkily.

I glanced around the car-filled and frost-covered car park and shivered. We apparently were the only eejits stupid enough to come outside and argue when it was below zero.

"No," Darcy replied, and hung his head.

"We got a call that a female and male fitting your descriptions were causing trouble inside the toy shop."

I widened my eyes and glanced back to the shop.

They called the guards on us?

I looked back to them and swallowed. "We had a disagreement, but I don't think we did anything wrong . . . not really."

Darcy scratched his neck and remained quiet.

Smart lad.

"Look, it's coming up to Christmas, and I don't want to arrest a couple for arguing in a shop, so in the future keep it private. Got it?"

I knew we were being let off the hook for our behaviour in the shop, but all I could focus on was that this man thought Darcy and I were a couple. I felt disgusted with his observation. Disgust, and a bit of irritation – I didn't have room for anything else when it came to him.

"Yes, sir," I replied in unison with Darcy.

The guards nodded to us, then went on their way back to their car. I didn't move a muscle, and neither did Darcy, until they drove out of the car park and out of sight. As soon as they were gone I took off running toward the bus stop.

"Neala!" Darcy hollered. "Damn it, woman!"

I didn't stop or look over my shoulder. I unleashed my inner lioness and ran. I kept my eyes on the ground so I could watch out for any black ice that would mess me up if I slipped. I heard Darcy let out a loud yelp, then a grunt of pain followed by a spew of foul curse words, and I smiled.

He'd fallen over.

I was breathless when I reached the roadside a few moments later. I was searching for a bus, but a blue taxi caught my eye instead. I instantly lifted my arm in the air and waved the car down. I prayed the driver saw me, and when I spotted his indicator flashing I squealed with delight. The driver was pulling over for me.

I ran up to the taxi, jumped into the back, and slammed the door shut. I rattled off my address and asked him to pull off right away. The man did as asked and I relaxed back into my seat before I turned my head and looked out the window.

I swallowed nervously when I spotted Darcy.

He was still standing in the car park with his hands folded across his chest in annoyance, staring after me and shaking his head. He was already ticked off, and since I had to have the last word and wanted to annoy him further, I stuck my middle finger up at him as the taxi pulled away. I turned my head forward when I lost sight of him, and I giggled to myself.

Neala: 1. Darcy: 0.

CHAPTER FOUR

I loathed Neala Clarke.
I growled in anger at just the thought of the thieving wench.

She had messed everything up for me. Finding that godforsaken doll for my nephew Dustin in Smyths was my last option; everywhere else was sold out of the stupid thing.

Any sites I found online that sold it wouldn't deliver until the New Year, which was no good because I needed it for Christmas Day. I had had the damn thing in my hands, twice, and she'd still managed to pull one over on me and take it away.

Any sane person would simply curse Neala and get over the toy store spat by finding an even cooler present for their nephew, but I couldn't do that.

It wasn't in me to let her away with pulling a fast one on me. She'd played that game back when we were kids: one second she was the centre of my world, and then the next she was a stranger.

She'd pulled a complete three-sixty on me and cut me out of her life without even giving me a damn explanation.

"Bloody woman," I snarled as I stared at the blank screen of the fifty-inch plasma-screen TV on the wall in front of me.

There hadn't been a single encounter with Neala Clarke over the past fifteen years that ended well. She just couldn't be civil with me – she had to be rude and physical, and had to one-up me on *everything*.

If I brought a girlfriend to a family party, she brought a new boyfriend who was always bigger than me and could probably kick my arse with ease. I was an easy-going man – I was more of a lover than a fighter – but if someone ever came at me with the intent to harm me I wouldn't back down. I would try to talk it out first, but wouldn't back out of a fistfight if it were for a good reason. I was a nice person who sometimes could be stubborn, but only when *she* was around.

I downed the last of my Coke and squeezed the can until it crumpled within my fist. I momentarily imagined it was Neala's head.

"Why are you grinning like that?" Sean, my best friend, asked me.

I was in his apartment. I had a key for emergencies, but I used it for random drop-ins, and as usual Sean was cool with it.

"No reason."

He raised an eyebrow. "Well, stop it. You're creeping me out."

I snorted and tossed the can onto the coffee table. "Sorry, man."

Sean fell onto his spot on the couch next to me and kicked his feet up. That was how I knew Jess, his fiancée, hadn't come home with him. He would never put his feet up on the coffee table if she were here.

"So, did you get Dustin's present?" Sean asked.

Here we go.

I grunted. "Almost."

"Almost?" Sean questioned.

I blew out a frustrated breath. "Yeah, almost. I had the fecking thing in me hands, then she appeared and took it away."

Sean turned his head so he could look at me as he asked, "She?"

"*She*," I growled.

Sean laughed. "Who is *she?*"

The Devil.

I looked to him and spat, "Your little sister."

Sean Clarke was my friend, but he was also the older brother of the bane of my existence.

Sean smirked and shook his head as he said, "Neala. I should have known."

He really should have.

"Exactly. Who else pisses me off like her?"

Sean considered this, and then said, "No one."

Exactly.

"Because she's a little shit."

Sean punched me in the shoulder for the insult. It was nothing new; he knew how Neala and I were. If I cursed her out, he would hit me for it and then it would be forgotten until I opened my mouth about her again.

He was my friend, but he was her brother first, and I respected that completely.

"She got the doll?" he asked, enjoying my situation.

I resisted the urge to rub my shoulder as I nodded. "Not fairly, though. She practically attacked me."

Sean bit down on his lower lip.

"It's not funny. She hurt me, man; me nipples are fucking killing me. I thought she made them bleed at one point. Either that or she ripped them clean off. She was like a wild animal."

Sean fell into me as his laughter erupted from him like a volcano.

"Nipple . . . twisters?" he asked through his laughter.

I lifted my hands to my nipples and flattened my palms over them. I was still in pain. The nipple twisters were unexpected, and that had made receiving them even more painful. I should have been ready for anything when it came to Neala, but in my defence I thought she was too mature now to resort to violence.

She hadn't come at me in years. I think the last time she hit me out of anger was when we were fifteen and I 'accidentally' spilled red fabric dye on her while she was wearing white jeans and told everyone she 'just became a woman.' I, of course, announced to our friends a few seconds later that I was only joking – I even showed them the bottle and made it clear it was a prank – but Neala didn't find it funny.

"Yeah, she twisted so hard I honestly thought they came right off."

Sean slapped his hand on his knee as he continued to laugh. I lowered my hands from my sensitive nipples and glared at him until he stopped, which wasn't for a solid two minutes.

"I'm glad you find this funny. I was robbed of the only chance I'll have to get Dustin that doll because *your* evil sibling fucked me over. Justin won't let me forget this."

I thought of my brother, older by seven years, and winced. I'd told him I'd get that damn doll for Dustin, and now I didn't have it. I was going to look like a shite uncle on Christmas Day when I had nothing to give Dustin.

He'd asked for this doll, and I had stepped up to the plate and said I'd get it even though there had been only two weeks until Christmas when he asked me.

Sean shook his head. "Jay will be cool about it."

I snorted and cracked my knuckles. "You're his best friend – I'm his little brother. He's gonna kick me arse for breaking me promise to his son and upsetting him."

Sean considered this, then laughed when he realised I was right: he knew just as well as I did that Justin would want to throw fists if I didn't get this done.

I didn't blame my brother for getting so easily annoyed with me over things when it came to his son. Selfishly, when I hadn't been working, I was so wrapped up in myself the last few years, with partying, bedding different women, and partying some more. I hadn't spent as much time with Dustin as I should have over the years, and I wanted this present to be a do-over for us. After the holidays I planned on taking him hiking with me, trail running, and fishing in the lake. Just the two of us. Man-to-man time.

It was a deal I had made with myself, and the doll was part of that deal. I didn't want to break my own word before I could even get a real chance to know my nephew, and that would happen if I didn't have that doll.

"So go over to Neala's place and get it back."

That was a suicide mission.

I grunted. "I can't, because she bought it . . . She'd probably attack me again and claim I broke into her apartment. I wouldn't put it past her to call the guards on me either."

Sean snickered. "I'd usually defend her and say she wouldn't do that, but she does change when you're around."

I'll say.

"It's because she likes me so much," I said, my tone laced with sarcasm.

Sean's mouth curved, and I didn't like it.

Not one bit.

"What are you smirking at me like that for?"

"No reason," he said, mimicking my early voice.

Dick.

"Well, stop."

Sean continued to smirk, then after a moment of thought he snapped his fingers and jumped to his feet. "I have an idea. Both of us can go over to Neala's and get that doll back for Dustin."

Was this clown serious?

I raised my eyebrow. "You want me to break into your *sister's* apartment, and steal the doll she just paid for to give to your *daughter* on Christmas Day?"

Is *that* what he was saying?

Sean laughed gleefully. "No, and no. We won't break in – we'll be invited in. You also won't be stealing an item belonging to her – you will take back the item that belongs to you. Charli is covered on the present thing; she will be too happy on Christmas morning with her million other presents to even notice a doll is missing. Trust me."

He was losing it, but I wasn't about to question him, because it meant I could possibly get the doll back from Neala if he helped.

That aside, I didn't know how he thought I owned the doll when I told him Neala had paid for the bloody thing.

"Man, I've no idea what you smoked, but I didn't pay for—"

"Neala's debit card is on the coffee table."

Was it?

I furrowed my eyebrows in confusion, and then sat forward. I reached out and grabbed the card he was talking about. I read the name on the card – *Miss Neala Clarke.*

How had I ended up with Neala's debit card?

"I don't understand," I muttered in confusion.

Sean sighed. "It's not that hard to realise what happened, man."

For him, maybe.

I grunted. "Enlighten me then, oh wise one."

Sean cracked his knuckles and said, "I'm guessing you and me sister both tried to pay for the doll at the same time, and the person behind the till paid for the doll with your card and gave it back to Neala; then you took her card thinking it was yours. Simple mistake."

I stared at Sean, and then looked back to Neala's card.

Holy shite.

"I own the doll?" I asked.

Sean grinned. "You own the doll."

Oh, hell, yes!

I smiled smugly as I let Sean's words sink in. I owned the princess doll. I fecking *owned* it, and all I had to do was get it back from Neala.

My smile dropped when I thought about that particular task, but after a moment I brushed it aside. I could do this – harder things have been accomplished.

I'd have to be vigilant and guard my nipples, but other than that it'd be fun . . . *right?*

CHAPTER FIVE

"A re you nervous?" Sean asked me as we walked down the hall-way of Neala's apartment building.

I swear I could hear my heart beating against my rib cage with every step that took me closer to Neala's apartment door, and this fool asked me if I was nervous? Try downright terrified.

"Nah, man," I lied. "This'll be easy."

I was well aware that sweat was starting to bead on my forehead, but if Sean noticed it he was being a good mate and not mentioning it. I could have hugged him for that, but since I didn't want to deal with gay jokes from him for the rest of the day I refrained from showing any sign of grateful emotion. I kept my face expressionless; it was extremely difficult, but I managed.

"Ah, here we are," Sean announced as we came to a stop in front of a door made from human skeletal remains.

Okay, it was oak, but it might have well been skeletons; Neala *was* the Devil, after all.

My breathing picked up its pace, my heart pounded faster, and the sweat turned from beads to droplets as they fell from my forehead down to my cheeks. I was very aware of how much of a pansy I was being, but I didn't care. I was on *her* territory, somewhere I had never been before. She could outsmart me here and I wouldn't be able to do a single thing about it.

This was the stuff Irish nightmares were made of. My nightmares, anyway. Neala was always the star of my nightmares.

"You could at least *try* to not appear so terrified," Sean muttered to me as he lifted his hand and knocked three times on the door.

Each pound of his fist against the varnished wooden door made me flinch.

"I'm not scared," I said after clearing my throat . . . twice.

Sean snorted. "Could've fooled me, man."

I scowled at him and straightened myself up to my full height of six feet three inches.

Stop being a bitch.

I repeated the thought over and over in my head until I was semi-calm. The door to Neala's apartment opened seconds later, and the feeling fled without warning. I was back to being a sweaty bucket of nerves.

Lovely.

"Hey, little sister." Sean grinned at Neala, who was looking at him with a raised eyebrow.

I wanted to laugh the moment her eyes slid to mine. Her whole demeanour changed: her hands balled into fists, her slender body tensed, her lip curled in a snarl, and her eyes narrowed to slits.

Oh yeah, she was pissed.

"*You*," she growled.

The nervousness I'd felt moments ago disappeared, and my usual snarky attitude returned, the one that came out when Neala was around. I was grateful for it. Being a dick to her was something I could play well; anything else was out of my comfort zone.

I grinned as I said, "*Me*."

"What are you *doing* here?" she hissed.

I blinked as a bad thought – deplorable, really – entered my head: Neala was hot when she was mad. *Oh God.* That was *not* cool, not cool at all. I only thought of things like dead puppies and homeless kittens when I thought of Neala, not her damn sex appeal.

I shook my head clear and said, "I'm with him," and jammed my thumb in Sean's direction. I felt like I suddenly couldn't speak, so putting the attention on Sean was all I could think of.

Neala switched her burning-mad gaze from me to her brother.

"Explain," she growled.

Always straight to the point.

I hated to admit it, but I liked that about her. It was probably the only thing I liked about her, besides her body— *Stop it!* I blinked away the sudden internal battle inside my head and focused on Neala and her brother's conversation.

"It's Christmas next week, and I know it's been tried before, but I figured it was time to finally squash this bullshit you and Prince Charming here have had for the last fifteen years. I'm not sitting through another Christmas dinner of awkwardness only for it to turn into an Irish remake of *Gladiator*." Sean glanced between Neala and me and shook his head. "The kids, *your* niece and *your* nephew, are old enough to understand the hate you have for one another, and I do *not* want it to rub off on them. Get your shite together and act like the adults you are."

What the hell?

I thought he was here to help me get back my property!

"But—"

"No buts, Neala. I will not have me child around you both when you're together, and since our families do everything together it means you *both* won't be invited to anything. Do you understand that? You won't be welcome at birthday parties, anniversary parties, engagement parties—"

44

"Engagement parties?" I cut in.

Sean looked to me and grinned, which in turn made me grin. I instantly knew he and Jess had finally picked a date for their engagement party. This news would come as a delight to my mother and Sean's. Our mothers were the best of friends, so it meant they did everything together, and I mean everything. They'd both been waiting to get Sean and Jess's engagement party out of the way so they could buckle down and start planning the wedding.

Hopefully the engagement party would lift Jessica's spirits, too. She had been down lately, since money hadn't been coming in for her and Sean like it used to, which was the main reason she didn't want to waste any on an engagement party. She worked in O'Leary's Pub in the village along with Justin's wife, Sarah, but their pay wasn't the greatest.

Me, I worked in construction as a contractor: I co-owned Clarke & Hart Construction with Sean and Justin. It was passed down to us a few years ago from our fathers, though unfortunately we'd had only one major job in the last year and a half – rebuilding the Holiday Inn hotel in the village.

The job brought us in a decent wage, but we had to be smart with the amount we continued to invest into the company, as well as our own paycheques, because we needed to survive too. Luckily, the owners of the hotel were going for bigger and better, so that meant longer work for our company, but we would ideally have liked to have more jobs to work on throughout the year to help distribute more hours for our employees.

Construction wasn't really in demand the last few months, though, so things were a little sparse. It killed me, my brother, and Sean – having to let our lads go when we didn't get enough work. Especially coming up to the holidays.

"You and Jess picked a party date, for real?

Sean nodded his head. "For real. She wants it before Christmas."

I widened my eyes. "Before Christmas? As in *this* Christmas on *Tuesday?*"

Sean laughed. "Yeah, she wants a small party in the local pub on the twenty-first. This Friday."

Today was Wednesday.

Talk about short notice.

Neala flung her hands up in the air. "Friday . . . That's in *two* days!"

Sean rubbed his neck and looked between Neala and me again. "I know, but this is what Jess wanted. You know she's stressed about cutbacks at the pub and us not getting another job since the Inn for the company, so she wants this to brighten everybody's spirits."

I was all for a party, so I slapped my hand against Sean's outstretched one and bumped my chest against his as we hugged. Neala quickly got over the short notice of the party and put a bright smile on her face when both Sean and I looked back at her. Her smile was for her brother, of course, never for me. If her lip was curled up in a disgusted snarl, then it would be for me.

"When was this decided?" Neala asked as she stepped into Sean's open arms.

"Last night. Jess rang Bob and asked could we have it this weekend. Since he needs the business, he said yeah without a problem, and since Jess works there we got a discounted rate on the food too – so that's a plus."

Neala chuckled at her brother's excitement and hugged him tightly.

I waited for the brother-and-sister moment to end before I made my play to move my plan along. I needed to get inside Neala's apartment, and I could only think of one logical way that wouldn't be suspicious to her.

"Can I use your bathroom, Neala Girl?" I asked, smiling wide.

Neala slid her green frosty eyes to me and growled, "No. Piss yourself for all I care."

I blinked.

Well . . . *that* made things difficult.

"Neala, don't be like that. We're here to quash childish drama, remember?" Sean said as he leaned his shoulder against her doorframe.

I glanced at him and shook my head, feeling like an eejit. This really was just another family ploy to try to force us to mend things. I'd thought the bastard was going to help me, but I should have expected the outcome. As if he was going to help me rob his little sister.

"Please, for me?" Sean asked, his tone soft.

I watched as Neala gave in to him before she spoke the words.

"Fine." She sighed and stepped aside as she gestured us into her apartment.

I let Sean go first, because I needed a moment to gather myself. I was about to enter her lair, and I was both excited and terrified for reasons I couldn't explain. I stepped forward when Neala cleared her throat. I glanced at her and grinned as I passed her by. I chuckled lightly to myself because if looks could kill, I would be dead and buried.

"The bathroom is down the hall and to the left, Darcy."

I always liked the way she said my name . . . even if she did spit it out of her delectable mouth each time she said it.

I blinked.

Delectable mouth?

Since when did I think *any* part of Neala was delectable?

"Thanks," I said after a long period of silence.

I didn't look at her or Sean as I turned and walked down the hallway in search of the bathroom. It wasn't hard; Neala's place was tiny, and apart from the bathroom on the left side of the hall there was only one other room, which I guessed to be her bedroom.

Perverted things entered my mind, much to my shock, the longer I looked at her bedroom door, so I quickly stepped into the bathroom. I went to the sink and turned the taps, then waited a few moments before I cupped my hands together, gathered some water, and splashed it over my face. I rubbed my eyes and took a few deep breaths to relax myself.

I could do this.

I could find the doll and take it from Neala.

It wasn't stealing when it belonged to me . . . *right?*

"Get it together," I grumbled, and splashed some more water over my face.

I dried my face and hands with a small towel before I exited the bathroom and re-joined Sean and Neala in her sitting room. They were both seated, Sean on the couch next to the Christmas tree and Neala on the lounge chair facing it. I took the spot next to Sean and cleared my throat.

"Nice place," I said as politely as I could.

Neala's lip quirked. "Thank you."

She said 'thank you,' but what I heard was 'fuck you,' and it made me grin.

"I bet you're both crying on the inside right now for being nice to one another," Sean said as he looked between Neala and me.

I snorted, but didn't deny the obvious truth. It *was* easier to be horrible to Neala than to be nice to her.

Did that make me a dickhead?

Probably.

"Is that why you're both really here?" Neala quizzed. "You want us to . . . get along?"

Sean looked to me, so I took the lead and lied through my teeth.

"Yep, I want us to get along, and God knows so does everyone else, so I'm taking the first step here. Literally. I came to try to come to some sort of truce between us."

Neala huffed and folded her arms across her ample chest.

"We aren't two countries at war, Darcy."

"No," Sean cut in, "but you are two people at war, and to be honest, when you both get together it's the equivalent of two countries fighting. Two highly weaponised and equipped countries."

I swallowed.

Were we really *that* bad?

Shite.

I knew we acted somewhat – okay, a lot – immature with our feud, but damn, Sean's words made me feel like crap. And the chances were good that when I took the doll back from Neala, and she realised I had it, it would spark a war like no one had ever seen before.

Why was I so excited about that?

I was sick in the head, that's why.

"What are you smiling at?" Neala's voice snapped.

I flicked my eyes to her and shrugged. "Just thought of something funny."

Well, funny in a twisted and demented kind of way.

Neala obviously didn't believe me: I could tell by the look on her face. But I didn't give her the reaction she wanted because I didn't want to fuel her suspicions of me; I wanted her to be at ease. Or as much at ease as she could be with me in her home.

"So . . . how are we supposed to do this?" she asked. "We hate each other, Darcy."

I stared at her for a long moment, unblinking.

She was actually considering mending things between us?

I wasn't expecting that.

"Um . . . I'm not sure," I said, then swallowed. "I know how we feel about one another, but I guess we could start by not attacking one another or cursing when the other person's name is mentioned . . . That could be a start to . . . tolerance?"

Neala was silent as she mulled things over in her constantly on-the-go mind. I knew her like the back of my hand, so I knew she would overthink this until she made up some story that I was out to get her. I wasn't giving her the chance to do that.

"Stop thinking that I'm playing you," I said.

I winced inwardly as I said that. I *was* playing her – not about the mending of our 'relationship,' because that would actually be kind of cool, but about playing the peace card, which was of course a trick that would help me get the doll back from her.

Damn, she was really going to hate me more than ever when she eventually found out what I was doing to her, but I had to focus on my reason for being so sneaky.

Dustin.

"I don't trust you, Darcy."

A wise decision.

"But I trust me brother, and me family, and if they think we can get to a point where we can tolerate one another then okay – I'll give it a shot. But know I'm doing this for our families, not for us."

Seemed fair.

"Noted." I nodded.

Neala nodded her head back to me then cleared her throat as she stood up.

"Can I get you both anything?"

I looked to her brother and waited to see what he would ask for, because if I asked for anything, even though she offered, she would probably bite a chunk out of my face. I could feel the anger radiating from her hot – pun intended – little body. She was open to the idea of us getting along, but she wasn't happy about it.

Sean shook his head, though, so I smiled and said, "A water, please."

After a curt nod she went into the kitchen, and Sean nudged me with his elbow.

"If you take that doll, she is going to kill you when she finds out that—"

"I know."

"And me for bringing you here—"

"I know."

Sean sighed and muttered, "It's gonna kill me ma."

While I waited for my water, I forgot about Sean and Neala and looked around the room. If she had the doll in her bedroom I was fucked, because there was no way I could come up with a viable excuse that would result in my having to go there. I looked around the sitting room, and my eyes locked on to the well-decorated Christmas tree next to me. I looked down and spotted wrapped presents. I glanced up to the kitchen door, and when I was sure Neala wasn't coming into the room I dropped to my knees and picked up each present.

None of the gifts had name tags on them, so I went for the ones that were a similar size to the box I'd held earlier in the day. I dismissed the first two I held because they were heavier than the box I was looking for. I reached for a pink box I spotted behind the other presents. I held the box in my hand, and I instantly knew it was the doll without even unwrapping it. It was the right weight, and as I ran my fingers over the wrapping paper I could feel the dents in the box that were caused by my and Neala's tug of war for it at the store.

"This is it," I whispered to Sean.

"So hide it," he hissed.

I spun around in a circle and realised I couldn't hide it without Neala seeing it, so in desperation I tiptoed quickly to the door and quietly opened it. I placed the box next to the doorframe outside and very carefully closed the door again. I quickly retook my seat next to a bemused Sean and tried to calm down.

"Why did you put it out there?" he mumbled.

So she wouldn't beat me to death with it after she got it back.

I swallowed. "So she wouldn't see it. I'll pick it up on the way out."

Sean raised his eyebrows. "But what if someone outside takes it?"

I froze.

I hadn't considered that.

"Then I'll hunt them down and kill them; then I'll take the doll back." My lip twitched as I spoke.

Sean snickered. "Okay, Rambo."

I chuckled and mentally thanked him for easing the tension that was building up again in the room.

I licked my lips. "Do you think she will notice it's gone?"

"No. Or at least not right away," Sean replied.

We'd have to leave soon, though, just in case she did notice it was missing. I'd die in this apartment if that happened.

"What the hell is she doing in there?" I muttered.

Sean snorted. "Probably talking herself out of killing you, and me for bringing you here."

That sounded like Neala.

I smirked. "I think you might be right."

We sat in silence for a minute or two, then sat up straight when Neala entered the room with a single glass of water in her trembling hands.

"I put ice in it," she mumbled, and looked down as she handed the glass to me.

I blinked.

Did she remember I only drink ice water, or was it a coincidence?

"Thank you," I said, and took the glass from her.

She nodded, moved across the room, and sat back down on the lounge chair. I didn't mean to do it, but I ran my eyes over the glass of water, inspecting it for any signs of foul play. It was Neala we were talking about, after all; she could easily have poisoned it for all I knew. I wasn't taking any chances.

When I was sure, or as sure as I could be, I took a sip of the water and swallowed. I sighed as the ice-cold liquid slid down my throat and quenched my sudden thirst. I took a large gulp, followed by another, and another, until the glass was drained of water and left with only ice cubes gathered at the bottom.

"Thirsty?" Sean asked from my side. His voice was teasing.

"Not anymore," I said, smiling.

I looked away from Sean and to Neala, who was watching me with interest.

"Is this where we set up a play date?" she asked sarcastically.

Sean laughed and stood up. "That doesn't sound like a bad idea, because we have to get going. I have to get Charli from her last day of school before the holiday break and this fella is giving me a lift, since Jess took the truck to work with her today."

Neala shot upright. "Okay, that's fine. Thanks for stopping by."

I smirked.

She couldn't wait to be rid of us, mainly me.

"It was nice . . . talking to you, Neala," I lied.

It wasn't nice; it was both torture and amusing as hell.

Neala swallowed. "And you, Darcy."

Bullshit.

She was physically sick just saying that.

I stood up, turned and walked to the door, opened it, and stepped outside. I quickly scooped up the pink-wrapped box and held it in front of me as I walked down the hallway, not waiting for Sean, who was still back in Neala's apartment, probably getting his arse chewed out for bringing me by.

I didn't care, though, because *I'd* pulled one over on Neala for a change.

I'd got the doll, and there was absolutely *nothing* she could do about it.

CHAPTER SIX

I stared at my hall door and wondered what the hell had just happened.

Sean was always weird and came over to my apartment at random times, but Darcy, that eejit, had never stepped foot in my place, for good reason . . . until today.

Why?

He had even been . . . nice to me.

He'd smiled at me a few times, too.

Not a grin or a smirk – an actual smile.

"I don't get it," I muttered as I locked my front door and backed away from it, as though Darcy might burst back through it at any moment.

Why was he here?

I knew it wasn't so we could 'start getting along with one another,' like he claimed. Even Sean, who was all for us getting along, had given Darcy a funny look when he said that. It was like he knew just as well as I did that what Darcy was saying wasn't remotely true.

I could see right through Darcy's bullshit, but I didn't understand why he'd said the nonsense he did. I didn't even understand why he had come to my apartment in the first place. Everyone, apart from Darcy, was sick of our feud. I was sick in the sense that I enjoyed it; it gave me something to do. I knew he definitely liked it too; he looked forward to seeing me just so he could piss me off. He was demented, just like me.

"Something's not right," I said aloud, and began to look around my apartment.

I had no idea what I was looking for, but I searched anyway.

I spent most of the evening looking for something, and after finding nothing, I gave up. I got a glass of water and drank it as I leaned against my kitchen counter.

Maybe Darcy *did* just want to try to smooth things over and I was just being paranoid.

I shook the silly thought away. There was no way in hell Darcy Hart would willingly want to befriend me. But I knew he had done something; I felt it in my bones.

The doll.

I blinked and felt tremendously stupid for not realising it sooner. It was too much of a coincidence for Darcy to show up wanting to make friends when I *knew* he wanted the doll. We had had it out in a toy shop over it, for goodness' sake.

I walked over to my Christmas tree and glanced down to the presents I'd wrapped earlier that day. I tilted my head and stared at them. The colours weren't right; I had three blue presents, one red, one yellow, and one pink. I pulled the presents out from under my tree in search of the pink-wrapped box.

Where the *fuck* was Charli's *Blaze* doll?

He wouldn't.

Wouldn't he? my mind taunted.

"Darcy!" I snarled, and pushed myself to my feet.

I spun around and placed my hands on top of my head and screamed.

56

He'd robbed me! The callous bastard had come into my home and robbed me blind . . . and I was pretty sure my bloody brother had helped him.

Neala: 1. Darcy: 1.

"Dead. They're both *so* fucking dead!" I growled in anger.

I was going to get that bloody doll back and destroy Darcy in the process. There wasn't a place on Earth he could hide from me. If he wanted a war, I'd bloody well give him one.

Let the games begin.

CHAPTER SEVEN

W hat do you mean, Darcy stole from you and Sean helped?"
I rolled my eyes at Justin Hart, Darcy's older brother,
even though he couldn't see me.

Justin was my brother's best friend, and pretty much my
adoptive big brother. I liked to call him 'Wise One' because he
was only seven years older than me and yet had the mind of a
pensioner. I didn't mean he was forgetful; he was just a very smart
man and knew stuff normal people in their thirties probably
wouldn't.

"I mean exactly that, Justin. Yesterday while I was at home
minding me own business, *your* bastard of a brother came into me
apartment with *my* bastard of a brother, and stole me Christmas
present for Charli!"

Justin sighed into his phone as he accepted what I said as
truth. This sort of thing wasn't a far-fetched idea when Darcy and
I were involved. In fact, things like this happened so often they
were probably tiresome for everyone else to hear.

Scratch that – I *knew* for a fact they were tiresome for everyone
to hear. Everyone who knew us was more than likely fed up with
our feud.

"Is it possible that he is just messing with you?" Justin probed. "It *is* Darcy, after all."

I scoffed. "No, we've been fighting over this present since yesterday—"

"What?" Justin cut me off. "Since yesterday? What do you mean?"

I groaned. "It's a long story."

Justin made his trademark God-save-me-from-Neala-and-Darcy sigh. "When you and Darcy are involved in something together, it usually is. Come over to me house and tell me about it – I'm chilling with Dustin until his ma is home from work."

I had nowhere better to go, so I shrugged my shoulders and said, "Okay, I'll be over in ten."

Justin lived only a few minutes down the road from my apartment complex in a small housing estate just outside the village. I visited often because I was out of work for the moment, so it meant I had nothing else to do. I wasn't a deadbeat; I had a job – a job I loved at the Holiday Inn as a receptionist – but the hotel was currently under construction. A year ago the owners had decided to rip the old hotel down and rebuild a brand-new bigger hotel in its place.

I'd get my old job back in the New Year once the hotel reopened on January 3rd, it was guaranteed, but until then I was seeking unemployment payment from welfare just to help me get by. It was shite money, but at least it was something.

I hated being on welfare, but after months of searching for just about any job close to home and finding nothing, I had no other choice. I was counting down the days until I could get back to work and earn my money instead of just having it handed to me.

I put on my coat, wellie boots, scarf, woolly hat, and gloves. It wasn't just the ice outside that I had to worry about anymore.

Since I'd got home from Smyths yesterday it had started to snow enough to stick to the ground and cause problems. There were already a few inches on the ground. It was unheard-of weather for Dublin – it only snowed once every five or six years – but the pending winter snowfall was forecast to be our worst in history. I hadn't paid much attention to the warnings, though; half the time the weather channel got it wrong anyway, so I never took what they said as fact.

I locked up my apartment, then headed out of the complex and onto the street. It took a little longer than usual to walk to Justin's house. The snow was so thick that I had to watch my step, because I wasn't sure whether there was ice under the layers of snow. It was better to be safe than sorry.

By the time I arrived on Fairview Road, where Justin and his family resided, it had begun to snow again, and it did nothing for my heated temper or my ice-cold limbs.

"You look frozen," Justin's laughing voice called out as I hiked my way up his driveway.

I grunted. "If I wasn't so stiff and cold, I'd stick me finger up at you."

Justin smirked as I neared him. "The death glare you're currently giving me is a grand replacement."

I couldn't help it; I smiled, or at least I tried to – I was so damn numb I couldn't tell whether my lips moved or not.

"You look like you're constipated," Justin mused as I stepped into his hallway.

I groaned as Justin closed his front door and the heat of his house surrounded me.

"Me face is frozen, you dick!" I said through my chattering teeth.

Justin laughed as he ushered me into his living room, where it was even warmer. I scurried over to the radiator under the window and pressed my arse and thighs against it. I sighed in delight and stayed put as the heat caused tingles to spread across my thawing skin.

"You sound like you're in a porno."

I kept my eyes closed. "Only you would think that, pervert."

I heard a giggle.

"What's a porno?" a small voice asked.

I opened my eyes and widened them to the point of pain. Dustin, Justin's son, was leaning against the doorframe of the living room with his arms crossed over his chest and a quizzical look on his face.

Justin was looking at Dustin with worried eyes, and after a few moments of silence he said, "Never mind . . . Don't repeat it to your mother, though."

Dustin smirked. "Is it something bad?"

Uh-oh. The kid had a blackmail look about him.

Justin awkwardly scratched his neck. "No . . . not necessarily. Look little man, just don't tell your ma I said that word, okay?"

Dustin tilted his head to the side as he thought about it, and I smiled. He was the double of Justin with his blond hair and big eyes, but looked like his uncle when he was thinking.

I shook away a sudden unwelcome stream of pleasant thoughts about Darcy, and focused on the cutie before me.

"What's in it for me?" Dustin asked his father.

I laughed. "He's your kid; there's no doubting that."

Justin grunted at me without looking away from his son. "I'll let you out of helping me wash the dishes for a whole week; how does that sound?"

Dustin considered it for a moment, then suggested, "A week without washing the dishes *and* a week of late-night snacks?"

Justin balked. "You're killing me, kid; your ma will have me arse if she knows you've had sugary snacks past bedtime."

Dustin stood up straight, a sign to me that he wasn't about to back down.

"That's the deal, Da. Take it or leave it."

I covered my mouth with my hand so I wouldn't laugh.

The kid had Justin by the bollocks.

"Okay, fine, you little shite – but not a word to your ma about the snacks, dishes, or the not-bad word I said, okay?"

Dustin grinned from ear to ear. "What word, Da?"

He turned and ran out of the room then.

"Hey, rude kid! Say hello to Neala!"

I heard Dustin's feet as he pattered up the stairs at lightning speed.

"Heya, Auntie Neala. Bye, Auntie Neala."

I laughed. "Hello and goodbye to you too, Dusty!"

I looked to Justin, who was grumbling under his breath as he sat down on the recliner facing me.

"You can't be mad; he isn't doing anything you weren't doing at his age."

Justin snorted. "You weren't alive when I was his age."

I rolled my eyes. "Give it a rest. You've got seven years on me, Wise One, not seventy."

Justin grinned, then nodded at the living room doorway and said, "Can you believe he is turning seven in July?"

I shook my head. "Nope, it's like yesterday he was born."

Justin smiled as he thought about that fond memory. "The kid is too smart for a six-year-old. I wasn't as advanced as him when I was his age; nor was I that much of a hustler."

I cackled. "He's picked up some new tricks, that's for sure."

"All at me own expense."

"Would you have him any other way?" I asked, smiling.

Justin looked at me and smiled. "No."

"That's what I thought." I snickered, then said, "I still can't believe you wouldn't give on his name. Justin and Dustin are confusing to me sometimes."

"I wanted him called after me, but his ma wasn't having it, so Dustin was a close second."

I moved away from the radiator now that I had feeling back in most parts of my body. I took off my wellie boots and other winter layers and set them by the radiator to dry; then I sat across from Justin and rubbed my arms with my hands.

"This winter is horrible." I grumbled.

Justin nodded in agreement. "It's going to get even worse, too."

God, I hoped not.

I leaned my head back against the chair. "Where's your baby mama?"

Justin pulled a face at me. "*Sarah* is working."

I snapped my fingers. "Right – you mentioned that on the phone. How's work going for her?"

Justin shrugged. "It's going as well as can be down the pub. She and Jess have pretty much the same shifts, so they have a bit of craic together."

"Good, glad to hear it."

Justin grinned. "Spit it out."

I smiled knowingly; nothing got past him.

"Spit what out?" I smiled.

"Why are you really here, kid? I know it's not to shoot the shit and rag on petty little things, so say whatever it is about Darcy that you need to say," Justin said, a warm smile on his face.

Time to get down to business.

I trained my gaze on him. "I'm here to enlist you into me army."

"Steady on, Lara Croft." Justin laughed.

I hissed. "I'm serious. I need you on me side in order to win this war."

Justin dropped his smile and stared at me in dismay. "War? Army? Who the hell are you fighting, Neala?"

"Darcy and Sean." I spat out their names. "Apart I can handle them, but together they form one working brain and can anticipate me every move. I need help to defeat them. *Your* help."

Justin blinked. "I don't like the vibe off you right now. You sound, and look . . . murderous."

I grinned evilly. "I am, and your brother is one of two on me hit list."

Justin screeched, "Fucking hell, will you blink already? You're scaring me, Neala!"

I snorted and batted my eyelashes.

"Better?" I asked sarcastically.

"No," Justin huffed. "You looked like that chick out of—"

"I don't care who or what I look like, Justin." I cut him off. "I really need your help. Your stupid little brother has crossed a line with me, and I intend to make the bastard pay."

Justin sat forward and scrubbed his face with both of his hands.

"Tell me." He sighed. "What *exactly* has Darcy done to upset you so much this time?"

I swallowed down my rage, and reminded myself that Justin wasn't the person I was angry with.

"He stole a doll from me."

Justin raised an eyebrow and muttered, "A *doll?*"

I nodded my head. "Long story short, we both fought for the same doll in Smyths yesterday. He wanted it for Dustin, and I wanted it for Charli. I won it fair and square." He didn't need to know that was a lie. "But that wasn't enough for Darcy. He came into me home pretending that he wanted us to be friends, and when me back was turned he stole the doll right out from underneath me nose. Who does that? That is me niece's Christmas present and he just took it! I knew better than to believe him, but Sean vouched for him, so I had no reason to doubt him, you know?"

I looked down to my fisted hands and willed them to stop shaking, but I couldn't make them stop. They weren't shaking from the cold anymore. I was so angry with Darcy, and hurt that he would do this to me. The hurt I felt disgusted me more than anything, because I had sworn a long time ago that Darcy's actions wouldn't faze me, and yet here I was close to tears over the idiot.

My brother's role in Darcy's messed-up game was upsetting, but I knew deep down Sean thought I enjoyed my tug-of-war games with Darcy, and to an extent I usually did. But not this time around. I'd taken a lot of crap from Darcy over the years but I refused to let him one-up me on this.

Justin frowned as he looked at me. "I agree he shouldn't have robbed you of the doll, but I don't think he intended to upset you. In his mind he probably thinks you're cooking up a plan to get the doll back from him. This is what you and Darcy do, kid. You play off one another."

I grunted. "Not anymore. He crossed a line by coming to me house spewing lies about false relationship mending. I hate liars and he knows that."

Justin chewed on his lower lip. "I feel for you, kid, and I want to help you even out the playing field, but I can't step in on this one. Orders from the head office."

The head office?

No. Way.

I gasped. "Our mothers!"

I don't know why I was even surprised at the mention of our mothers being involved in this situation – those two knew everything. They had eyes and ears all over the bloody village.

Justin grinned at my outburst. "They never told me what was going on, but they warned me not to get involved because they don't want to encourage any drama between you two that will roll over to Sean and Jess's engagement party tomorrow night."

How did they even know what Darcy and I were up to?

Did someone in Smyths let on what happened to them? Damn our small town – everyone knew your business.

"Those meddling cows! How come Darcy gets Sean's help and I have to go it alone?"

Justin winced, and I guessed it was because of how unfair everyone was being to me.

"Maybe they know your cleverness and wit is worth ten of Sean and Darcy put together, and that you don't need the extra help to outsmart them both?"

I couldn't help but smile. Justin was a smooth talker.

"You're such a lick-arse." I chuckled.

Justin smiled. "I know what to say in certain situations; it's a nice trait to have."

"Well, if you aren't going to help me bring down Dumb and Dumber, then keep mum that I know Darcy has the doll, okay? I want him sweating with worry on when and how I'm going to strike back."

Justin winked. "You got it, and for whatever it's worth, kid, I'm rooting for you to come out on top on this one. Literally."

That sounded more than a little suggestive, and I was about to call Justin on it when a shout came from upstairs.

"Da, I'm starving!"

I rolled my eyes at Dustin's dramatics.

"What do you want to eat?" Justin shouted back.

"Pizza!" came Dustin's quick response.

I snorted as Justin reached for his phone and said, "Don't judge me. I don't like cooking."

I motioned with my hand over my mouth that my lips were sealed.

Justin smirked. "You staying for dinner?"

I shrugged. "Sure. Plotting my plan of attack against your brother over pizza sounds perfect to me."

Justin shook his head as he pressed on the screen of his phone and then lifted it to his ear. "Poor little brother. He doesn't realise he's opened the gates to Hell."

CHAPTER EIGHT

How do you ignore a person who's bought you something nice? Easily – you don't look at them.

"Which one do you want to wear tonight at the party? The red one or the blue one?" my mother questioned me, as she held up two identical skin-tight dresses, only in different colours. They were gifts from her, since I hadn't bothered to go out and get anything new to wear for the party.

"Can you at least *pretend* you're excited about going to Sean and Jessica's engagement party?" My mother frowned and lowered the outfits to her side.

I raised one eyebrow. "I am excited . . . for Jess, anyway. No comment on me feelings towards Sean right now . . . or towards you and the other meddling cow, for that matter."

My mother huffed. "For goodness' sake, Neala. It's not a terrible thing we did. Marie and I just don't want you or Darcy to ruin the party with your arguing. We're your mothers; we know what you're both capable of."

Way to place the blame!

"Oh, thanks very much."

My mother groaned. "I don't mean it like that—"

I cut my mother off. "Then, pray tell, how did you mean it?"

My mother shook her head as she gently laid both outfits over the back of my lounge chair. She folded her arms across her chest and stared me down.

"Everyone knows what you and Darcy are like when you're caught up in a fight: neither one of you cares how it affects the people around you. Justin was told not to get involved because we didn't want the current dilemma to build up and explode tonight in front of the entire village."

I gasped. "We're two people, Ma, not bloody ticking time bombs!"

My mother rolled her eyes. "You're both the equivalent of chemical warfare during an argument, Neala."

Talk about dramatics.

"That's ridiculous," I stated, waving her off.

"No," my mother calmly stated. "What's ridiculous is your and Darcy's behaviour of late."

I could feel my temperature rise.

"Darcy stole from me, and me so-called brother helped him. Why is everyone failing to see that *they* are in the wrong here?"

I hated that my eyes filled with water – and my mother hated it too, from the saddened look she gave me. I held up my hand and shook my head when she made a move to come over to comfort me.

"I'm fine; I just hate that everyone is siding with *him*."

My mother's frown deepened. "Honey, we aren't picking sides here. We just don't want what normally happens with you and Darcy to happen at the engagement party . . . Is that so horrible?"

I thought about it and decided that it wasn't. I didn't want to ruin anybody's party, but I wasn't letting Darcy think for a moment that he had gotten away with what he had done. No way.

"No, it's not. You're right. I'll behave. I will just stay away from Darcy at the party so nothing will happen," I said, and stood up from the couch.

I passed my mother, picked up the blue dress from the back of the lounge chair, and smiled. "I like this one." As I walked up the stairs to my old bedroom, my mother's words halted my steps.

"Just so you know, sweetheart, I'm always in your corner. Always."

I smiled as I entered my room and closed the door behind me.

I would do as my and Darcy's mother wished – I would stay away from Darcy and I wouldn't cause trouble with him. I smirked to myself then as a wicked thought entered my mind.

I didn't need to be near him to mess with him.

I was suddenly excited about the engagement party tonight. *Very* excited.

∾

"Neala!"

I looked around for the source of the voice calling my name, and when I found Jessica Waters, my soon-to-be sister-in-law, walking toward me I smiled wide.

"Jess, hey! You look gorgeous!"

She had on a knee-length wine-coloured lace dress. It was stunning and her figure with its never-ending curves did wonders for her and the dress. She looked sexy as sin.

"Me? Look at you! God, I'd bloody kill for your legs!" she gushed as she crashed into me and hugged me tightly.

I laughed and hugged her back and kissed her cheek for good measure, but I felt uneasy. I didn't do the friend thing very well; Darcy had made sure to ruin that for me at a young age. After our initial falling-out when we were ten, and our other spats throughout the years, I had never put myself out there with anyone else. I didn't even attempt to find another best friend, always worrying that history would repeat itself. I had friends in school, but no one I confided in.

I hated to admit it, but Darcy had once been very special to me, and I just didn't think a new friendship could compare to the one we used to have.

Despite all this, Jess was a friend of mine, and even though I couldn't trust anyone enough to tell them my deepest and darkest secrets, I *could* trust her enough to lightly vent to.

"So, you and Darcy . . . What the hell happened? Sean told me he may not live long enough to see our wedding if you get your hands on him anytime soon."

It wasn't something to laugh about, especially because Jess looked genuinely concerned, but I couldn't help it. It was funny.

"I shouldn't be laughing, because I'm seriously pissed off at both Darcy and Sean, but it's nothing that payback can't wait a few days for . . . for Sean anyway." I smirked.

Jess widened her eyes. "You plan on getting Darcy back for whatever he did . . . tonight?"

Shite.

She looked worried.

"Yes, but I promise it won't cause a scene or put a dent in your engagement party."

Jess waved me off. "I don't mean that. I mean Darcy got to you so much that you want to seek revenge right away? You usually wait until he isn't on Neala Alert."

Neala Alert was a two-word code Darcy had made up when we were ten after the incident with Laura Stoke and a certain skipping rope. He used it to let people know not to distract him because he was completely focused on his surroundings and on the lookout for me. Neala Alert usually happened to Darcy after he'd pulled a prank on me or if he'd just pissed me off.

I shrugged. "He crossed a line this time."

Jess stared at me and waited for me to explain.

I sighed. "It may sound stupid, but he stole a doll from me that I bought for Charli for Christmas a few days ago at Smyths, and your soon-to-be husband helped him. I'm sort of mad about it."

Sort of . . . Okay, I was livid.

"This is all over a doll?" Jess asked, her tone now amused.

No.

I huffed. "It's not about the bloody doll. It's about the fact that he stole something from me that was mine, and I don't plan on letting him get away with it."

Jess frowned. "You seem . . . upset?"

"I am," I nodded.

"No." Jess shook her head. "I mean you seem upset, like *really* upset, not just annoyed."

I shrugged my shoulders. "He went too far this time; he tried to trick me into thinking he wanted to be me friend again."

Jess blinked her big blue eyes. "I'm sorry, babe."

I didn't want to lose my cool and dwell on my silly feelings, so I forced a smile and waved the conversation off.

"It's nothing a bit of payback won't fix." I devilishly smirked.

Jess grinned. "You're hard-core."

"In all aspects of me life," I teased.

Jess laughed and pulled me into another hug. When we separated, Darcy's mother, Marie, was in front of us with a very large camera in her hands pointed directly at us.

"Smile, lovelies." She beamed.

Jess and I straightened up and put an arm around one another's waist and smiled wide into the camera lens. The flash spotted my vision for a few moments. When my eyes refocused I instantly narrowed them.

"*You,*" I growled.

Darcy was standing behind his mother, grinning knowingly at me. He was actually using his mother, the woman who'd carried him for nine months and birthed him, as a human shield. He was a bloody wimp!

"You both *promised* you wouldn't start any fights tonight," Marie said as she looked back and forth between Darcy and me.

I continued to glare at Darcy as I said, "I know, and I'm not going to start anything."

Darcy winked at me and said, "Me either."

I clasped my hands together to try to kill the slap-Darcy itch that had gathered on both of my palms.

"Is it too much to ask for a picture? The last one we have of you both together is from when you were both kids."

Lie.

"We're in tons of pictures—"

"They are family pictures," Marie cut me off. "Not any of just the two of you in a picture on your own . . . not smiling, anyway."

I swallowed the rejection I had planned when I saw Marie's face; she looked so hopeful that I couldn't say no to her, even though I really wanted to. She was like a mother to me, and I hated seeing her upset.

"Okay," I grumbled. "Take a picture."

Marie quickly grabbed a reluctant Darcy's arm and all but threw him at me.

"Arm over her shoulder, Darcy, and arm around his waist, Neala. Somebody get Clare; she needs to witness this. It might never happen again!"

I rolled my eyes. We weren't a bloody comet that only passed by the Earth once in a millennium.

I wanted to get the picture done, but Marie wouldn't move until Clare, my meddling mother, was next to her.

I put my arm sharply around Darcy's waist and left it hover there, making sure to barely touch him.

I refused to look at him as the side of his warm, hard body moulded against mine and his intoxicating scent surrounded me.

Damn.

Why did he have to smell so good?

"We haven't seen this type of picture in nearly a decade!" Marie suddenly stated, making Jess, who had come up beside her, laugh.

"You both look great together," Jess commented just as my mother appeared.

My flesh and blood, a.k.a. my cow of a mother, squealed, "Oh, don't they just."

To which I growled, "*Don't.*"

Jess smirked, my mother ignored me, and Marie pretended the camera suddenly wasn't working just so Darcy and I would have to stand next to one another longer. She thought she was being clever, but she was just being obvious.

Well, to me she was, anyway.

Darcy suddenly grunted. "Come on, Ma, you turned it off. So just turn the fecking thing back on."

I mentally snorted.

Okay, so he knew what she was up to as well.

"Don't rush me. I birthed you so I can unbirth you just as quick!" Marie snapped at Darcy, making Jess laugh.

I glared at Jess, who only continued to beam in our direction. It was honestly starting to freak me out, so I switched my gaze to my mother, but when I saw water pool in her eyes I quickly made Marie my focal point.

Bloody women.

"Okay, both of you smile," Marie said in a cheerful voice, then huffed, "and don't force it, Neala!"

I inwardly rolled my eyes but did as asked and smiled wide – and because Darcy didn't get told off I imagined he did the same. I flinched a little after the flash went off, but I quickly snapped out of it.

"Oh, my goodness!" Marie beamed. "It's beautiful. I'm framing this!"

"Me too!" my mother gushed.

"Oh, my God," I grumbled as I quickly dropped my arm away from Darcy and took a step to the left.

My freedom was short-lived, though. My mother shot forward and pushed me back against Darcy, which surprised me and caused me to stumble. I was even more surprised when large hands gripped my waist and kept me upright and on my feet. The feeling of his hands on me caused my pulse to spike and my heart to race.

"Careful," Darcy murmured, his voice surprisingly soft, as he pulled away from me once again.

I brushed myself off with my hands and mumbled, "Thanks."

I blinked when I realised those were the nicest things Darcy and I had willingly said to one another in years.

Wow.

My mother's giggle got my attention.

"Sorry, baby, but I want pictures with both of you . . . with Sean."

I glared at my mother. "You're pushing it."

She just smiled at me like she had no clue what I was talking about, but of course she did, because she knew everything. The witch knew Darcy and Sean were on my hit list and she wanted me in close proximity with both of them? She really was testing a girl's restraint.

"Sean!" my mother shouted.

I don't know how he heard her over the punters in the pub, but Sean popped up behind Jess and rubbed his neck as he said, "Yeah, Ma?"

My mother snapped her fingers at him. "Picture time with Neala and Darcy now."

Sean hesitated as our eyes locked.

He swallowed and shook his head. The worry on his face made me happy. He was scared, and he should be.

"Sean, don't make me ask again. Get in the picture with Neala and Darcy."

Sean paled visibly as he stepped around a laughing Jess and walked in our direction.

"Please don't hit me," Sean muttered as he came up against my left side.

I gritted my teeth. "No promises."

My mother was exasperated as she gave the lads orders on where to put their hands on my body. They were both told to place their hands on my back and lean into me, because I was considerably shorter than both of them. I blew out a breath when their hands pressed against me. Someone told us to smile.

Sean's hand was in the middle of my back, and Darcy's was on my lower back. I knew this because I was acutely aware of how close to my arse it was.

"Stunning!" Marie gushed.

Suddenly Justin's voice sounded in my ear, and I could feel the lads start to pull away.

"Don't forget me."

Our mothers squealed with delight.

Justin placed his hands on Sean's and Darcy's shoulders and rested his chin on my head.

"Smile!" Marie shouted proudly.

We did as ordered, and when the flash went off I couldn't help but groan.

"Was that the last one?" I asked.

I felt a hand nudge my back. "Don't complain about getting in pictures with family, kid," Justin said.

I didn't want to seem disrespectful, so I kept my mouth shut.

"No, it's not the last one," Marie stated. "Now one with you all and Jess, since she is legally joining the family in a few short months."

I smiled to myself. Sean and Jess were a brilliant couple, but had worked hard to get to where they were. When they met, they'd had a one-night stand and Jess had got pregnant with Charli right away. They had decided to stay together and make a go of a relationship for Charli's sake, but they soon fell in love and seven years later they were still together and on their way to marriage.

"Where is Sarah?" Marie's voice cut through my thoughts. "I want a group photo of all of you together."

I growled at my mother as Jess pranced over to Sean's side. My mother shouted Sarah's name, and like Sean she appeared out of nowhere and stood behind me with Justin.

"Okay, big smiles, everyone. This is one for me wall," my mother said excitedly.

I couldn't help but smile at my mother's excitement.

Her 'wall' was the one along her hallway in her house. She had a pretty big house; the hallway was very long and pictures covered its entire wall. It looked beautiful, but only the nearest and dearest pictures went up onto the wall – and if you were in one that made the cut, you knew you were being honoured by my mother – and by Marie, because behind every decision my mother made was Marie, and vice versa.

After the final flash from the camera I stepped away from Dumb and Dumber and surged towards my mother. "Where is me da?" I asked.

She waved towards the back of the pub where the plasma screens were. "Back there – he's watching some football manager's documentary. I don't know."

Without a word to anyone I took off in search of my father, because he had something I needed, something I'd asked him to bring. Something that would *partially* get Darcy back for what he'd done to me over the past few days, and also something that would lead to my getting the doll back.

I found him right where my mother said he would be, watching a football documentary with his friends while drinking – it was a pub we were in, after all.

I moved over to my father and leaned down. "Did you bring it?" I asked.

Darcy's father, Jimmy, smiled and shook his head as my father discreetly reached into his shirt pocket and took out a strip of tablets.

"No more than two. You'll cripple the lad otherwise," my father said without looking away from the plasma screen.

I smiled; he was all for me getting revenge on Darcy, but he didn't want him severely hurt. My father loved Darcy; he thought of him as a son. But I was his baby girl, so when I'd rung him in tears (fake ones, by the way) and explained how Darcy and Sean had robbed me of Charli's Christmas present, meant for his precious granddaughter, he was bothered and more than ready to help me get revenge – and also get the doll back.

He came up with a deadly idea, and even though it was old-school, it was still gold. It wouldn't harm Darcy, only his pride, and it would help me get the doll back. All I had to do was execute my plan perfectly.

Jimmy laughed out loud, which got my attention. "Feck him. He deserves whatever's coming to him after the stunt he pulled. I'm with you on this one, Neala."

I high-fived Jimmy, lovingly patted my father on the back, then turned and went searching for Darcy so I could put the laxative tablets to work. My plan was to give Darcy the shits for two reasons.

One, he deserved crippling stomach pain and ring burn for stealing the doll from me. Two, it would guarantee he had to go into the toilets and stay there for a *long* time.

Once Darcy was resigned to a painful night in the pub toilets, I would then happily head to his lodge farther up the mountains, break into said lodge – let's see how he liked it – and get the doll back.

Everybody wins.

Well, everybody except Darcy.

Darcy didn't get to win at all.

CHAPTER NINE

I scanned the pub for the tenth time in the thirty minutes since the forced picture-taking had ended. Actually, being next to Neala wasn't too bad, because it meant I could keep my eye on her, but now that I couldn't see her chocolate brown–haired head anywhere, it made me uneasy.

It was Neala's turn to strike, and that meant I couldn't drop my guard.

I was one hundred percent certain she knew I had taken the doll from her apartment. I just didn't understand why she hadn't outed me to everyone, or at the very least got me on my own to attack me over it. Christmas was in four days' time, and I knew she needed that doll for Charli, so she couldn't afford to wait around; she had to come at me sooner rather than later for it. The when was a question, but the how was an even bigger one that played on my mind.

I had no clue how she would seek revenge on me and try to get the doll back. It was chilling to think about, because Neala could be creative – *very* creative – with her methods of revenge. Each and every single one of her revenge plans over the years had left me wallowing in the shreds of my crumbled pride. I was well aware that she could bring a grown man to his knees . . . I was living proof of it. But as apprehensive as I was, I would be lying if I said the thrill of it didn't excite me, because it did.

Neala was an adrenaline rush for me; she was something I craved and feared at the same time.

I'd never admit that out loud, though; it killed me just admitting it to myself. I shouldn't want anything to do with her; she had left me high and dry when we were kids. When I'd needed her as we got older, she hadn't had the time of day for me.

She'd cut me out of her life because I didn't agree with her hitting a girl when we were ten. It was stupid, petty, and plain childish, but it had somehow developed into us being how we were now as adults.

I continued to scan the room for her, but instead of her pale face I saw other familiar ones. One particular face I spotted was one I'd come to know well over the past few years; it was Laura Stoke's pretty one.

The same Laura Stoke that Neala despised.

She was tall, not as tall as my six foot three, but taller than most girls, at five foot eleven. She had freckled, pale white skin, long, thick strawberry blond hair that touched the small of her back, and an arse that made my cock stand at attention with one sway.

Laura was, to put it nicely, my fuck buddy. Like me, she wasn't looking to settle down with a relationship; she was simply up for fun whenever I was up for it – pun intended.

I had had a long sample of Laura only a few days ago. I licked my lips, grinning at the memory.

"Laura," I called out.

Her head turned in my direction, and a knowing smirk curved her red-painted lips. I allowed my eyes to slowly trail over her sizzling-hot body as she sashayed towards me through the small crowd, and as always, the thought of what I could do, and had done, to that body caused me to harden.

"Darcy Hart, fancy seeing you again . . . so soon," Laura purred as she reached me.

She leaned in and placed a chaste kiss on my lips.

"You look edible," I growled down at her, and swallowed when she snapped her teeth at me.

Laura took a step back and looked down at the hot-pink pencil dress she had on.

"What? In this old thing?"

I groaned as she slowly twirled, giving me a full view of just how tightly that old thing hugged her slender body in the sexiest of ways.

"Yeah," I hissed as she turned and pressed herself fully against me.

Laura smiled at me seductively. "I've never turned you or your cock down before, Darcy . . . Quite frankly, because you give me amazing orgasms. But no orgasm, no matter how good, is worth the wrath of Neala Clarke."

I sobered, and my dick softened at the mention of *her* name.

"What the hell has Neala got to do with us shagging?" I asked.

Laura smiled. "This is her brother's engagement party, and I've been around you enough to know explosive shite happens when you're both at the same function. I don't want to jump to the top of her hit list by being on your arm tonight. She hates me; it wouldn't take much for her to target me."

I growled in annoyance. "Neala doesn't get a say in who I fuck."

"No," Laura agreed, "but when she's mad at you, she will get you back no matter who you're fucking – and she is *always* mad at you. I don't fancy her pulling some stunt while we get down and dirty in the bathroom. She'd be more than happy to make a show of me."

This wasn't happening.

"Don't do this to me, Laura. I need you tonight," I pleaded.

Yeah, I was pleading with a woman to have sex with me. So sue me. I wasn't the first man to do it, and I wouldn't be the last.

Laura smiled that sexy smile of hers and gave me one more chaste kiss before she whispered against my lips, "Until next time, Wicked Mouth."

She turned and broke the pulsing heartbeat in my cock as she walked away. I looked at her arse and instantly narrowed my eyes at the torturous hump.

Did she really need to sway so much?

"Women," I grunted, and looked away from Laura's arse and up to the ceiling of the pub.

I took a few deep breaths.

I grunted again, this time in annoyance as I thought of *her*.

Neala Clarke.

The malicious little menace had managed to work her way into my sex life. She had just singlehandedly cock-blocked me . . . and she didn't even fucking know about it.

"Bloody woman!" I snapped.

The noise of the punters in the pub filled my ears until a familiar voice got my attention.

"What's the matter, little brother?"

I sighed as I looked to the concerned gaze of my older brother. "Laura just turned me down because of Neala."

I spat out her name like it was poison in my mouth.

Justin's eyebrows jumped. "Why?"

I shrugged. "Something about her being worried Neala would target her for being with me."

Justin laughed, and it annoyed me.

This wasn't funny.

"Care to explain why you're being a dick and laughing at me?" I quizzed.

Justin chuckled. "Why does everyone make Neala out to be something she isn't? She's probably the sweetest girl I know, and just happens to have an attitude every now and then. Sounds like every woman I've ever met, if I'm honest."

I gawked at my brother.

"Neala Clarke is the Devil in disguise, brother. You had better realise that. Sweet is the *last* word I would use to describe her . . . She is evil incarnate."

Justin cracked up again, and like before, it pissed me off.

"Fuck you, man."

Justin waved his hand at me. "I'm sorry," he said as he tried to calm himself down. He managed, but only after another minute. "I understand you both have history," he went on, "but I love that she gets to you this much. You actually freak out about her."

I furrowed my eyebrows. "You find it funny that a woman pisses me off?"

"No, I find it funny that she gets under your skin and you like it and hate it at the same time."

What the hell?

"I don't like—"

"Don't lie. Don't say you don't like Neala, because you do. You hate her because you want her so much. It's obvious, to me anyway."

"There is something wrong with you. I don't want Neala in *any* way."

Justin smirked but said nothing, and it bothered me.

"What?" I snapped.

He laughed. "Nothing, bro, nothing."

I shook my head. "You're a dick."

Justin clasped his hand on my shoulder and squeezed. "I may be a dick, but I'm an honest one."

With that said, he walked off and greeted some of the other locals. I stared after him, feeling utterly confused. This was the first time he'd ever mentioned that he thought I liked Neala, but he was very wrong.

I didn't like her.

I hated her.

I just enjoyed messing with her from time to time.

Sure, I sometimes felt like I needed the Neala adrenaline rush to keep me sane, but that didn't mean I liked her; it meant I liked her reaction to my bullshit. That's all. I didn't like her. Not one bit.

"You look absolutely horrified about something."

I blinked my eyes, turned my head to the right, and saw Sean standing next to me.

"Justin thinks I like Neala," I said, and shook my head.

Sean remained silent, so I turned to face him.

"Don't tell me you think the same thing?" I asked, shocked.

Sean shrugged, but remained silent.

"For fuck's sake. I *don't* like her. I can't stand the witch!"

Sean laughed, but continued to look at me as he held his tongue.

"Say something or I'm going to sock you one!" I warned.

He licked his lips and said, "Don't hit me . . . but I agree with Justin."

Oh, Christ.

"What the hell? But it's not true. I don't like her!" I stated.

Sean raised an eyebrow at me and grinned. "You're possessive of her. You never let anyone pick on her growing up. You—"

I cut Sean off. "Because she was mine to torture."

"You wouldn't go to any parties unless she was in attendance. You—"

I jumped in and cut Sean off again. "Because they weren't any fun unless she was there so I could wind her up!"

Sean lightly chortled. "You punched Kenny *and* Luke Spencer in the face because they said she was hot at her sixteenth birthday party. You—"

"Because I didn't want to deal with a boyfriend when I was torturing her . . . How can you not see any of this?"

Sean shook his head, still not convinced.

"You admitted that seeing her makes your day."

"Because I know I drive her mad every time I see her, and *that* makes me happy."

Sean pinched the bridge of his nose. "You never shag brunettes, even though you told me they are your preference – you only get into blondes, redheads, or black-haired girls."

"Because the only attractive girls in this bloody village happen to have blond, red, or black hair!"

Sean burst out laughing, "You're so deep in denial you can't see past it."

I badly wanted to punch Sean in the face in that moment, but it wasn't worth the wrath of my mother, or Sean's, if I made him bruise at his engagement party, so I settled for punching him in the arm instead.

"You're being a real bastard, you know that?"

Sean rubbed his arm. "I'm aware of it, yes."

Arsehole.

I lifted my hands to my face and scrubbed. When I lowered them I looked around the pub again and grunted.

"Where is she? I know she's biding her time to get back at me, and not being able to keep me eye on her is scaring me."

Sean laughed. "You're scared of Neala?"

I growled. "You'll be scared too when it's her turn to strike you. She thinks you aided me by getting me into her apartment; I'm sure of it."

Sean opened his mouth to speak, but quickly closed it and nodded in agreement. "What are you going to do? Stand here all night and search for her?"

I sighed and shrugged.

"I don't know. Maybe."

Sean was about to say something when my mother appeared with two glasses filled with what looked to be an alcoholic liquid.

"These were meant to be vodkas and Coke, but the barman gave us whiskey instead. Do you both want them?" my mother asked.

Sean shook his head, but I took both drinks.

"Thanks, Ma," I said, and downed them both.

I scrunched my face up as the liquid burned a pathway down my throat and to my chest. I hadn't planned on drinking tonight. I needed to be on Neala Alert, but it was essential that I be relaxed for that, and that was exactly what the whiskey did.

"Why don't you both go and see your fathers?"

I raised my eyebrows. "Why?"

My mother huffed, "I don't really care where you go, Darcy; just stop standing here and glaring at our friends. You look . . . odd."

Sean laughed. "He's on Neala Alert."

My mother smirked, and it caused me to roll my eyes.

"Don't start, Ma."

With that said I brushed by my mother and went in search of my father. Sitting with him was probably the safest thing for me to do right now. Neala loved my father and wouldn't try to hurt me when I was in close proximity to him . . . I hoped not, anyway.

"Darcy, where are you going?" my father called out to me thirty minutes later.

"Bathroom," I rasped.

I thought I heard laughter coming from my father, but I couldn't be sure. I didn't really care, though, because I needed to get to a bathroom as soon as possible. My stomach was absolutely killing me, and I felt like my insides were about to spill out from my arsehole.

If it sounds disgusting, you can only imagine how I felt.

"What the hell did I eat?" I groaned in pain as I stumbled down the small hallway of the pub.

I tried to think of anything I had eaten earlier in the day that could make me feel so ill, but the only thing out of the norm was the buffet of pub food that Sean and Jess had made for their party. I'm not fond of spices, and that was all the buffet consisted of. Spices and herbs.

Never, ever would I touch either one again; my stomach churned just at the thought.

I reached the men's toilet and sighed out loud as I pushed the door open, only to stumble into the wall when I saw all three stalls had pieces of paper with 'OUT OF ORDER' on the door.

"This can't be bleeding happening to me!"

I made a decision in a split second to use the ladies' room. I would apologise to every woman who came in and heard or smelt me, but I couldn't *not* go to the bathroom. I quickly moved to the right to go into the ladies', but like the men's room, the door wouldn't open. I looked up and punched the door when I spotted the same 'out of order' sign hanging on the door.

"*None* of the toilets work?" I shouted.

Bollocks.

I had to leave.

I had to go home where I could go to the toilet, and die in peace.

I would never usually leave a party, especially a family one, but I had to, and I couldn't stop to say goodbye to anyone. I ignored everyone around me and made a beeline for the pub exit.

Of course I wasn't blessed with making a quick escape; the hand that clamped down on my shoulder made sure of that.

"Where the hell are you waddling off to?"

I turned to face Sean. "I need to go."

"Go where? And seriously, you're walking like a penguin. What's up with that?"

I ignored his laughter and said, "I need to leave."

"What do you mean, you have to leave?" Sean asked me.

I understood his annoyance. I was part of his wedding party, and here I was bailing on the long-awaited engagement celebration. Not only that, I was also his friend. But I couldn't help it; I *had* to leave.

My arsehole demanded it.

"I have to, man," I said, then hunched over as another horrible cramp somersaulted in my stomach.

I felt a hand on my back. "Darcy, are you okay?"

I really wasn't.

"No," I hissed in pain. "I think the food isn't sitting well with me. Me stomach is killing me."

Sean helped straighten me up and smiled and nodded at the punters of the pub, who gazed at me a little too long.

"You don't think the food is bad, do you?" Sean asked, his tone worried.

I shook my head.

"No, no, it tasted delicious. I think the spices are just affecting me the wrong way tonight."

Sean winced as he caught my meaning.

"Go on home, man. Make friends with your toilet. I'll tell everyone your arse is on fire and you had to leave. They'll all understand, trust me."

"If I wasn't hurting so bad, I'd knock you out."

Sean laughed and patted me on the back, hard. "Lucky me then."

"Aye," I grumbled as he wished me well and trotted over to his beautiful soon-to-be bride. "Lucky you."

I turned and waded through the group of familiar faces. I grew up in Tallaght Village, so there wasn't a face I didn't know, or a name I didn't recognise. Right now I hated it more than anything, because multiple people tried to stop me for a quick chat or a picture along my way out of the pub, but I had to turn them all down.

I heard a familiar laugh from somewhere to my left, and when my eyes caught hers I narrowed them. Neala was perched upon a stool at the bar. For a moment I found myself staring at her legs, but I shook myself out of it and growled in her direction. She was looking right at me and she was smirking.

She had done this to me.

I didn't know how I knew she was responsible for my sudden pain and desperate need for a toilet, but I just knew it was all because of her.

I froze like a statue and widened my eyes in horror as she got up from the stool, turned away, and got lost in the crowd. I swallowed down the bile that rose in my throat, and forced myself to push on through my friends and my family's friends until I was outside in the freezing cold.

Did she know I took the doll or was this just her getting me back for the antics in Smyths the other day?

I didn't know, and it freaked me out.

I forced all thoughts of Neala aside as I slipped and slid down the pathway on my way to the car park. The crippling pain in my stomach was so bad that at one point I considered crawling along the path.

What the hell was happening to me?

I was breathless and sweating like a pig by the time I got to the car park and found my Jeep. I fumbled with my car keys as I pulled them from my pocket, but I managed to open my car door and climb inside.

"Home," I whimpered. "I need to get home."

Be a man.

I sucked in a huge amount of oxygen, then forced my eyes to stay open as I drove along the slippery back roads that led up to my cherished house. I loved nature, which is exactly why I had my house in the middle of it. I loved the calm that came with nature and the space surrounding it, but right now I didn't care for any of it.

Holy Mary, mother of God.

I had never felt a pain like the one that had taken up residence in my stomach. It was so bad I wouldn't wish it on my worst enemy. That's right – I wouldn't even wish this upon Neala, and she was *malicious.*

"Please, God, help me!" I whimpered as another cramp crippled my abdomen.

This wasn't happening to me.

I pressed down on the accelerator and prayed to God above that I wouldn't crash, get stuck, or slide dangerously along the road. I prayed for my safety, and for a toilet.

God, I needed a toilet badly.

The journey was ten minutes too long, and it was dangerous. A few times I lost control of my car on the slippery road, but I managed to make it up to my house in one piece. When I was in my driveway, I shut off my Jeep and opened the door. I fell out and dragged myself through the snow and over to my porch.

I growled deep in my throat as stabbing pains attacked my rear.

"No! Christ, no!"

I fumbled with the keys in my hands and I opened my front door.

"It's coming! It's coming!" I yelped, and shouldered my door open when the key finally turned in the lock.

I stumbled down my hallway in the dark and opened the bathroom door just as it happened. I let out a whimper when the realisation – and smell – hit me.

I'd shit myself.

I'd literally shit myself.

I was going to bloody *kill* Neala Clarke when I got my hands on her.

CHAPTER TEN

I couldn't believe what I had resorted to in order to get to Darcy's house. All to get the doll back on what had to be the coldest day in the entire history of Ireland.

Freezing my arse off on my mission wasn't enough, though. To make matters worse, I'd had to pay some bratty kid fifty Euros to 'take a lend' of his mountain bike! The little shite had made sure to let me know his mother knew my mother, and would tell her I'd hit him and stolen his bike unless I got it back to him in the condition he gave it to me in. The stupid bike wasn't even worth fifty Euros; he'd practically hustled me.

"Bloody kid!" I growled as I pedalled uphill as hard and fast as I could.

No matter how hard or fast I pedalled, though, the wheels of the bike just spun in the slushy snow. I wanted to scream and cry. My legs were on fire, my lungs were seconds away from collapsing, and I couldn't feel my body. No really, I couldn't feel it. I was numb all over. The below-freezing temperature and stupid snow made sure of that. I'd thought about nothing else but this plan over and over since I'd found out about the engagement party two days ago. I'd plotted everything out . . . except my stupid attire!

I was in a blue dress, black blazer, and black heels.

That was it.

There was a picture of my face next to the definition of stupid on the Internet, I was sure of it.

"Stupid, stupid, stupid!" I screamed in anguish.

I was tired and cold, and just wanted to get the doll back from Darcy, but I was still several hundred metres away from his house. As I neared it, I looked up and noticed it was still in darkness, but his garden and some of the surrounding area was well lit.

Darcy had surprisingly great street lighting for being up in the mountains, where the back roads were usually dark and dangerous. The road up on this side of the mountain was still dangerous, but not dark, which was probably the only stroke of luck I'd had all evening.

Well, the second stroke, if I'm being honest. The first stroke of luck by far had been when Darcy had drunk both the whiskeys I'd spiked with the laxative. That had gone off without a hitch. It really was a thing of beauty watching him accept the tainted drinks from his mother, then swallow the very thing that would make him lose the doll to me.

The thought that I would soon have the doll comforted me somewhat. It did nothing for my freezing body and tired limbs, but it helped put my mind at ease, at least.

I tried once more to pedal the stupid bike, but when the wheels spun endlessly in the snow I gave up. I put my foot down and lifted my other leg over the bike, but I lost my balance and fell backwards. I screamed, then groaned in pain when my arse hit the hard, cold ground under the blanket of snow. The pain from the impact sent shockwaves up and down my body, and because I was ice cold it hurt that much more.

I fought back tears as I struggled to my feet. I wanted to give up, but I could do nothing except stick to my plan and walk in the direction of Darcy's house. I couldn't turn away now. I still didn't have the doll, and that was my reason for being here.

I abandoned the kid's bike, and decided I'd deal with that headache at a later time.

Ten minutes of careful, slow-paced walking later, I reached Darcy's front garden. I noticed Darcy's car in the driveway, but dismissed the vehicle when I guessed that he walked down to the pub, or got a lift there.

I silently thanked God I'd made it, because just as I stepped foot into the garden, it started to snow again.

"Stupid bleeding weather!" I snapped, then flung my hands over my mouth.

Shite.

I had to keep quiet.

Darcy might not be home, but I didn't want to draw attention to myself.

I carefully walked over to Darcy's porch and tiptoed up onto the decking. I gently tested the front door handle and found it to be locked. My heart sank a little, but I didn't let it completely dishearten me. I knew the chances of my having to literally break into his house were high, but I had been kind of hoping a door would be unlocked.

I shook away the disappointment, walked down from the porch, and made my way around to the side of the house. I tested the first window I came up against and found it to be locked tight.

Crap.

I pressed on through the snow, and found myself gasping for breath as it became increasingly difficult to walk through. I was so cold that I couldn't feel anything, so for a moment I thought maybe walking through the snow was hard because my legs were starting to give out. But I quickly realised why walking was suddenly harder: it was snowing even more heavily. Each flake was large and thick and made my task even more energy consuming.

"G-give m-me a b-break!" I said to Mother Nature, in the vain hope that she was listening.

A large gust of wind hit me seconds later, and I took it as her telling me to feck off.

What a bitch.

I hiked through the snow in my five-inch heels, and just when I was at the back of Darcy's house and almost safe on his back decking, I tripped and fell. I think I screamed, but I wasn't sure. I had to quickly use my hands to push my body up so I could lift my head out of the snow, because I couldn't breathe.

"Th-this w-was a b-bad b-bloody id-dea," I said to myself as my body began to shake violently.

I stomped my way out of the snow and across the deck, and then walked as carefully as I could to his back door. I closed my eyes and prayed to God that the door would be unlocked. I opened my eyes and lifted my hand to the door handle and slowly pulled it down.

Click.

"Oh, m-m-my G-god," I whispered through chattering teeth when the lock clicked and the door opened.

I was in. I had made it successfully into Darcy's house all on my own.

Yes!

I tried to control my breathing, because it had sped up dramatically in the last twenty seconds. I was scared, and now that I was inside I had to find the doll and not get caught. It was mission impossible in my current state. I was shaking from the cold weather, and I couldn't feel my body.

I gently closed the kitchen door, then reached down and pried my high heels off and left them by the back door. Darcy's kitchen wasn't dark, but it wasn't bright either. The light on the fan above his stove was switched on, so it meant the room was somewhat lit.

I looked around the kitchen and nodded in approval. A high-gloss cream kitchen with black granite countertops.

Nice choice, Darcy.

Co-owning Clarke & Hart Construction had clearly paid off for him.

I didn't know why, but I searched the entire kitchen for the doll. I had to check everywhere just in case Darcy had put it somewhere that most people wouldn't think to look. I wouldn't leave his house without the bloody doll, so I'd make sure to check every cupboard, drawer, and wardrobe. Luckily, all the movement I was doing caused my shaking to ease, and it even gave me some feeling back in my body. Thank God.

I glanced to the door at the end of Darcy's kitchen; it wasn't a nice door that had glass in the frame like the other door in the room, so I guessed it had to be some sort of storage room. I tiptoed towards it, but a hiss from my right halted my steps.

What the heck was that?

The area of the kitchen where I was looking was darker than the rest of the room, so naturally I stepped forward to see what the hissing was. I squinted my eyes at a dark blanket that was thrown over some sort of box that sat on a stand high up in the air. Everything in me told me not to pull on the cover to see what was under it, so I turned and walked to the wooden door and opened it.

I was right; it was a small storage room.

I reached inside the dark room, placed my palm flat on the cold wall, and moved my hand around in search of a light switch, but decided against it in case Darcy came home earlier than expected and saw the light. Just as I dropped my hand, the low hissing came from behind me again. I jumped with fright and spun around.

"What *is* that?" I whispered.

I stepped closer to the dark cover and carefully reached out with my hand. I hesitated when I touched the cover, but without a second's thought I pulled it and gasped when something began flapping about in a cage.

It made a noise that instantly identified the creature as a bird.

A memory hit me then of Sean telling my mother that Darcy had bought an African grey parrot. The parrot continued to hiss at me and it freaked me out. I didn't know birds could bloody make noises like that.

"Shhh," I whispered. "Be quiet."

"Shut up," the bird said, then made the creepy noise again.

I froze to the spot and stared at the bird.

Was I losing my mind or did that bird just say what I think it did?

"What did you just say?" I asked.

"Water . . . You want some waterrr, baby girl?" the bird chirped.

I narrowed my eyes. "That's not what you said before."

"Nealaaaaa."

I stood rooted to the spot, and blinked.

The bird said my name.

"How do you know me name?" I asked, even more freaked out.

"Fuck off, Neala!"

What the hell?

"Be quiet!" I hissed and pointed my finger at the bird.

The bird hissed back. "Darcy, Darcy, Darcy."

Oh, my God.

The bird was ratting me out.

"Shhh, you little bollocks!" I snapped, and thumped the cage.

It was a bad idea, because the bird went fucking crazy and squawked like it was being murdered.

"I'm sorry," I pleaded in a whisper, "Please be—"

I froze midsentence when the light in the kitchen was suddenly flicked on.

"What are you doing, Clarke?"

Oh Christ.

I screamed with fright and stumbled backwards until I tripped and fell flat on my arse into the storage room. I groaned as I looked up, and widened my eyes when Darcy's half-naked body came into view.

"You know I heard you coming up the driveway, right? I unlocked the back door so you wouldn't freeze to death."

I couldn't believe it.

What the hell was he doing here?

Darcy grinned. "Don't look so surprised; you weren't exactly quiet, Neala."

I shook my head and opened my mouth to speak, but nothing came out.

Darcy chuckled. "Cat got your tongue? I'm sure an hour or two in here will change your mind."

What?

"What are you— Darcy!"

He closed the door of the storage room and turned the lock.

"Use this time to think about what you've done."

"Darcy!" I screamed. "Let me out or I'll fucking kill you!"

"Goodnight, Neala." Darcy laughed.

He left. The bastard left me locked in his kitchen storage room. I was going to kick his arse when I got out of here.

CHAPTER ELEVEN

D ARCY! LET! ME! OUT!"
I opened my eyes and smiled.

"Music, sweet music." I beamed.

I heard Neala scream in anger as she began to beat on the storage room door for the tenth time in the last few hours. I was originally just going to play a trick on her and leave her in the storage room for only a few minutes, but she cursed and banged on the door for a solid thirty minutes, and to be honest, I wasn't opening the door while she was in that state. She would have just attacked me.

I did eventually open the door when she stopped banging and screaming, an hour after I'd put her in there, and I found her rolled up on the storage room floor lying on multiple tea towels, snoring like an old man. I didn't want to move her for the simple reason that my hourly trips to the bathroom were her fault – I had no proof, but I knew she had given me diarrhoea – and I wanted her to suffer a little. I didn't want her to get sick, though – I wasn't as heartless as she was – so I got my spare duvet cover and some pillows and put them in the room with her during the night.

She didn't move a muscle while I tucked her in, probably because she was exhausted from hiking up to my house in below-freezing weather wearing only a dress, blazer, and high heels while it was snowing. The girl wasn't the brightest crayon in the box.

"Darcy!" Neala bellowed once more from my kitchen.

I sighed and got up from my bed. I stretched, then put on a pair of comfy trousers.

I shook my head just thinking about last night. After shitting myself I'd spent thirty minutes cleaning up my bathroom, and bagging my soiled clothes and cleaning rags.

I threw them out into my bin out back, and that was when I heard the little criminal cursing up a storm in my driveway. She was wearing the wrong clothes to break into someone's house when it was snowing outside, and she was so loud I could hear her from the back of my house.

Stealth definitely wasn't her forte.

I couldn't call her too much of an idiot, though; she *had* managed to pull one over on me and make me shit myself. I don't think my pride will ever recover from *that* moment that she caused.

My stomach had only settled around five o'clock this morning. Unfortunately my arsehole still felt like it was in the fiery pits of Mount Doom, except I didn't have to trek to Mordor.

Oh, and if having crippling stomach pain and a flaming arsehole wasn't enough, my nose suffered terribly with the smell that had taken up residence in my bathroom.

I had gone through *two* bottles of bleach and a whole can of air freshener, and the smell of death *still* lingered in the room. I'd closed the bathroom door and had to leave the built-in ceiling fan on all night as an added method to air the room out. The smell might never leave, though – I wouldn't be surprised if it moulded onto every surface at the molecular level.

I'm sure that's what Neala wanted in the first place.

"The vile specimen," I muttered as I exited my bedroom and walked down the hallway to my kitchen and Neala's temporary prison.

I opened the kitchen door and winced when the love of my life made a whimpering sound.

"Baby girl, what's wrong?" I asked, and rushed over to my African grey parrot.

She was my baby – she was seven years old and the boss of my house.

"Darcy, is that you? Open the door and let me out; the bird is driving me bleeding mad!"

I ignored Neala, opened the birdcage, and stroked my baby's chest when she climbed onto my hand.

"What's wrong with you, Einstein?" I asked.

I heard a frustrated wail come from the storage room.

"I *told* you, I want you to—"

"I wasn't talking to you, Neala. I was talking to me bird." I cut Neala off as I continued to stroke Einstein's chest.

Neala was silent for a moment; then she laughed.

"You called your parrot *Einstein*? Why?"

I opened my mouth to speak, but Einstein cut me off.

"Shut up, Neala."

I beamed and scratched my Einstein's head. I glanced at the storage room door, then laughed. Neala had gone silent in her makeshift prison.

"I named her Einstein because she is *very* smart, as you can tell." More silence.

I smiled smugly. "What's the matter, Neala? Why are you quiet all of a sudden?"

I could practically feel her mind turning as she thought.

"You taught your bird to tell me to shut up?" she asked, low.

I taught her much more than that.

I simply laughed and said, "Yeah."

"Why?"

I shrugged even though she couldn't see me.

"I thought it would be funny for Einstein to tell you off if you ever came up here, and I was right. It's hilarious. This prank was set in motion years ago."

Neala banged on the door in outrage.

"You're a class A arsehole!"

I couldn't disagree with that statement.

"Waterrr . . . apple."

I looked down to Einstein and lifted my hand up so she could get on top of her cage and nibble on the fruit that I'd put onto different sections of her cage yesterday. She had access to her water bottle there, too.

I turned away from Einstein and walked over to the storage room, where I paused as I reached for the door handle.

"Promise you won't attack me if I open the door."

Neala laughed.

"That doesn't give me any reason to let you out, Neala."

She quieted down and muttered, "Okay, I won't hit you."

She didn't sound the least bit truthful.

"Try again, and this time make me believe you."

I could feel Neala's hate for me radiate through the storage room door, and it only caused me to grin. The next while after she was free from the storage room would be interesting, that was for damn sure.

"Darcy," Neala started, "please let me out of this storage room. I promise *not* to attack you if you do."

It was forced, but possibly honest.

"Okay, good enough."

I leaned forward, turned the lock on the door and pressed down on the handle. I had every intention of apologising for keeping her in the storage room and explaining why I had done what I did, but suddenly all of my thoughts went out the window, and I jumped back like I had been burned when the door was kicked open and a disoriented and wild Neala emerged.

She squinted at the light in the room and lifted her hands to shield her eyes from the beams. She lowered them only after she blinked a few times and allowed her eyes to adjust. When her vision was clear, she quickly glanced around the room. The moment her eyes landed on me I tensed. Her eyes were narrowed and her teeth were now bared. She gripped a tea towel that was in her hand and hissed at me.

Fuck.

She was fuming mad.

"You promised!" I yelped, and stumbled backward.

Neala's eyes bored into mine as she rolled the tea towel in her hand as tightly as she could and snarled, "I lied."

Oh, shite.

"What are you going to do with the tea tow— Ow!"

I looked down to my leg and gritted my teeth. She'd whipped my thigh with the tea towel, and it bloody hurt!

A lot.

"You locked me in your storage room all night; you practically held me hostage!" Neala snarled, her eyes wild with rage.

I held my hands up in front of my chest and slowly started to back away from her and toward my escape – the kitchen door.

"You broke into me house, *and* you gave me the runs – that out-does anything I've done to you in the last twelve hours!" I snapped right back.

Neala hesitated in advancing on me; she folded her arms across her chest and grinned impishly. "I *knew* you would take those drinks from your ma and down them. It was a beautiful thing to watch, really."

Holy crap.

The deception hit me like a freight train.

"You drafted me *mother* onto your side?" I accused.

How bloody dared she co-opt my unknowing mother into her villainous scheme? That woman had *birthed* me!

"No, not necessarily." Neala smirked, her face a mask of wickedness. "I paid one of the bartenders to give us the wrong drinks; I only *suggested* to your ma that you liked whiskey and would be glad of *both* of them. It was a piece of cake. Your ma didn't want them to go to waste, and since I knew none of the women at the table would drink them I knew she would do as I suggested and bring the drinks to you."

I narrowed my eyes at the she-devil. "I cannot believe you. I can understand using my mother as a pawn in your satanic plan if it was for something less than this, but you upped the ante this time around. You all but twisted my insides, Neala. I've *never* messed with your body. What you did to me is just deplorable."

I blinked my eyes when Neala threw the tea towel at my face and screeched, "Liar! You gave me food poisoning at Sean's twentieth birthday party. I was bed bound and puking for days!"

I winced.

I had forgotten about that.

"I didn't do that on purpose, though; I really thought that chicken was in date. What you did to me was planned down to a tee, you vicious pig!"

I wished I'd used a different word instead of pig when Neala's face twisted in rage. I stepped away from her in case she decided to unleash her building fury upon me.

"You kept me hostage all night, had your parrot insult me all morning, and now you're calling me *fat?*"

Oh, Jesus.

I was going to die today.

I didn't answer Neala; nor did I try to explain that I wasn't calling her fat. Instead, I turned and ran out of the kitchen so fast I left a smoke trail behind me. I didn't care if it made me a coward, a bitch, or anything else. No one else knew how hard Neala could punch, and from the look in her rage-filled eyes, I knew she would aim for my balls if given the chance. I wasn't giving her that opportunity.

"Darcy!" she bellowed from behind me.

I could hear her feet smack against my tiled kitchen floor, and for a moment I wished she would slip and fall so she would be preoccupied and wouldn't come after me.

Was that mean?

"Shite!" I yelped when what could only be described as a semi–heavy-set monkey jumped on my back.

I instinctively reached up and grabbed Neala's arms when she tried to wrap them around my neck. I was ready for that move this time around.

Not today, Clarke. Not today!

"Are you crazy?" I snapped, and tried to wriggle her off my back, but she clung onto me for dear life.

I tried to wriggle her off some more, but when those efforts failed I grunted and staggered into my living room, where I tried to forward flip her off my back and onto my couch. When *that* didn't work I got annoyed and decided to play dirty. I let go of her arms, reached behind my back, and tickled her sides all the way down to her outer thighs. This was one hundred percent effective because Neala was ticklish, *extremely* ticklish.

"Bastard!" she screeched, and let go of me.

She fell backwards and landed on her back on my red oak floor with a mighty thud.

I winced as I turned around and looked down at her.

I placed my hands on my hips and sighed. "Are you okay, Neala Girl?"

Neala made a noise that wasn't exactly human, and it freaked me out. I was afraid to lean down in case she was faking and grabbed at me, so instead I reached out and nudged her with my foot to make sure she was still alive.

"Darcy," she growled through her pain. "Get your disgusting foot away from me right now."

I grinned inwardly at her threatening outburst.

She was fine.

"Still afraid of men's feet?" I asked, and raised my leg so I could wriggle my foot around in front of her face and annoy her further.

She screeched and pushed herself away from me.

"Not afraid, just repulsed," she spat.

I looked down at my foot, then back up to Neala's curled lip, and smirked.

She growled at me, "Don't even *think* about it."

I raised a curious eyebrow. "Think about what?"

"Whatever nasty thing is going through your tiny mind right now."

She never missed a chance to insult me.

I raised my hands in the air. "I'm not thinking about doing anything; therefore I'm not going to do anything . . . *You*, on the other hand, are."

Neala slowly got to her feet.

I swallowed as her dress rose a little higher up her thighs than it should have. I swallowed again and looked away when she gripped the hem and tugged it down.

"What am I going to do?" she asked, her voice strained as she shook away the pain from her fall.

I looked at her face and grinned. "You're going to get out of me house."

Neala stared at me with unblinking eyes. "What?"

"You are leaving me house. Right now, actually," I said, and reached up to scratch my head.

I ruffled my hair a little to help get rid of the just-out-of-bed look. Neala moved slowly as a zombie as she trained her gaze on me and followed my movements, staring at me a little longer than normal. She even bit down on her lower lip as she scanned her eyes over me in a leisurely matter.

Interesting.

"Neala," I called, and snapped my fingers to get her attention.

She jumped a little, then narrowed her eyes when she saw my smirk. She knew I'd caught her checking me out. I could also see the moment her expression turned to one of disgust at herself.

"Why are you in just a pair of trousers?" she snapped, and made a big show of looking away from my chest and stomach.

I laughed. "Maybe because your banging on the storage room door woke me up and didn't leave me time to pull on anything more?"

Neala scoffed, "Whatever. Just . . . just go put some more clothes on."

And miss her being this flustered?

Not a chance.

"Nah, I like wearing just these trousers. The fabric is thin and I like feeling the crisp morning air tickle me balls."

Neala reached down and grabbed a cushion from my couch and flung it at me.

I caught it and laughed loudly.

"Stop being a dick!"

"Never." I grinned.

Neala screeched in annoyance and left the living room. She didn't go in the direction of the kitchen, though; she took a right turn, which would lead her to my bedroom, dining room, or bathroom. And the bathroom was off limits for at least another two or three hours. Even though I'd cleaned up and the room was spotless – I wouldn't risk my lungs in that room just yet. It was under biohazard quarantine until further notice.

"Neala!" I called out, and quickly began to follow her. "Where are you going?"

"To the bathroom. I've been in your bleeding makeshift prison all night; I need to wee," Neala snapped.

Oh, my God.

"Uh, Neala, I wouldn't go in there if—"

"I'm not listening to your bullshit anymore, Darcy. Just tell me which door is for the bathroom and I *won't* murder you!" Neala snapped, her voice close to a growl.

I leaned against the living room doorway and eyed the she-devil.

Feck it, she didn't deserve my warning; what she deserved was to inhale a lungful of toxic gas, since she was the cause of the stench in the first place.

"The first door on the left, before you near the last door along the hallway," I said, smiling.

Neala didn't thank me; instead she turned, walked a few paces down the hall, and stood before the bathroom door. She opened it and stepped inside, slamming the door after her.

Three seconds passed before she screamed.

"DARCY!" she bellowed.

I burst into a fit of laughter. "That's what you get for giving me the shits – *smell* what you caused!"

She screamed and cursed for twenty solid seconds; then the toilet flushed and she all but sprinted out of the room, her fingers plugging her nose.

"That is fucking vile!" she hollered in my direction. "What the fuck? It smelt like something crawled up inside your arse and died!"

I continued to laugh as Neala stormed down the hallway by me and into the kitchen. I followed her and watched as she took off her blazer and threw it onto my kitchen table, then picked up the tea towel she had thrown at me a few minutes before. I grinned as she moved to the kitchen sink and scrubbed her hands and up her arms with water and hand wash. She washed her face with water and then soaked the tea towel in water and rubbed it under her arms, then leaned down and rubbed it up and down her legs.

I reached over and shut the door then so she could have some privacy and clean her lady parts. I shook my head as she continued to curse up a storm in the kitchen.

"I can't believe I've to freshen up in your kitchen with your pervy parrot looking at me vagina like it's a foreign object!"

I laughed out loud and shook my head.

She was brilliant.

After a few minutes passed by, Neala opened the kitchen door and glared at me with a plastic bag in her hand.

"What's in there?" I asked.

"The tea towel I used to clean myself, and me knickers," Neala snippily replied.

Her knickers were in that bag?

I swallowed as filthy thoughts surged through my mind.

"You're going commando?" I asked, shocked.

Neala continued to glare at me. "I could hardly leave me under-wear on; I wore them all day yesterday and all of last night . . . I need a fresh pair, but since I don't have any I have to go commando. Is that okay with you?" she snapped.

I shrugged. "I don't care what you do with your knickers," I replied, then cleared my suddenly dry throat.

"Good," Neala grumbled as she turned and walked over to the bin in the kitchen and thrust the plastic bag into it. I was silent as she did the task and turned back to face me.

She huffed as she walked out of the kitchen and passed by me to go down my hallway.

I sighed. "Where are you going *now?*"

"Where do you think? I'm going in search of the doll that *you* stole from me!"

Thank God, something to take my mind off her bloody knickers. Or *lack* of knickers.

"I was only taking back an item that belonged to me in the first place," I replied.

Neala froze just as she reached for the handle of my bedroom door. "What do you mean, 'belonged to you in the first place'?"

I shrugged my shoulders. "I own the doll."

Neala looked like she'd swallowed something sour – her face scrunched up and her mouth dropped open. She lifted her hands to her temples and massaged them.

I was hurting her head.

Good.

"I don't even know what to say to that."

I snickered. "I'm not going crazy. I really *do* own the doll. You used my debit card to pay for it. I have yours inside me bedside locker."

Neala blinked her wary eyes at me, then narrowed them to slits.

"Show me!" she snapped.

I gestured for her to open the door she stood facing, and with a glare my way she stepped inside. I walked right by her and headed straight to my bedside locker. Opening the top drawer, I took out Neala's debit card, then turned and extended it to her.

Neala stared at me for a moment, then hesitantly stepped forward and snatched the card from my hand. She looked at the name and number on the card, then flipped it over to the back where her signature was. She flipped the card back and forth a few times, as if to make sure it was real and not a fake.

When she looked at me I saw hate and anger in her eyes, but that was a normal thing.

"I'm not lying to you," I said, just to clarify I wasn't messing around.

She swallowed. "I don't care. So you technically own the doll – big deal. I asked the lad in the shop for it first. He went and got it for me and then *you* took it away."

I blinked when Neala sniffled. She quickly wiped under her nose and brushed her hand over her eyes, but it wasn't quick enough. I caught the light build-up of water that gathered in the corners before she brushed away the evidence. I felt like I was suddenly going to walk over to her and do something crazy like *hug* her, so I had to take a step back.

I felt . . . bad, and I didn't know what to do about it.

I had never felt bad over Neala, but seeing her genuinely confused and upset did nothing except make my chest hurt and my stomach feel sick.

What the hell was that about?

"Neala Girl—"

"*Stop* calling me that, Darcy." She cut me off and wiped at her eyes again.

I frowned. "I can't. It's your name."

Neala shook her head. "It hasn't been me name for a long time."

I smiled lightly. "Of course it has. It always will be. You're my Neala Girl, after all."

Neala widened her eyes, and so did I.

I hadn't meant to say that out loud.

Or at all.

"I don't mean *my* Neala Girl. I just meant that you will always be known as Neala Girl to me. That's all."

Neala raised an eyebrow, and I could tell she wanted to say something but she didn't.

Not a single word, which wasn't like the big mouth at all.

Silence filled the room, and I momentarily wished she would shout or curse at me, just to take the sudden awkwardness away, but she didn't; she just stared at me.

"You aren't getting the doll, *Neala*," I said firmly.

It was the only thing I could think to say that would put some fight back into her and make her stop looking at me like I was an alien from outer space. It would also kick the silence and sudden awkwardness out of the room.

As predicted, the statement worked like a charm.

Neala's left eye twitched. "I'm leaving here with that doll whether you like it or not, Darcy."

Was that so?

I snorted. "Good luck finding it."

I walked out of my bedroom and headed back into my living room, where I sat down on my couch and placed my hands behind my head. I heard Neala mutter curse words as she searched for the doll, and it made me smile, because all she would find in my room was clean clothes, dirty clothes, condoms, and possibly even a used condom if she looked in the rubbish bin.

"You dirty bastard! Ever heard of emptying your bin every so often?" Neala screeched.

I smiled broadly.

"I swear, Darcy, you're a dog!"

Ruff, ruff.

I sighed as I relaxed into my couch. I glanced around the room and noticed how shit the Christmas decorations looked. I had my tree up, but the ornaments to go on the branches were in a box on the floor next to the base of the tree. The light-up Santas, snowmen, and other Christmas characters were all over in a corner of the room. I'd bought them because they were battery operated, which meant no wires and no high electric bills, but I was too lazy to even sort them around in various places in the room. I liked Christmas – it was my favourite holiday – but decorating everything was not my scene at all.

I guess you could say I was a lazy bastard.

I sighed to myself, closed my eyes, and chuckled lightly when Neala stomped out of my bedroom and went down the hallway and into the kitchen.

"Darcy!" Einstein squawked.

"Shut up, you stupid animal."

I opened my mouth to tell Neala to leave Einstein alone, but it turned out my bird could hold her own.

"Fuck you, Neala."

I burst out laughing.

"I *hate* this bloody bird!" Neala screeched.

I loved that bird.

I had a big smile on my face when Neala stormed back into the living room. She stood in the doorway with her hands on her hips.

"Tell her to shut up!"

I chuckled. "I can't. She doesn't know what the words mean. She is only repeating things she has memorised, that's all."

"*That's all?* You taught a parrot to tell me to fuck off!"

I burst out laughing, "Yeah, I know."

Neala scowled at me. "You're unreal; do you know that? I thought you couldn't surprise me anymore with your stupid pranks, but yet again you've proved me wrong."

Yeah, the way she was looking from my eyes to my stomach showed how much she couldn't stand me.

"Then leave. The door is right there. I don't want you here anyway."

Neala snorted. "I don't wanna be here either, *sweetheart*. As soon as I find the doll I'll be on my merry way and you can get back to semi-naked Saturdays with your parrot."

Oh, feisty.

"I can get fully naked right now if you want a more full-on naked Saturday?"

"Spare me," Neala said with her hand held up. "I don't want the sight of your bare body to make me sicker than I already am."

My body made her sick?

"Oh, is that what that look on your face is?" I mused.

Neala straightened. "What look?"

"You keep staring at me stomach, me trousers, and me chest. I must be *very* repulsive for you to keep looking at me the way you do," I said sarcastically.

Neala swallowed. "I wasn't looking—"

"It's not nice to lie, Neala Girl. You of all people should know that."

The jab about lying brought me right back to when we were kids. Anytime I pulled a prank on Neala and got caught, I would make up a lie and blame it on her, and ever since those times she had hated liars and lying in general. I always enjoyed pointing out when she was lying, or trying to lie.

The look on her face was priceless.

Neala closed her mouth, blew a large amount of air out through her nostrils, and shook with anger as she glared at me. "I'm not lying, and *stop* calling me that!"

Never.

I grinned. "Weren't you leaving?"

Neala snarled, "I will *after* I find the doll."

I winked. "Good hunting."

It was just after two in the afternoon when Neala started what would turn out to be a two-hour hunt in the house in search of the Fire Princess doll. We had woken up very late, but I usually slept to the afternoon after I had had a few drinks.

After an hour or so of listening to her complain and curse me, I went into the kitchen and made some breakfast. I asked Neala if she wanted me to make her some food, but she just told me to fuck off, so I did just that and had my own meal. She eventually came into the kitchen when she was hungry, though; she stopped long enough to have some cereal, but it was only a mini break she was taking, she said, and then she would get back to her search – her words, not mine.

After breakfast I was stuffed and felt drowsy. A large meal always made me sleepy, but I was mainly tired from not getting much sleep during the night, so when I went back into my living room and settled down on my couch I closed my eyes and dozed off within seconds.

I opened them when I heard a loud bang, then Einstein's squawks. I sat upright and rubbed the sleep out of my eyes. I wasn't sure how long I'd slept, so I glanced to the clock on my living room wall and shook my head. It was after half six in the evening.

Was sleeping for three hours considered a nap, or a coma?

I wanted to go back asleep, but Neala's cursing in annoyance and shouting at Einstein kept me up. I didn't stand up from the couch, though; I was comfortable, and when the house fell into silence again I closed my eyes. Moments later, I snapped them open once more when I heard Neala gasp, then squeal in delight.

She had the doll.

I don't know how I knew she had it; I just did.

How the fuck had she found it? I didn't have it out in the open like she did at her house – it was tucked away in my goddamn attic, for crying out loud.

Wait.

"Are you up in the bleeding attic?" I shouted.

Silence.

Neala was dangerous when she made noise, but she was lethal when she was silent.

I stood up from my couch and slowly walked over toward the sitting room. When I reached the doorway, I was about to call out Neala's name when she suddenly sprinted by me with a pink box tucked under her arm. She was running for my front door. Her escape was in motion, but I wouldn't let her get away.

Not on my watch.

I ran after Neala and collided into the back of her just as she opened the front door. I grunted as she fell back and took us both to the ground. She wasn't a big girl, but she wasn't as light as a feather either, so when her weight slammed down onto my stomach, I dry-heaved with the force of it.

I moved Neala off me and groaned in pain. I hissed as I felt an ice-cold ache stab my bare feet. I pushed myself back away from my front door and looked up to see what cold and painful thing was touching me. What I saw caused me to widen my eyes and stare in horror.

"Jesus, Darcy! You didn't have to jump on me— Omigod!"

Yeah. Omigod.

"Darcy, what is that?" Neala whispered.

I stared at the six-foot-tall wall of thick snow in front of me and licked my lips.

I blinked, then swallowed. "It looks like snow, Neala Girl."

Neala gasped. "Does . . . does this mean what I think it means?"

I groaned as a slight pulsing pain formed in the base of my head.

"Yeah, Sherlock, it does." I sighed and looked at my unwelcome houseguest. "We're snowed in."

CHAPTER TWELVE

No. No. Bloody. Way.

I was *not* snowed in with Darcy *inside* his house.

I was *not* trapped here alone with him.

Just . . . *no!*

I scrambled back away from Darcy and the wall of snow and pushed myself to my feet. I turned and ran down the hall and into the sitting room. Rushing to the window, I opened up the blinds and gasped.

The snow was built up and completely covered the glass. If the living room lights hadn't been on the room would be shrouded in darkness. I'd noticed it was unusually dark even with the lights on inside, but it never occurred to me that it was because snow was blocking out the sunlight.

"What are you doing?" I heard Darcy ask from behind me.

Trying to find a way out of here.

"The window is blocked too," I said, and turned to face him.

I looked to his hands and growled.

He had the doll box.

"Give that to me," I said.

Darcy rolled his eyes, leaned over, and put the doll box on a table next to a lamp. I was momentarily confused; he had sort of complied with me, but why? I found my answer when I looked at his face and found his eyes almost popping out of his head.

He was about to lose it.

"We can't be trapped in here. No way . . . Check all the windows and doors. There *has* to be a way out of here!"

I blinked as he took off running down the hall in the direction of the kitchen, then jumped when I heard him spew out a number of foul curse words. I guessed the kitchen door and windows were blocked with snow, too.

I picked up the doll box and hid it behind the couch; then I walked out of the living room and headed down to the dining room. I frowned when I realized I didn't even have to go to the window to know it was blocked by snow as well. The blinds were open, and the snow was pressed against the glass plain as day.

I stared at the glass as my stomach churned.

This could *not* be happening.

"Please, Jesus, don't do this to me!" Darcy shouted from the kitchen. "Trap me with anyone else but her, *please!*"

I rolled my eyes.

He was such a dickhead.

I walked out of the dining room and down the hall back into the living room at the same time as Darcy.

"What have I done to deserve this?" he asked me as I sat down on his couch.

I blinked. "You were born."

"I didn't ask to be born," he hissed. "I had no say in the matter!"

I couldn't help it; I laughed.

"You're laughing?" Darcy snapped. "You think us being snowed in together is *funny?*"

I continued to laugh as I shook my head and said, "No, but if I don't laugh, I'll scream or cry . . . Is that what you want?"

Einstein shouted from the kitchen, "Fuck off, Neala!"

I glared at Darcy.

He winced. "No, I don't want you to scream or cry. Panicking is the last thing we need to do."

I nodded. "Exactly. So sit down and shut up. We'll think better in silence."

Surprisingly, Darcy did as he was told and sat down on the other end of the couch.

I looked at him, and quickly looked away. "Darcy, put some clothes on . . . You'll get sick."

It sounded like I cared about his well-being, but I didn't. I just didn't want to stare at his body any longer, because he was surprisingly very well built and I was definitely noticing.

Who knew Darcy had a six-pack . . . and obliques?

Darcy looked down at his body then back up to me. "Did you just say something about me obliques?"

Did I say that out loud?

"No," I said sheepishly. "I didn't even notice you had one."

I felt Darcy's smirk as I spoke the white lie, and it irked me. But what got on my nerves even more at that very moment was both that I'd been caught and that I had looked in the first place.

"I don't know why you're smirking, but knock it off."

Darcy adjusted himself on the couch so he was now turned to face me. "Nah, let's talk about you liking me incredibly ripped body."

Oh, here we go.

"Let's not," I said, then snickered. "I wouldn't say you're ripped either."

"I thought you didn't check me body out?" Darcy questioned.

"I didn't."

"Then how do you know if I'm ripped or not?" Darcy asked, sporting a shit-eating grin.

Well . . . crap.

"Shut up, Darcy," I muttered.

Darcy cackled. "Not a snowball's chance in Hell, Neala Girl. I don't get the opportunity to tease you over liking me body every day, so I'm going to enjoy this."

I scowled. "You're a real moron, you know that?"

I looked at Darcy and became infuriated when I noticed he was nodding.

"I hate when you do that," I hissed.

Darcy grinned. "Do what?"

"Agree with me when I'm trying to insult you."

He snickered. "Not an insult if it's true, but yeah, I mostly agree, because you get this look on your face like you're going to bite me or something."

I snorted. "And you think that's funny? Poking the lioness when she's angry?"

Darcy winked. "I'm sure if you came at me I could handle you."

Oh, really?

"In the last week I've come at you twice, and I recall I've done well *both* times."

"Yeah, but both times my back was turned, so that doesn't count," he said, keeping direct eye contact with me.

He was enticing me to come at him now that we were facing each other, and I could tell he was trying to make me uncomfortable, so I decided to flip the situation on him.

I batted my eyelashes. "Darcy, are you flirting with me?"

He blinked, then swallowed and shook his head, indicating he wasn't.

I leaned in closer. "Sounds to me like you are . . . Do you want me to come at you now while we're facing one another? It might be a bit dangerous, though; you have so little clothing on, after all . . . What if I *scratch* you? The thin fabric on those trousers of yours won't protect you."

Darcy's jaw dropped open, and I couldn't contain the belly-rumbling laugh that escaped my mouth.

"Gotcha."

Darcy scowled. "Don't do that; I really thought you were about to try something with me."

I cackled. "Darcy, you're the last man on Earth I would ever have sex with."

That wasn't a *complete* lie.

I'd have sex with Darcy if his mouth was sewed shut.

Darcy reared back at my jab like I'd slapped him.

"Yeah? Well, that's a shame. I know no lad in the village has touched second base with you, let alone pulled off a home run, so if not me, who would you lose your virginity to?"

It was my turn to pull back and stare at him.

He did *not* just say that.

"I'm not a virgin, Darcy."

I wanted to kick myself, because for someone who hated lying so much I seemed to be doing plenty of it, but this time it was to hide something personal, so it didn't mean anything. I mean, I *was* a virgin, but how the hell did Darcy know that?

Do I have it stamped on my forehead or something?

"Yes, you are," Darcy argued.

What the hell?

"Explain to me how you came to that conclusion. I've apparently got nothing but time here with you, so go ahead," I said, and made a big deal out of getting comfortable.

I probably looked at ease, but what Darcy couldn't see was that my heartbeat had become erratic. My palms were sweaty, and my breathing was uneven.

I didn't know how he knew something so personal about me, and I hated that I'd asked, because deep down I didn't want to know, but at the same time I did.

Darcy looked at me, *really* looked at me, and shook his head. "Never mind."

He went to stand up, but I grabbed his wrist and held him put. "No, tell me."

Darcy again shook his head. "Drop it, Neala."

There was no trace of a smile on his face.

"No. Tell me."

He growled, "You don't want me to, trust me."

What did that mean?

"Darcy, will you just *tell me*?"

He shook off my hold on him, and dropped his head to look at the ground. "Fine," he grunted. "Do you remember when we were sixteen, and Laura Stoke had her eighteenth birthday party down in O'Leary's pub, but it went on to the early hours and we all went back to her house?"

I swallowed. I *did* remember that party. Laura Stoke was, and still is, Darcy's fuck buddy or secret girlfriend. I still didn't know why I had gone to the party, or why I was even invited. It was no secret Laura and I didn't like one another, but I had gone anyway just to say I went to a party. But the party had turned out to be different than I'd thought it would be.

Very different.

I would never forget that night, but I did a damn good job of trying to.

"Yeah, I remember. What about it?" I muttered.

Darcy swallowed, then said, "It was around two in the morning, and Sean asked me to go check on you. You told him you were going to the bathroom before we took you home, but you were taking your time. He figured you were somewhere with Jess and Sarah drinking and shite like that."

I sat in silence as he spoke.

He laughed lightly. "I thought you were off somewhere in the house and that you just didn't want to be near me. But to appease your brother I went upstairs to check on you, and I heard you inside the bathroom . . . I heard him too."

I froze in my seat.

"W-what?" I whispered.

"I know, Neala," he replied, his voice barely audible.

Oh, my God.

He knew?

That was the worst night of my life, my only secret, and Darcy *knew* about it?

"I heard you laughing, then slurring so I knew you had somehow got some drinks into you," Darcy said, then balled his hands into fists. "I heard Trevor Nash, the fucking wanker, telling you to give him head, and then I heard you comply. You said okay. I wanted to stop you, but I knew it was your mistake to make, and if I intervened you would have just hated me even more than you already did."

He sat back then and leaned his head against the couch.

"I don't know why I stayed outside the door; something in me gut told me to, so I did. It was lucky I did, because when Trevor told you to pull up your skirt and you said no, I heard the noise of the slap he gave you. I didn't hesitate; I kicked the door open, and the sight of you on the ground with Trevor standing over you undoing his jeans enraged me. As you can expect, I punched the shite out of the prick." Darcy kept his eyes averted as he spoke.

My throat closed up at the admission. I stared at Darcy blankly, blinking.

He had saved me?

I wanted to cry, hug him, thank him . . . but I couldn't move. I felt frozen.

"I only stopped hitting him when I heard you starting to cry. I picked you up, and when I tried to bring you downstairs you begged me not to, because you didn't want Sean to know what had happened. You were pretty out of it, so I had no clue if you knew it was me you were talking to. It was weird. You asked me not to tell anyone because everyone would think you were a slut for giving Trevor head even though you were really a virgin."

I blinked back hot tears when Darcy turned his head to the side and looked at me. He didn't look through me like he usually did; he looked at me and saw me.

"So I didn't tell anyone, and to this day I haven't. I brought you down the hall and sat down with you until you fell asleep. Trevor stumbled out of the bathroom and out of the house without anyone noticing during your slumber. You woke up about thirty minutes later, and instead of being upset, you shouted at me for being so close to you. You remembered what Trevor did, I could tell by the look on your face, but you didn't remember any of what I did. I didn't know if it had anything to do with what you drank or if your mind had blocked it out, but you had no idea what I did for you. It didn't matter that I didn't tell anyone what he was about to do to you either, because karma got him back later that night."

The karma he was referring to was the accident Trevor had got into after he stole a car with two of his friends after he left the party. A drunken Trevor had crashed the car – he was driving at such a speed down the mountain that he'd wrapped the vehicle around a tree. Literally. The crash instantly killed all three of them. I couldn't say I'd been sad to hear it either.

I felt for Trevor's family, and the families of his friends, but that was it.

I remembered the look on his face when I'd told him no, and I remember knowing that he was going to try to force me to do what he wanted me to do. If he'd got the chance, he would have raped me that night.

But he didn't, and now I knew why.

Darcy had stopped him.

"Darcy . . . I—"

"Don't. Don't thank me for something anyone would have stepped in to stop."

I swallowed the lump that still sat in my throat. "You stopped him from *raping* me. I don't think you realise the years of hurt and pain you saved me from."

Darcy looked back up to the ceiling and sighed. "I don't think that's true. I've put you through some crazy shite over the last few years."

I wiped my eyes as I unexpectedly snorted. "Our fights were the best thing for me back then; they gave me something to focus on so I wouldn't focus on what . . . what almost happened."

Darcy gave me a one-shoulder shrug. "I know. It's why I hassled you so much. It let me know you still had fight in you."

That was almost romantic.

"Thank you, Darcy," I said, and meant it.

He sighed. "You're welcome, Neala Girl."

I didn't know what to do then. I had never been in a situation before with Darcy where we were civil, so I flipped it around to familiar territory.

"You have really hassled me this week. The doll, remember?"

Darcy groaned. "You're never going to let that go, are you?"

I shook my head.

"Well, I hope you enjoy disappointment, because you aren't getting it."

What?

"Excuse me?"

Darcy looked at me and raised his eyebrows. "What's the shocked look for?"

"You just revealed something so deeply intimate to me. You just told me you stopped me from being raped when I was a teenager . . . and yet you *still* won't give me the fucking doll?"

He blinked at me. "I didn't think telling you what you *asked* to hear was an invitation for you to think you had a claim on the doll."

"You're unbelievable."

Darcy shrugged. "Tell me something I don't know."

I glared at him. "You still didn't answer me question. You said I was a virgin, but how would you know that? I was a virgin back when I was sixteen, but I'm twenty-five now."

"So?"

"So, I'm not a little girl anymore."

Darcy did something that caused my insides to jump: he looked down to my body, then back up to my eyes. "I can see that, but so what? Your body grew, but you're still the same girl I've known all my life. You took what happened very seriously, like any person would. You wouldn't get with just anyone back then, and even more so now. I don't know for certain if you're a virgin, but I'm pretty damn sure you are. You're guarded; you don't get close to people. Your idea of a night on the town is a trip down to the pub with our families. You aren't an *out there* kind of girl, so I can't imagine you just dropping your knickers at the drop of a hat for anyone."

"Like Laura Stoke, you mean?" I widened my eyes right after I said it.

I didn't mean for that thought to slip out.

Darcy chuckled. "Yeah, you're nothing like Laura Stoke, Neala Girl."

Wow.

Talk about a low blow.

Laura Stoke was everything I wasn't. She was tall, slim, had a big arse and big boobs. As much as I hated to admit it, she was beautiful and had naturally long, thick, strawberry blond hair. Darcy saying I was nothing like her shouldn't have hurt or upset me so much, but damn it, it did.

"You know what? Fuck you, Darcy!" I snapped, and stood up off the couch and stormed out of the room. "And I *am* a virgin," I shouted, "but so what?"

"What the hell did I do?" Darcy blurted as he followed me out of the living room and into the kitchen.

I stormed all the way into the storage room and slammed the door shut behind me.

"Neala, are you seriously escaping me by going back into the storage room?"

I was *trying* to escape.

I pounded my fists on the door. "Leave. Me. Alone."

He was silent for a moment; then a little thud came against the door and I didn't know if he was leaning against it or not.

"I don't know what is wrong with you, and you can bet your arse we'll be talking about it, but if you wanna sulk in there like a child for a while, go ahead."

Don't take the bait.

"I will."

"You do that." Darcy laughed.

I screeched, "Go. Away!"

God.

"No, this is *my* house, remember?"

He just couldn't leave me alone!

I grunted in defeat and kicked the door open; it hit Darcy, who was standing behind it, and he yelped like a girl. That made me feel a little better. I stepped out of the storage room and walked out like nothing was wrong. I made sure to ignore Darcy and stupid Einstein.

He grabbed my arm in the hallway and spun me around to face him.

"Okay, *what* is wrong with you?"

I deadpanned, "You don't know?"

"I really don't, so enlighten me."

"You called me fat and ugly."

Darcy stared at me with wide, unblinking eyes. "You've officially lost your mind."

I scoffed, "How do you figure that?"

He placed his free hand on my other arm and shook me.

"I did *not* call you fat or ugly. I never even mentioned the words."

"You didn't have to; it was implied."

Darcy looked so confused that I almost pitied him.

Almost.

"Neala . . . What the fuck?"

I blew a large amount of air through my nostrils and said, "You said I was *nothing* like Laura Stokes. She is perfect, if there is such a thing. She is gorgeous, tall, and skinny, and everything else that I'm not. I don't care that I'm not, but you didn't have to *say* it."

Darcy's shoulders slumped a little.

"You got mad because I said you aren't like Laura?"

I shrugged. "Call me crazy, but no girl, even an enemy, likes hearing they're *nothing* like a girl who could easily pass for a supermodel."

He stared at me for a long moment, and then the bastard burst out laughing.

I was instantly furious.

"You're an insensitive piece of—"

"You're crazy if you took what I said as an insult instead of a compliment." Darcy cut me off, still laughing.

Come again?

"Wait a fecking minute; I'm supposed to be *flattered* you think I'm nothing like Laura?" I clarified.

Darcy nodded.

"How do you figure that one?" I snapped.

He just shook his head and laughed.

"Answer me," I demanded.

Darcy tilted his head back and sighed before he lowered his head, and his gaze, back to mine.

"Do you want to stand here and talk about this, or do you want to get *out* of this house?"

Topic change.

I hesitated for a moment, then said, "Get out of the house."

Darcy nodded once. "That's what I thought, so help me figure a way out of here."

I'd let it go for the moment, but as soon as we weren't in a survivor panic mode I would be back on his case, demanding to know what he meant.

"Okay, so all the doors and windows are blocked up with snow. The smart thing to do now would be to ring someone to help get us out of here."

I chewed on my lower lip for a moment, then gasped. "I left me phone in the pub with me ma last night!"

At the time I hadn't wanted to bring it with me, because I had no pockets on my blazer or my dress. It would have been awkward to hold when I realised I needed a bike to get up the mountain, too. I then thought about the bike, and the kid who had loaned it to me, and groaned inwardly. He was so going to tell his parents I stole the stupid thing from him.

"Good thing I have mine then, isn't it?" Darcy quipped, then turned and headed down the hall to his bedroom.

I pulled a face at the back of his head as I followed him. Leaning against the doorway of his bedroom, I watched as he retrieved his phone from his bedside table. He turned to me and smirked as he waved it in my direction. I stuck my middle finger up at him, to which he shook his head.

"Nice." He snorted and pressed on the screen of his phone.

The lights in his bedroom went off.

I yelped, and so did Einstein from the kitchen.

"It's okay, sweetie!" Darcy called out.

I gripped the panel of the doorway. "I'm okay, Darcy."

Silence.

"I was talking to Einstein."

I glared into the darkness. "You're more concerned for your *bird* than you are me?"

Darcy snorted, "Uh, *yeah*."

Dickhead.

I stumbled back when something hard collided with my chest.

"Bloody hell, Neala. Where are you?" Darcy snapped.

He'd walked into me, yet *he* was the mad one.

Typical.

I grunted and extended my arms, grabbing at thin air searching for him. I clutched onto what felt like his bare arm, patting my way down it until I interlocked my fingers with his.

My heart pounded at the skin-to-skin contact.

"Okay, you won't bump into me now. Lead the way."

Silence.

"Darcy?" I pressed.

He cleared his throat. "I heard you . . . I'm just wondering why the power went out."

I thought about it, then grumbled, "The weather, maybe? It seems to be fucking up everything else, so why not the electricity?"

Darcy groaned. "Bollocks. We have to get out of here, man. My central heating system requires power. We're fucked."

"Just ring one of our brothers to come and get us."

I looked to Darcy's phone when the screen lit up.

"Oh, shite," Darcy muttered.

That didn't sound good.

"What is it now?" I asked.

Darcy shoved his phone in my face. "I've only two percent battery left."

That was all?

"So charge it."

I felt Darcy turn his head to look at me. "The power is out . . . remember?"

I cringed and felt stupid for my snotty suggestion.

"Forgot," I mumbled.

Darcy snorted lightly as he pressed on the screen. Justin's picture came up as Darcy's phone tried to connect. He brought it to his ear when Justin answered.

"Justin? Bro, you have to help me and Neala. We're snowed in at my house, and we need— What do you mean, you're snowed in too? You can't be serious!"

My stomach sank. I clutched Darcy's hand more tightly, and he gave me a squeeze back, which both surprised and reassured me – slightly.

"Is it bad everywhere? The snow, I mean," Darcy asked.

I strained to hear what Justin was saying, but his voice was very muffled, so I couldn't hear his reply.

"Justin? Hello? I can't understand what you're saying. Bro, can you hear me?"

That didn't sound good.

Darcy cursed as he pulled his phone away from his ear, and I could see that the home screen was visible, indicating that the call to Justin had ended. I was about to suggest he redial Justin but the screen suddenly went black; his battery was drained. I gripped Darcy's hand again as darkness consumed us once more.

"We're never going to get out of here," I said, and gnawed at the inside of my cheek.

Darcy grunted from my side. "We will. If our families can't come and help then we'll just have to help ourselves and get out of here."

I laughed humourlessly. "We're snowed in, you bloody gobshite!"

Darcy growled. "I'm going to get us out of this house even if it kills me."

I pulled my hand free from Darcy's when he moved away from me. I heard him make his way into his bedroom. I snorted once or twice when he cursed because he stepped on something or walked into something. He was making a lot of noise, and just as I was about to ask what he was doing a candle's light appeared in the hallway.

"I'll look for a torch, but for now I've a bunch of candles we can light to brighten the place up. Hold this one."

I took the candle from Darcy, and when I inhaled, a sweet vanilla scent filled my nostrils.

"Scented candles? Really?"

Darcy playfully shoved me as he passed me by. "Go ahead, laugh it up. Vanilla scented candles smell lovely, and if you disagree, hold your breath."

I chuckled. "*I* like them. I just didn't think *you* would."

"Why, because I'm a man?" Darcy asked.

"If I say yeah, will you think I'm sexist?"

"Yep."

"Then no." I grinned.

He laughed. "Typical."

I smothered a warm smile and forced down the giddy feeling that, since the conversation between us a few minutes ago, things were . . . changed. I didn't know if it was Darcy's admission of what he had done to help me when we were teens, but I could say I didn't one hundred percent hate him anymore.

That freaked me out more than a little.

To get my mind away from my thoughts I focused on the situation at hand.

"So . . . what's your plan to get us out of here?" I asked, and leaned my shoulder against the wall in the hallway.

Darcy looked to me and smirked.

I didn't like it, not one bit.

He cracked his knuckles, then his neck. "The time on me phone before it died said it was close to seven in the evening. We woke up late; the temperature is already on its way to dropping so I can't execute my plan now. Instead, first thing tomorrow morning when I wake up I'm going to dig me way out of here, and *you* are going to help me."

I laughed, but Darcy didn't, and it caused my stomach to sink.

We were going to dig our way out of here?

Well . . . crap.

CHAPTER THIRTEEN

Neala was gone.

I'd woken up roughly five minutes earlier, and after I went to the now safe-to-enter bathroom to relieve myself, I opened the sitting room door and popped my head around to see whether she was okay, but she wasn't there – which was weird. When I'd gone to sleep last night she was snuggled up on the couch, but now she, and the spare blanket I had given her, were nowhere to be seen.

It was darker than last night because a few of the candles were blown out, but I relit them to brighten the room up. I had a large lit candle in my hand as I walked around the living room and checked behind the couch and every other part of the room where Neala could be sitting or lying down, but there was still no sign of her.

There *was* a sign of the doll box, though, so I picked it up and brought it into my room, where I put it in the top drawer of my dresser. I wasn't thinking of keeping the doll from her; I just wanted it in a safe place. I resumed my search for my unexpected house-guest. I checked my dining room, and like the living room it was empty.

"Neala?" I called out.

No reply.

I didn't like silence when Neala was in close quarters with me; it would be a foolish and dangerous move to assume she wasn't up to something.

"Neala?" I called out again.

I knew she wasn't in my room, but went back and thoroughly checked it again anyway. When that room was in the clear, I went back out into my hallway. I don't know why, but I went to my front door. A vision of Neala somehow getting through the wall of snow flashed through my mind, so I rushed forward and opened the door. I breathed out a sigh of what felt like relief when I saw the wall of snow perfectly intact.

I reminded myself that I wasn't relieved that she was still here somewhere, just that she wasn't out there dead and encased in a block of ice. Her ma would kill me if she'd died while I slept.

I closed the door and turned around. I walked down the hallway and stopped at the bathroom. I hadn't looked into my bathtub while I was in there, so I knocked on the door and called out Neala's name again. Again, no reply. I opened the bathroom door and shivered; the vent in the ceiling definitely wasn't clogged with snow, because cold air from outside was flowing through it perfectly fine.

I closed the bathroom door and continued to walk down my hallway. Pausing at my kitchen door for just a moment, I reached for the handle, opened the door and stepped through the doorway.

"Neala?" I murmured as I poked my head around the door.

No Neala.

Where the hell was she?

I stepped into the room and frowned. It was pretty dark, so I used my candle to light the ones on the counters. When the room was lit I was about to shout Neala's name as loud as I could when I heard the faint sound of a snore. A smile stretched across my face when my eyes locked on the door of my storage room. I walked over to it and knocked on the door.

"Clarke! Are you in there?"

Another snore.

I smirked to myself as I placed my candle on the kitchen counter, then moved back to the storage room and used both of my hands to bang on the door as loud as I could. I stopped when Neala screamed, and then laughed when I pulled the door open and found she was sleeping against it. I watched as she fell back.

"You're a bastard!" Neala moaned from the floor, her voice raspy from sleep.

I couldn't disagree with her, so I didn't.

"Are you okay, Harry Potter?" I asked as I looked down at her.

Neala cleared her throat. "Harry lived in a cupboard under the stairs, not a kitchen storage room."

I shrugged. "He had no option; you, on the other hand, had a perfectly good couch to kip on, and yet you came in here to sleep . . . Why?"

Neala rolled over onto her back and stared up at me. "Your house makes funny noises at night-time and it kept me up . . . so I came in here. Einstein talking every so often made me feel a bit better . . . like I wasn't alone."

I hated that I felt bad.

"Why didn't you come into my room if you were afraid?" I asked curiously.

Neala grunted. "Because I knew you would have told me to get into your bed and go to sleep."

I blinked away the image of Neala spread out on my bed, tilting my head as I looked down at her.

"How did you know I would have said that?"

She shrugged. "Because you don't like me being scared out of me mind, unless you're the reason for it."

She had me there.

I gnawed on my inner cheek as I looked her in the eye. "You're right; I would have told you to get into me bed, but it would have been just to sleep. No funny business."

Neala snorted. "I know that."

I frowned. "So why did you come in here then?"

She sighed. "Me pride wouldn't let me go to you for help."

I smiled. "You're going to need me eventually, Neala, whether it's for a tin of beans, a bottle of water, or even a light for your candles."

She looked away from me. "I'll avoid needing you until absolutely necessary."

I laughed.

Typical Neala.

"Okay, well, I wasn't joking about what I said yesterday evening. We're digging our way out of here."

Neala groaned. "That's *not* a good idea. The snow has had Friday night and all day yesterday to set; it's going to be hard as ice, and all we have to dig through it is spoons and forks. Trust me, I checked."

I opened my mouth to correct her, but when I realised all my tools and shovels were outside the house in a shed, I closed my mouth and huffed. I had a big house, but hardly any furniture to fill it. I had bought only what I needed when the house was finished being built.

I didn't know how to cook; the extent of my culinary skills was putting a pizza in the oven, then taking it out when the timer went off. And since I didn't cook I had no use for anything in my kitchen except for knives, forks, spoons, a few plates, cups, and the odd bowl for cereal.

"Well, spoons and forks will just have to do."

Neala cackled. "You're crazy."

"Excuse me, but *I'm* not the one lying on a cold floor laughing like a hyena. Nope, that would be *you*, nut job."

Neala kicked at me, so I jumped back away from her. "Less of that!"

Neala continued to laugh as she got up to her feet. I frowned when she picked up the duvet from the storage room and wrapped it around herself. I hated that it was so cold and I couldn't just turn on my heat and make it all better.

"Do you want some of me clothes to wear?" I asked. "They'll be big, but they will keep you warm."

I could have sworn a blush crept up Neala's cheeks, but I couldn't be sure.

"I'm fine," she replied.

She wasn't fine; she was freezing.

Neala suddenly snapped her fingers and jumped up and down in a circle around me with nothing but fake enthusiasm. "Let's get to it, boss. Let's dig our way out of here."

I didn't appreciate her sarcasm.

"If you don't wanna help then don't; I'm not going to force you," I snapped.

I turned and walked out of the room.

I hoped I seemed rugged and manly, but I was holding a scented vanilla candle to see where I was going, so I doubt I looked as tough as I wanted to.

Neala followed me and snickered. "Don't get your knickers in a twist, Miss Daisy. I'm going to help."

I rolled my eyes. "Help me by shutting up."

Neala scoffed from behind me, "You shut up. *You're* the one who never stops talking."

"Everyone we know would disagree; you could talk for Ireland, chatterbox."

"I'm *not* a chatterbox!"

Yes, you are.

"Okay," I said as I set my candle down on the floor. Neala leaned against the hallway wall and snarled as I walked by her. "Don't just say okay to appease me."

I grinned as I entered my living room. "Okay."

"Darcy." Neala grumbled in annoyance.

God, it was so easy to wind her up.

"I'm only messing with you, Neala," I said, hoping she would hear truth in my voice.

There was, of course, no truth, because she *was* a chatterbox – she never stopped talking. Everyone in our village could vouch for me when I said that.

"I don't believe you . . . What are you doing?"

I sighed as I picked up the lit candles. "Bringing these out to the hall so it will make things easier to see when I dig us out of here."

"When *we* dig us out of here, you mean."

Yeah, right.

"Yep, I meant we."

Neala grunted. "You're such a bad liar, Darcy."

I smiled to myself as I walked by her and headed back out into the hall.

"Could you grab a few other candles from the living room for me? I'll get the spoons and forks."

Neala muttered what I could only guess were rude curse words to herself, but she did as asked and went into the living room to gather more candles. I headed into the kitchen and got some spoons and forks from the kitchen drawers. I looked around for something bigger that would make digging easier, but found nothing. I regretted not letting my mother buy me a bunch of kitchen shite when I first moved in here; anything would help us right now.

I sighed to myself. Einstein squawked, so I walked over to her cage. I opened up the cage door and let her out so she could stretch her wings and have a bit of a walk around. She loved her cage, but she loved walking around on top of it even more.

"Shut up, Neala!" Einstein shouted.

I smiled at Einstein just as Neala venomously shouted, "I *hate* that bloody bird!"

I snickered and rubbed Einstein's head. "Good girl," I whispered lovingly.

I left the kitchen armed with my digging tools and headed back to my front door . . . which was filled in with snow.

"It's weird how the snow hasn't caved into the hallway. The door has been open a few times and nothing has happened," Neala said as I came up beside her and stared at the doorway filled with snow.

"It hardened while the door was closed, not exactly to ice, but enough for it not to cave in when some space became available."

Neala swallowed. "I can't believe this is happening; we never get this much snow."

I looked at her and raised my eyebrows. "I'll agree that we never usually get this much snow, but for weeks we have been warned that this winter was to be our worst in over fifty years. That's why I, and everyone else, stocked up on tinned food and bottled water in case of a blackout or if the roads weren't safe enough for driving."

Neala shrugged. "I heard the warnings, but the weather people usually get things wrong. They forecast clear skies and sunshine and instead we get cloudy skies and heavy rain. The odds were just in their favour this time, since they turned out to be right."

I shook my head. "Well, it's done now, and it's caused us to be stuck in here, so let's change that. You stand back and I'll get to work on digging us out."

I stepped forward, only to be jolted back by the small hand that encircled my forearm. "Don't treat me like some unstable little woman, Darcy."

"You're an unstable— Ow!" I yelped when Neala grabbed hold of my earlobe and twisted.

"Finish that sentence. I dare you." She twisted harder.

I cried out, "I'm messing, I swear!"

Neala smirked at me and let go of my ear, so I quickly placed my fingers over my earlobe and rubbed. The throbbing remained when I removed my hand, but the initial stinging pain went away. Thank God.

I focused on Neala and glared as hard as I could at her.

"Do that again and I'll have no mercy as I tickle the life out of you."

Neala blinked at me, and for a moment she looked shocked . . . That is, until she laughed.

"Wow!" She cackled. "For a second there you looked serious."

I didn't move a muscle in my face.

"I am serious."

Neala stopped laughing and stared at me, unblinking.

"Oh. Well, okay, then. I won't touch you ever again."

Excellent.

"Good, now stand back and let me start digging a tunnel. I'm not blowing you off on this; you can help. We'll just take shifts . . . Okay?"

I went into my room and put on a few layers of clothes to warm me up and help keep the cold from the snow out. When I was dressed, I went back out to the hallway and handed Neala some spoons and forks. I kept two spoons for myself, just to make raking through the snow a little easier. I gave Neala a curt nod, but she wouldn't look at me, so it went unnoticed. I sighed and turned to the doorway of snow and narrowed my eyes.

I had this.

I got down on my knees and started to scrape a large circle. Once it was outlined I started to scoop out spoonfuls of snow and piled them by my side. Ten minutes of this and I had barely made a dent into forming an actual tunnel, and an impatient Neala started to huff behind me.

"You're taking forever."

I halted my digging.

"I don't need your pressure right now, Neala."

With that said I began working on the tunnel again, and Neala went back to being silent. After about an hour, she complained about feeling cold, so she went and got her blanket from the storage room and wrapped it around herself, then went into my living room and kept herself busy with something. I didn't ask what she was up to or go and check on her because I was revelling in the silence. It didn't last long, though; when she was bored she decided to come back out to the hall and open up her mouth again.

"It's my turn. I've nothing to do, and making sure the candles don't blow out is stupid."

My God, woman!

I had a decent tunnel in the making and she *still* had to complain.

Ungrateful witch.

"Keeping the candles lit is an important job!" I turned my head so she could hear me.

She kicked my leg. "Then *you* bloody do it."

I was fuming mad – so much for her never hitting me again. She couldn't just let me finish the damn tunnel so we *both* could get out of here and away from one another.

"Fine!" I snapped, and began to wriggle my body to back my way out of the tunnel.

My shoulders hit off the sides with each inch I moved backward. I halted when a noise from above me sounded. Just as I turned my head to the side to look up and see what was happening, snow caved in around me.

The cold stabbed me like needles, but what was worse was that it weighed me down and pressed me to the floor of the tunnel. I tried to move, but I couldn't. I tried to take deep breaths to calm myself down, but breathing became difficult with the snow surrounding me.

Fuck.

This wasn't good.

CHAPTER FOURTEEN

It all happened in slow motion.

Darcy was shouting at me from inside of the tunnel one minute, and the next his upper body disappeared as the roof of the snow tunnel literally collapsed on top of him, and now he wasn't moving.

At all.

For at least twenty seconds I did nothing but stare at him; then my senses kicked into overdrive.

"Darcy!" I screamed, and threw my blanket off my body as I rushed over to him.

I stared down at his legs with wide eyes, my limbs shaking. My heart was slamming into my chest, and each pulse got louder and louder; my ears rang with the noise.

"Darcy!" I shouted, hoping he would make a noise from under the snow or at least move his legs.

Nothing.

Not a sound or kick from him.

I really started to worry then; the thought of him suffocating crossed my mind. I mean, snow was made of water so while it looked fluffy and beautiful, in reality it was very dense and heavy. I didn't have much time before Darcy smothered to death.

Fuck.

I had to save him.

I dropped my candle to the ground and ignored it as the glass bowl that encased it smashed, causing the flame to blow out.

It was darker now, but the rest of the candles along the hallway were still lit, so I could see pretty well.

"Darcy, don't worry!" I shouted. "I'm gonna get you out of there!"

I dropped to my knees and began to scoop handfuls of snow off his body. I threw it off to my right onto the pile Darcy had created while digging the tunnel, but I had to stop, because my hands hurt with the cold. I instead moved to Darcy's legs, gripped them, and pulled with all of my might. The idiot's body moved only slightly.

"Move!" I shouted, and pulled at his legs again.

I held on to Darcy with every fibre of strength I had and pulled again, and by the grace of God, his body moved.

It actually moved.

I was strong!

"Yes!" I cheered.

I scrambled up to Darcy's back when his shoulders became visible. I placed my hands on both of them and pulled as hard as physically possible; the wet floor under him made him slide, which made things so much easier for me and my arms.

"You're out!" I cheered.

Darcy was gasping for air. I rolled him over so he could suck in as much as he needed. His eyes were closed, but his body was shaking. I instinctively placed my hands on his arms, directly on his biceps.

His firm biceps.

Stop it.

I began to rub up and down very fast, hoping to generate some heat for Darcy to ease his shivering. All the rubbing was pointless, though; unless I got him up off the cold wet floor he would just get sick.

"Darcy, stand up," I said.

He didn't move; nor did he reply to me.

That worried me.

I looked to Darcy's face and found his eyes were still closed. I looked down to his chest and saw it was moving up and down, which relaxed me immensely.

"Darcy!" I said loudly, shaking him.

"Darcy!" Einstein called from the kitchen.

I screeched, "*Shut up*, Einstein!"

Stupid bloody bird.

I looked back down to Darcy when I thought I heard him chuckle, but I was mistaken, because he was motionless, with his eyes still closed. He was still breathing, but it wasn't right that he was so motionless. This wouldn't do; I had to wake him up because we'd be stuck in this house if he didn't fix the tunnel and continue to dig so we could get out of here.

Was that selfish?

"Darcy!" I shouted, and shook him again, hard.

He groaned and it caused my pulse to spike.

"Neala?" he croaked.

He was alive!

"Yes, Darcy, it's Neala. I'm here. It's okay. I saved you."

I was so proud of myself.

"Neala." He gasped my name again, and this time it was followed by a cough.

I frowned down at him.

Why was he coughing?

"Are you okay?" I asked, genuinely concerned for his well-being.

Darcy coughed again. "I don't think so . . . Everything is fading."

Oh, my God.

Fading?

As in fading to black?

"Don't you die and leave me here alone!" I snapped at him.

I may still have hated him close to ninety percent, but I didn't want him to *die* . . . I also didn't want to be left on my own with his corpse and just Einstein for company.

"I'm . . . I'm dying . . . Neala."

Oh, no.

"You can't be; you weren't under the snow for that long – Darcy!" I screeched, and shook him when he started to go limp.

"Neala." He gasped. "Come closer."

I couldn't believe what was happening.

This was not how things were supposed to end; we were supposed to get out of here . . . *together.*

"I'm here, Darcy," I said, and swallowed back a sob that wanted to escape.

Darcy's breathing slowed. "I can see the light," he whispered.

Like the light of Heaven? Surely he was Hell-bound.

I shook my head clear and said, "Go to the light, Darcy."

Darcy gasped for breath; then all of a sudden everything stopped.

His movement.

His breathing.

His everything.

Oh, no.

"Darcy?" I whispered.

Nothing.

Oh, my God.

"Please don't be dead," I said, then released the sob that was dying to be let out.

I stared down at Darcy's face, and I couldn't believe what had just happened.

He had died in my arms.

What was I going to do?

I'd never even told him I was sorry for giving him the runs, or for all the other times I was a bitch to him, and now I would never get the chance.

I felt like dirt.

I began to cry, but Darcy's body suddenly twitched; then he inhaled sharply and loudly.

I blinked, then widened my eyes in shock.

"Darcy?" I whispered.

Darcy blinked open his big brown eyes.

He was alive!

"Am I in Heaven?" he asked.

He thought he was dead!

Darcy blinked his eyes a couple of times; then he flicked them to mine and stared at me for a long moment before he sighed.

"Nope, not Heaven. This must be Hell if you're here," he said, his face as serious as if he'd just told me someone had had a heart attack.

I stared down at him, then narrowed my eyes.

Ex-fucking-cuse me?

"What?" I asked, completely confused.

Darcy looked at me, then burst out laughing.

Laughing!

I gasped and dropped him to the floor.

He grunted in pain, but continued to laugh.

That . . . that fucking bastard!

He'd played me.

"You joked about *dying?*" I screeched.

Who does that?

Darcy's only response was another fit of laughter.

"You evil prick!" I hollered, and dove on him.

I grabbed handfuls of the snow from the pile to my right and tried to kill the bastard for real this time by pushing it into his mouth and nose. Darcy turned his head from left to right and grabbed at my hands to stop me.

He laughed the entire time.

I was so mad.

I pushed myself up off him.

"I *knew* you really cared about me!" Darcy shouted through his laughter, then mimicked my voice. "Darcy, *Darcy*! Please don't be dead."

"I hate you!" I screamed, then turned and stomped down the hallway.

I felt my eye twitch as I slammed Darcy's living room door and separated myself from him, but it was no good; I could still hear the dickhead laughing. I stormed over to the couch and sat down. I folded my arms across my chest and glared at the living room door.

Who pretends to die?

That was *not* funny.

"Darcy! Go into the light, Darcy," Darcy cried out in the hallway, then burst into laughter again.

I was going to kill him before we made it out of this house.

CHAPTER FIFTEEN

Nealaaaa?"
Fuck off.

"Come on, Neala." Darcy chuckled. "You *have* to talk to me at some point."

I bloody do not.

"Neala Girl," Darcy sang, his voice merry. "Oh, you decorated the room."

Yeah, I decorated the room.

While he had been making the tunnel this morning I'd opened the box of tree decorations and hung them on the branches, taking the bare look off the tree. When I was finished it looked nice.

I'd even placed the Christmas light-up characters around the room. The fecking things were battery operated, which meant when they were all turned on they completely lit up the space, and we had been using candles since yesterday. Darcy was an idiot for not thinking of them when the power went out.

I was pulled from my thoughts when Darcy called my name again. I growled and turned deeper into the couch, hugging myself with my arms to stop my body from shivering. My blanket was in the hallway still and it was wet from the snow that was thrown around when I tried to make Darcy eat it.

"Neala." Darcy sighed long and deep. "You're freezing – I can *see* you shaking. Will you just get up and come into my bedroom, where you will be warm and comfortable in me bed?"

Ha. Yeah, fecking right.

That was the same tune Darcy had sung over and over since he'd faked his own death this morning. I wasn't having any of it. I would not speak to him or go into his bedroom no matter how dire things got for me. Darcy sighed from behind me, then chuckled to himself.

"I'll bring Einstein in here unless you come into my room," Darcy threatened.

He wouldn't dare.

"I *will* bring her in here, Neala. Don't doubt me."

I widened my eyes.

Could he read my mind?

Fuck you, Darcy.

Silence.

Nah, he couldn't read my mind; he'd just guessed what I was thinking.

"Come on, Neala. You're going to get sick in here. The room is soaking." Darcy's tone had changed to one of annoyance.

I wasn't falling for it.

The room was wet *because* of him; it was completely *his* fault.

After he'd faked his death and I'd closed myself off from him in the living room, the fucker had opened the door and thrown snowballs at me. Yes, *snowballs.* He was obviously never taught *not* to throw things inside the house, especially fucking snowballs. He'd completely soaked my dress and blazer and the furniture, because he had the worst aim in the history of mankind. The snowballs had melted, of course, and all but destroyed the furniture, what little furniture he had, when the wet soaked into them.

He was lucky he hadn't messed up the tree; I would have kicked his arse if he had. The moron hadn't even noticed I'd done up the room earlier when he attacked me, because I'd turned the light-up characters off to save the battery power, but now that they were lit he was noticing.

The bloody gobshite.

"Speak to me, Neala," Darcy pleaded. "I'll get upset if you don't."

I lifted my right hand in the air and stuck my middle finger up at him.

Darcy's sudden wail frightened the shite out of me. I quickly turned to face him just as he dropped to his knees and dramatically began to crawl over to me.

"Shut up!" I shouted, covering my ears with my hands as I got up from the sofa. "You're giving me a bleeding headache, you eejit."

He wrapped his arms around my legs and wouldn't let go.

"Stop it!"

Darcy ignored me, and Einstein started to freak out and wail too, and even though she was in the kitchen I could hear her as plain as day. She was even louder than fucking Darcy.

"You're upsetting Einstein; stop it!" I snarled down at Darcy.

He blinked up at me.

"Darcy!" I shouted, and bent down and slapped at his arms.

He wouldn't let go.

"For the love of God, will you let go of me and stop!" I snapped.

Darcy stopped his fake wailing and looked up at me. "Will you do as I ask?"

"No." I hissed.

He opened his mouth and sang, "Jingle bells, jingle bells, jingle all the wayyyyyy. Oh, what fun it is to ride in a one-horse opppeeeennnnnn—"

"Okay!" I screamed. "I'll do as you ask!"

If he'd stop acting and singing stupid carols like a five-year-old I'd do just about anything.

Darcy smiled up at me, then let go of my legs and jumped to his feet.

"Excellent. Now follow me."

I narrowed my eyes at his back as he turned and pranced out of the living room.

He was so bloody full of it.

I shook my head and reluctantly followed Darcy down the hallway and into his bedroom. I stood at his doorway, hesitating to go inside. Darcy looked over his shoulder at me and laughed, which made me want to smack him.

"I'm not going to jump you – I'm trying to *help* you."

Ha. Yeah, right.

"Help me how?" I asked curiously.

Darcy turned and walked over to his wardrobe. Opening the door, he pulled out a few items of clothing. He walked over to his dresser and pulled out something else, then turned and dropped the items on his bed and gestured at them with his arms.

"Trousers, a t-shirt, boxers, and socks. Have at them."

What?

"I don't understand," I said with furrowed eyebrows.

Darcy cleared his throat. "Your clothes are soaking. You can't stay in them because you'll get sick, so I'm giving you some of mine to wear."

Butterflies exploded in my stomach and I had to fight myself not to blush. I should have been annoyed with the clothing offer, because I couldn't stand Darcy, but I wasn't.

I was oddly excited.

"I'm not wearing your clothes," I said, simply to keep my excitement undetected.

Who the hell gets excited over wearing a lad's clothes?

Apparently me.

"Do I have to throw another tantrum?" Darcy asked.

I wasn't looking at him, but I could *hear* the smile that was sure to be plastered over his stupid good-looking face.

I looked up to him, ignored said smile, and glared. "You're threatening me."

It was a statement, not a question.

"You're a clever cookie," Darcy teased.

I grunted. "You'd rival a toddler with that bloody tantrum."

Darcy smirked. "Thank you."

It wasn't a compliment and he knew it.

"Fine. I'll wear your clothes."

Darcy winked.

I wanted to thump him.

He was really doing me a favour by offering me clean, dry clothes to wear, but he made it out like I was doing him a favour by wearing them.

"The boxers are brand-new; so are the socks. The t-shirt and trousers aren't though."

I felt heat flush my cheeks, so I walked over to the bed with my head down.

"Thanks," I muttered.

"What was that?" Darcy asked, loudly.

I hated him.

"Thanks," I repeated a little louder.

"I can't hear you."

Was he serious?

I set my jaw. "Thank. You."

Darcy pressed his hand against his chest and faked getting emotional.

"You don't need to thank me, Neala," he said, and fanned his face. "You're so welcome."

I blinked in boredom.

"I'd punch you, only I don't wanna get moron on me hand."

Darcy cut the act and laughed from behind me and patted my shoulder. "I'm finished, I swear. I'll be in the kitchen if you need me."

"I *won't* need you," I said to his back as he walked out of his room, snickering to himself.

I scowled at Darcy's now-closed bedroom door, then looked down at his clothes.

I forced the smile off my face and shook my head.

"You're pathetic," I muttered to myself.

I stripped out of my damp and cold clothes, folded them and placed them on top of Darcy's dresser, then pulled on Darcy's socks and boxer shorts. I had to use one of my hair ties to tie a knot on the band to keep them from falling down.

They were both big on me, but they felt nice, so I continued and put on Darcy's trousers and t-shirt. I had to tie the track suit bottoms tight with the string so they wouldn't fall down, and I also had to roll them up a few times because they were pretty long. The T-shirt was my favourite item of clothing. It was like a tent on me, but a warm, cuddly tent that smelled fucking amazing.

I inhaled deeply and groaned out loud.

Darcy. Smelled. Awesome.

I looked down at his T-shirt, and when I realised how creepy I was being I put my hands on my face and mentally chided myself.

I was turning into some sort of Darcy fangirl, and the worst part was . . . I liked it.

I possibly liked . . . Darcy . . . a tiny bit.

I think.

I had one thing to say to that tiny thought: WHAT THE FUCKING FUCK?

"I'm so screwed," I muttered to myself.

I walked mutely out of Darcy's bedroom and headed down to the kitchen.

Darcy was over at Einstein's cage finishing eating a tin of beans. I glanced at him, but when he turned in my direction I focused on washing my hands in the sink and not anything, or anyone, else.

"You look good in . . . clothes," Darcy commented as he put the now-empty tin in the bin.

I raised my eyebrow and looked at him. "I was in clothes before these . . . They were just wet."

Darcy gave me a 'get real' look. "That dress and blazer didn't cover much; what you're wearing now are *proper* clothes."

I inwardly smiled.

"Yeah, well . . . whatever."

Darcy chuckled. "Is it killing you to wear clothes that belong to me?"

No, and that's why I was annoyed.

"They'll do," was all I said.

I didn't want to lie, because I was tired of lying, so not directly answering his question was my only option.

"What time is it?" I asked.

Darcy looked to the wall behind Einstein and said, "Half eleven."

I widened my eyes. "At *night*?"

Darcy nodded. "It's Christmas Eve tomorrow."

I frowned. "I don't want to miss Christmas."

Darcy tilted his head as he looked at me. "We won't; our mothers will come up here and dig us out with their bare hands before they'd let us miss a Christmas."

I laughed and shook my head.

I wouldn't put it past *either* of our mothers to do something so drastic.

"So . . ." Darcy said.

I wanted to smile, because he was rocking back and forth on his heels as he looked at me.

"So what?" I asked.

Darcy shrugged. "So . . . it's late. Bedtime."

"You're putting me to bed?" I asked, teasing.

He shrugged. "Depends. If you walk into my bedroom freely then no, but if you run from me then yes."

My stomach flipped, my heart pounded against my chest, and I could feel a pulse between my thighs. The pulse frightened me most, because I'd never gotten that sensation for Darcy . . . until now.

"I'm, uh, good with the storage room," I said, and tried to walk by him.

Darcy clucked his tongue at me and caught me around the waist with his arms when I tried to pass him by. He pulled me back to him until my back was flush against his front. I could feel the heat of his body on mine.

Christ.

Why was I reacting to him like this?

This was *Darcy*.

The same Darcy who drove me absolutely mad.

The same Darcy who was my enemy, and had been for fifteen years.

The same Darcy who had chosen another girl over me – his *ex*–best friend.

The same Darcy who hated me as much as I hated him.

My body, and now my mind, seemed to not care about any of that, because I liked his closeness, and his touch.

I fucking *liked* Darcy holding me this close to him.

What the hell do I do now? Admit myself to an asylum?

"No more sleeping in the storage room, little woman. You're sleeping next to me in *my* bed tonight. You don't have to be scared; I'll even let you build a pillow fort between us so you don't have to look at me."

I giggled.

Yeah, I bloody *giggled.*

"Was that a *giggle* I heard?" Darcy teased.

I tried to smother my laughter as I said, "No."

Darcy brought his mouth down to my ear and said, "Are you coming willingly or not?"

Because I wanted to see what he would do, I said, "Not."

"I didn't want to have to do this, but you've left me no choice," Darcy said then, his voice raspy.

What was he— "Omigod!" I screeched as Darcy turned me to face him, then proceeded to bend, grip me behind the knees with his hands, and pull. I was flipped over Darcy's shoulder and hung there as he straightened himself up.

"Hi-ho, hi-ho, it's off to bed we go," Darcy sang as he marched out of the kitchen.

He turned slightly as he left the room and my head hit the kitchen door.

"Ow!"

Darcy winced. "My bad."

I cracked up as I hung over his shoulder. I smacked his arse a few times just to show some sign of protest, even though I was loving every second of his caveman act.

I yelped when I was suddenly flung back over Darcy's shoulders. But instead of hitting a hard surface I fell onto a soft mattress.

I was still laughing as Darcy jumped onto the bed beside me. I sat up and shoved him. He looked at me and chuckled. I was smiling as I found myself looking into his eyes, then to his mouth.

I caught the moment Darcy saw what I was doing, and I noticed his sharp intake of breath. I swallowed nervously and cleared my throat.

"Thanks . . . I don't agree with your method, but I appreciate your wanting me to have somewhere comfortable to sleep," I said, then turned and crawled up the bed and got under the covers, facing away from Darcy.

"No problem," Darcy said, then lingered for a moment before he moved and got under the covers also.

There was silence until he said, "Goodnight, Neala Girl."

My heart thudded in my chest and my stomach burst into butterflies.

"Goodnight, Darcy."

I closed my eyes and prayed sleep would come easily – even though my mind was screaming that something had definitely changed between Darcy and me, and I wanted to think about it. Surprisingly, I fell into a deep and relaxed slumber.

Which was utterly destroyed the next morning.

I woke up before I opened my eyes.

I didn't want to, because I was warm, comfortable, and completely content with the pillow I was hugging so tightly to my body. I snuggled into it and had just started to doze off again when movement under me interrupted my snooze.

What was that?

I groaned out loud and it caused whatever was under me to tense.

161

Since when can pillows tense? Since when can they do anything?

I became aware of everything in that moment as my mind fully awoke.

Oh, no.

"Oh, my God," I whispered as I opened my eyes and came face to face with a light pink nipple.

It was practically pressed into my eye socket.

I slowly reached up and pressed my hands against the chest around the nipple, carefully peeling my face away. I swallowed as I looked down and found my leg cocked over Darcy's body. I was so far into Darcy's space that I was practically straddling him.

I widened my eyes as a sharp pulse between my thighs caught me by surprise.

I was getting turned on?

By almost *lying* on Darcy's hard body?

I was fucking losing it.

I tried to retract my leg as slowly as I could, but when a slight moan rumbled up Darcy's throat, I froze. I didn't know what to do, so I stayed perfectly still until I was sure he hadn't woken up. I looked back down and slowly began to pull my leg away once again, but the moment it moved over his pelvis and slid over what can only be described as a speed bump, I felt tingles burst free all over my body.

Darcy had an erection . . . and my leg was currently resting on top of it.

Oh. My. God.

I wanted to clench my thighs together when the pulse between said thighs got a little too intense for me to deal with calmly, but I couldn't. I was mortified that I was having this sort of reaction to Darcy and he was doing nothing but sleeping.

I felt like a major pervert.

I quickly moved my leg away from Darcy's groin area, but the movement made my leg grind over the erection, and Darcy must have felt it, because he moved. My heart jumped as I took a peek up at him.

His eyes were closed, but he had a small grin on his face.

Oh, Jesus.

I gasped. "You're *awake*!"

Darcy opened his eyes and laughed. "I'm sorry; you trying to get off on me undetected was too entertaining to interrupt."

I was so embarrassed.

"I was trying to get off you, not get off *on* you."

He smirked. "My mistake."

The dirty bastard.

I scoffed and shoved his chest with my hands as I pushed away from him. I rolled off him and huddled into the covers on my temporary side of the bed because the entire section of the mattress was freezing.

I winced.

I must have being sleeping on Darcy for a long time.

Damn it.

"Neala." Darcy laughed. "Don't hide over there. I don't mind if you want to spoon me . . . or lie on me. If you're cold, don't be afraid to use my body to warm you up."

Bloody hell.

"Stop it. Stop talking to me; just go back to sleep," I pleaded, and buried my face into the pillow my head rested on.

"But I can be your heater, baby," he sang.

I couldn't even smile. "You just butchered a great song."

I was absolutely mortified. I didn't want Darcy to notice, because he would just tease me some more, so I tried to play it cool, and that meant I had to be a bitch.

"Are you embarrassed?" Darcy asked, chuckling.

Cool, play it cool.

"Why would I be embarrassed?" I said, and then cleared my throat. "I can't help what I do in my sleep. It's out of my control if my body moves when eighty percent of my brain is dormant."

Darcy cackled. "Same here, so my hard-on shouldn't freak you out so much. Men get morning wood all the time and it's out of our control."

I hadn't even mentioned his erection!

"Stop. Talking," I growled.

Darcy sighed. "You're freaked that you cuddled with me, but you're more freaked that you touched my cock . . . I mean penis."

I could hear the grin in his voice, the fucker.

"It doesn't freak me out. I'd just rather not touch any part of you. Especially your coc— penis."

Damn it.

Darcy snorted. "A little feisty, aren't you?"

I was never going to be able to calm myself down if he kept talking.

"Keep it up, and I'm heading out to the sitting room," I threatened.

Darcy chuckled. "Okay, Okay. I'll quit teasing you."

Thank God.

Darcy stopped talking, and after a few minutes his breathing slowed and I knew the fucker had fallen back asleep, which wasn't fair. My body was on high alert and I was still mortified.

I couldn't stay in his bed any longer, so I quietly got out and snuck into the sitting room. Some areas were still damp, so I went into the kitchen and got tea towels to dry everything up. It gave me something to do and focus on . . . for a few minutes.

My mind kept going back to touching Darcy's boner, and then him laughing because he knew I'd felt it.

I was so embarrassed.

I didn't want to look at him, or talk to him, ever again. I wanted to bury my face in the mountains of snow outside and cease my existence.

With Darcy, though, things were *never* that simple.

CHAPTER SIXTEEN

It was Christmas Eve, and I was *still* stuck in Darcy's house.

We had been trapped inside this hell-hole of evil for three and a half days already.

Three and a half days! (I was counting Friday night as half a day because it felt that long.)

It got worse too, because it seemed that there was no end in sight for this . . . ordeal.

I looked to the doorway of the sitting room when a noise got my attention. When I saw it was Darcy leaning against the doorway I flushed with embarrassment and looked away. I was grateful for the dimly lit room, because I could *not* take Darcy teasing me right now, especially not after what had happened this morning.

I'd avoided him for most of the day, staying in the sitting room while he stayed in his bedroom for the most part. I forced myself to endure a freezing cold bath for a while to clean myself up. I missed warm water terribly, but I needed to give myself a good scrub. It was a perfect excuse to stay away from Darcy for an extra couple of minutes.

I'd interacted with him only when I needed fresh clothes; he'd silently handed me another set, just like the ones I had before. I'd thought I would get away with not speaking to him at all, but now it was late in the evening and he was making me face him.

It was horrible.

I'd woken up this morning spooning Darcy, and I'd touched his . . . boner. That wasn't even the worst part. The worst part was that I kind of, *sort of*, liked it.

It was soul crushing.

I was so confused about my sudden feelings for Darcy. I didn't know what to do with them or myself. I was freaked by how intense they were for something so new. I didn't know how to process it.

"Go away, Darcy," I grumbled, and drew my knees up to my chest.

"I come bearing gifts, though."

I peeked at him and saw he had a bottle of wine.

A *large* bottle of wine, which was exactly what I needed.

I held my hand out and he handed me the opened bottle. I took at least five deep gulps and handed it back to him. He took a few sips as well and then put it on the floor next to the couch and walked right over to me, but I still refused to look up at him. I shook my head as the heat flowed through my body, and after a moment I pressed my face back against my knees as Darcy chuckled.

"Why are you being like this?"

I remained still.

"Being like what?" I mumbled.

I tensed when I felt him lean towards me.

"Like this. You're acting like a little girl who just saw her first coc—"

"*Don't* say that word," I growled, cutting Darcy off before he could finish his sentence.

He laughed as he fell onto the couch next to me. "You don't like that word?"

I didn't mind it, but when Darcy said it, it sounded dirty . . . dirty in a good way.

"No, I don't."

Darcy chuckled lightly. "Okay, you're acting like a little girl who has never seen a *penis* before."

I elbowed him in the stomach and he coughed and then laughed, hard.

"You're such a dickhead, Darcy Hart," I grumbled.

I tried to get up from the couch, but his arms closed around me, making that impossible.

"I'm sorry. I won't laugh anymore."

Yeah, like I'd believe that.

I sighed in defeat. "I don't care; laugh it up."

Darcy released me from his hold, but left one arm draped around my shoulder. I was very aware of it. The hairs on the back of my neck stood up.

"I'm only playing with you, Neala Girl. You know that, right?"

I did, but it was still embarrassing.

"Did you come in here to talk about this morning? Because if you did, you can feck off."

Darcy shook with silent laughter.

"I wanted to make sure you were okay. You've barely looked at me since this morning, and that is odd, even for you."

I leaned my head back on Darcy's arm and looked up to the dark ceiling.

"I know you couldn't help it; it was just your body and not you. I *know* all that, but still . . . it *touched* me, Darcy."

Darcy lost it and burst out laughing, and then quickly wrapped both his arms around my body as I tried to get up from the couch once more. He howled with laughter and yelped and screeched when I pinched his arm in an attempt to make him let me go, but he didn't. He held on to me tightly, and I hated that I loved every second of it.

"I'm sorry." He wheezed with laughter. "I'll stop . . . Just give me a second."

He was such a moron – he laughed at everything.

I muttered obscenities to myself until Darcy calmed himself down, which wasn't for at least three minutes.

"Okay, I'm okay," he said.

I tilted my head back and looked to my right at him. "Are you sure?"

He smiled wide. "Just don't say me hard-on touched you again in that horrified tone and I'll be perfectly fine."

I rolled my eyes and looked back to the ceiling. "You're an eejit. You know that, right?"

"Yes."

I couldn't help it; I laughed.

Darcy nudged me lightly until I looked back at him.

"You know what this reminds me of?"

I was intrigued.

"What?" I asked.

"When we were little, before the drama started between us, you would lie against me like you are now and you'd happily stay that way for hours. It was as if you felt safe in my arms, like you knew I would protect you from anything."

I melted. "You *would* protect me from anything back then, Darcy. I knew you would."

He nudged me. "I *still* would."

I swallowed and looked forward.

What the hell was I supposed to say to that?

"I'm not sweet-talking you. I've just never told you that even though we have hate for one another, I *still* have a lot of love for you. Even though we are at each other's throats all the time, you're a huge part of me life. Now that I really think about it, you take up half of it, to be honest."

I was half of Darcy's life?

"Wow," I whispered.

He chuckled. "I surprised myself with that one too."

"I'm not sure what to think. This is the weirdest conversation we've ever had."

Darcy chortled. "It's called being civil to one another."

I pretended to be disgusted. "I don't like it."

He pulled a face at me and pinched my side, making me squeal and him laugh.

"Do you think being stuck here together will change us?" I asked, trying to change the subject.

It was a question that had been sitting in the back of my mind since Darcy had told me what he'd done for me when we were teenagers.

He thought about it for a moment, then nodded. "I do. I mean, it has. Look how different we are with one another and it's only been a few days. Sure, we've still had spats here and there, but we're both alive, which speaks volumes . . . I mean, do you even remember why we acted the way we did for all those years?

Was that a serious question?

"Yes, I do. You picked Laura Stoke over me. I remember everything about that day, Darcy."

He blinked down at me. "You remember that day?"

I nodded my head. "It was the first time someone had ever broken my heart; of course I remember it."

Darcy widened his eyes as he stared at me, and I mirrored his expression, because I had not meant to say that out loud.

"I broke your heart?" he asked.

I shrugged, but didn't respond.

His fingers touched my chin as he turned my face in his direction.

"I broke your heart?" he repeated.

I swallowed, and slowly nodded.

He blinked his big brown eyes and opened his mouth to speak, but quickly closed it.

After a few moments of silence I smiled weakly. "It's okay." I lied. "It was a long time ago."

Darcy frowned at me. "It's not okay. I shouldn't have let my crush on Laura blind me from the truth that day."

"Then why did you?" I asked.

He sighed. "I showed up just as you punched her. I got a fright because you were never in a fight before, and I liked Laura. I did a shitty thing: I chose a girl over my best friend."

I stared at Darcy with wide eyes.

He caught my expression and gave me a sad smile. "I loved you, Neala Girl. You were my best friend. No one else's. Mine. I didn't like myself after I sided with Laura, and it's why I became so angry. You said you hated me. You wouldn't talk to me; you were just done with me and I felt thrown under the bus at that, but it doesn't excuse what I did. If I'd sided with you in the first place, like I should have, then our stupid feud wouldn't have happened. Is it too late for me to apologise?"

What. The. Hell?

What was happening right now?

Darcy was *apologising* to me?

This was too much to take in.

"You look like you're about to freak out," Darcy mused.

"I am," I replied honestly.

Darcy chuckled and hugged me to his warm body. "It appears to be honesty hour. We may never get another chance like this, so I want everything between us to be out in the open. Okay?"

I nodded.

"Does my honesty scare you?" Darcy asked.

Scare me?

No.

Thrill me?

Yes.

"No, I'm just a little . . . shocked? I don't really know. I never expected you to say anything like this to me, Darcy."

He nodded. "Trust me, I never planned on it, but it just feels right. I don't know why, but it does."

I gnawed on my inner cheek, then said, "Maybe you have cabin fever and the isolation is starting to drive you mad."

Darcy looked at me and burst out laughing.

The tension that had built up in the room fled within that moment, and I was very grateful for it.

"Be serious." He chuckled and nudged me.

I cleared my throat. "Deadly serious?"

Darcy nodded.

"Okay, it *does* feel right. I think because it's just us here together and we don't have our families around us trying to force us to be nice. We're being nice on our own terms, which is sort of a miracle in itself. I mean, did you ever imagine us ever being even remotely friendly to one another?"

He grinned. "No, but I hope today is the first day of many we're friendly."

I turned in Darcy's arm and raised an eyebrow at him. "Are you suggesting an indefinite truce between us?"

"Would that be so terrible?" he asked.

I thought about it and could come up with only one answer.

I smiled. "No."

"Then yes." Darcy beamed. "That is what I'm suggesting."

"Say it." I chuckled.

He playfully sighed. "Neala Clarke, can we live out the remainder of our lives in peace?"

I pretended to think about it, and Darcy shoved me, making me laugh.

"Yeah." I giggled. "We can be friends."

"Friends." He nodded.

Wow.

Talk about a strange turn of events. Father Christmas himself couldn't have predicted this.

"So we're friends . . . What do we do now?" I asked.

Darcy slumped down a little and said, "I've no idea."

I looked at him at the same time he looked at me and we both laughed.

"I shouldn't have been so pig-headed and childish. I should have let you explain yourself instead of acting out. I shouldn't have said the things I did, knowing they would hurt you. I'm sorry, too," I said and watched him smile at me.

I wanted to burst with excitement, but I somehow kept my cool.

"Our mas are going to be so happy," I said, amused.

Darcy snorted. "I'd bet money they'll cry."

I nodded in agreement. "That's an easy win; they'll sob for weeks."

He snickered. "Our brothers will be delighted; they won't have to break up our fights anymore."

I grinned. "They were getting too old for it anyway."

Darcy shook his head. "And our das? I don't even think they'll notice."

I gnawed on my lip. "They'll at least high-five; it means they don't have to listen to our mas go on about us anymore."

His mouth curved in a grin. "I think the entire village will rejoice. Birds will sing, mothers will weep, cripples will walk—"

I cut him off with my laughter.

He hugged me tightly to him. "Does touching my penis creep you out so much now?"

Really?

Did he *have* to bring that back up?

"Darcy!" I whined, and covered my face with both of my hands.

He cackled. "I'm only teasing."

"Well, don't. I've never been so mortified in me entire life as I was this morning."

He had both his eyebrows raised when I looked at him.

"Really?" he asked. "Touching me hard-on was worse than walking home naked from the Elite Swimming Pool after we graduated from school?"

I felt heat rush up my neck to my cheeks.

"Oh, my God. That day was all kinds of horrible, and you . . . *you* caused that!"

Darcy winced. "That prank *did* go a little too far. When I realised how insensitive it was, considering what almost happened to you the year before, I tried to stop Emmet, but I was too late."

I growled at Darcy.

The horrible incident he was referring to was the day I graduated from secondary school. It was the year after the situation with Trevor. I wasn't into drinking or acting a fool, so I'd tagged along with a few lads and girls from my graduating class.

We all decided to go to the local swimming pool – one of the lads in class got keys to it because his father was a lifeguard there. We had the pool all to ourselves, and it was a brilliant night – that was until Darcy, my brother, Justin, and some of Darcy's stupid friends showed up.

Once I saw Darcy at the pool in his trunks I knew I had to leave. I couldn't *make* him leave, because he'd just graduated too, so he had as much right to be there as me. I wanted to leave because he would probably try to drown me, but if I was honest with myself, the main reason I wanted to leave was because it was the first time I had seen Darcy in a new light, and it freaked me out.

Usually the sight of him turned my stomach, but I'd never forget the moment I realized that looking at Darcy made me feel something other than ill. He made me feel . . . hot. I put this down to being shocked at seeing his body in his swimming trunks. We both would be turning eighteen in the summer of that year and it was around that time Darcy stopped being skinny; he'd started to fill out and I noticed.

Every girl noticed.

I tried to discreetly leave the pool, but it was never that easy with Darcy. The dickhead gave one of his friends ten Euros to follow me into the girls' changing rooms, and whilst I was showering, he'd stolen my clothes and swimsuit. The stupid lad tossed them into the pool, and laughed his head off when I went out to the pool wrapped in a towel with a furious look about me.

I remember Darcy being in Emmet's face, and that he said he was very sorry, but I was too wrapped up in my thoughts to process it.

"You and Sean flanked me the entire walk home and threatened death upon anyone who looked at me twice," I mused.

Darcy leaned his head back and laughed. "That was a bad day. I felt like crap when I saw your clothes in the pool; then I saw your endless legs in that tiny towel. God. I wanted to kill everyone who looked at you – even your brother, which is saying something, because he socked me one when he found out what I did."

I smiled to myself as I asked, "Why did you want to hit people for looking at me?"

He looked at me and rolled his eyes. "You know why."

I really didn't.

"Nope, you'll have to enlighten me."

He groaned. "You enjoy torturing me, don't you?"

I smirked sadistically.

"Devil woman," Darcy growled.

My insides jumped at the delicious sound of his voice.

"Fine," he muttered. "I fancied you. There, I said it. I don't think I realised it at the time, though."

Darcy had fancied me?

Me?

What the ever-loving hell?

This was huge news to me. Darcy had fancied me! But . . .
'fancied.' Past tense. So was all the attraction I'd been fighting for
the past few days just one-sided, just me, or was he feeling it too?
Again? Whatever? Fuck!

My heard started to spin again.

"Past tense? You don't fancy me anymore?" I asked, and then
flinched when heat stained my cheeks.

Oh, hello, boldness.

Darcy glanced at me, and he looked as shocked as I felt.

The poor lad.

"I do," he said, then cleared his throat. "Do you . . . do you
fancy me? Or like me in *that* way?"

If he had asked me that question last week I would have said
no, even though I had always thought he was attractive.

I had never put a lot of thought into anything further than that,
because we always fought, but now, if the butterflies and rush of
heat when I saw him were anything to go by, then I would go with
a definite yes.

"Yeah . . . I do fancy you, and like you in *that* way," I admitted.

I couldn't believe I'd said it.

I couldn't believe it was the truth.

"Are you serious, Neala?" Darcy asked, his tone rough. "Because
if you're playing with me it's not funny."

He seemed irritated.

I put my hand on his arm. "I'm not joking. I'm serious."

Darcy looked at me, and then tilted his head back so he could
look up at the ceiling.

I settled back against his chest and I felt a shudder run through
my body at the familiarity.

"Do you know what else this reminds me of?" Darcy murmured.

I closed my eyes and smiled.

"What?"

"Your fourteenth birthday. You were out with Daryl Maine. I knew he fancied you, so I told him that you were a closet lesbian, and he wouldn't kiss you because of it. You drank your da's whiskey out of anger at me and got shitfaced. I had to mind you for a few hours until you sobered up so I could bring you home and you could go to sleep."

I burst out laughing, surprising myself again. "I actually remember a bit of that."

It was one of my best memories, even if it was foggy in parts.

Darcy gave me a little squeeze. "I brought you down to the river and we sat there for hours just throwing stones into the water, seeing who could out-skip who. We didn't fight or curse at one another – we forgot we hated each other and just had fun hanging out together. Just like we did when we were little."

My heart swelled and my eyes watered.

"I miss those times," I admitted.

Darcy was silent for a moment before he said, "Me too."

I turned and looked up at him. He was already staring down at me.

"Tell me no," he murmured as he lowered his head to mine.

My heart began to pound against my chest.

"What?" I whispered.

Darcy licked his trembling lips. "Tell me no. I'll kiss you if you don't."

His warning fell on deaf ears.

"Darcy, before I answer you, will you tell me something?"

He blinked. "Yeah?"

The conversation we had the other day was sitting on my mind, and I just had to ask the question that had been bugging me.

"What did you mean when you said I should take you calling me the opposite of Laura Stoke as a compliment and not an insult?"

Darcy stared into my eyes, the corners of his own eyes crinkling slightly as a smile curved his lips. "Laura in her own right is sexy, but you . . . you, my Neala Girl, are beautiful. Anyone can be sexy, but not everyone can be beautiful."

Oh, my.

My stomach exploded into butterflies, and tingles shot up and down my spine.

"Yes," I breathed.

Darcy swallowed. "Yes what?"

"Yes, I want you to kiss me."

I felt Darcy's body shake as he lowered his mouth to mine.

"Don't be scared," I whispered seconds before his lips touched mine.

CHAPTER SEVENTEEN

I opened up all my senses to Darcy.

I could feel him, taste him, hear him, smell him, and see him. I wanted him.

All of him.

I lifted my arms and slid them around Darcy's shoulders until I clasped my hands together behind his neck. I pulled his head closer to mine until our faces were pressed against one another. I opened my mouth and welcomed Darcy's warm, wet tongue. I mimicked his actions with my own. After a long moment I switched things up by nibbling on his lower lip with my teeth, and I could tell he liked it because he growled.

Darcy has growled at me enough over the years for me to decipher whether it was a good or bad growl, and this growl was good. *Very* good.

I groaned when his arms came around my back and he hoisted me up onto his lap. I moved my left leg and turned my body until I was straddling him. Straddling Darcy turned out to not be the best option, because the longer and harder I kissed him, the more my core ached and begged to be touched. I moved my hands away from Darcy to the back of the couch, where I gripped it.

"Neala," Darcy breathed against my mouth.

He pulled away and kissed along my jaw and down to my neck. He nuzzled there for a moment, then kissed the spot just under my ear, and it caused me to buck against him. I groaned out loud, and Darcy latched onto my neck and sucked.

"Darcy!" I cried, and ground my pelvis against his.

What the hell was going on me with me?

I was acting like a wild animal.

Get some self-control, woman!

It was extremely difficult, though, because it felt like I *couldn't* control myself, and that I had to have Darcy in every way possible.

"Neala Girl," Darcy murmured into my neck.

I moaned in response and pushed toward his mouth, making him chuckle.

"Are you okay?" he asked me.

I pulled back and growled at him. "If you stop touching me, we'll have a problem."

Darcy blinked at me. "I've never seen this side to you before . . . It's sexy as fuck."

I grinned. "Not beautiful?"

Darcy reached up and brushed his thumb over my cheek. "You're always beautiful, but baby, you're proving you can be sexy, too."

Baby.

I liked that.

I looked at Darcy and swallowed.

I felt like I was floating only to smack down hard on the concrete. This was Darcy, *my* Darcy. I had loved him a long time ago, and I hated him for years, but I'd also had an odd attraction that had solidified into a crush over the past few days. I'd never realised it, but Darcy was someone who was constantly on my mind, and seeing him made my day – even if it was just going to be filled with the pair of us arguing.

I think I had a serious *thing* for Darcy.

Shite.

I ground my pelvis against his once more, and this time I *felt* him.

"Neala Girl, don't do that. I don't want to upset you, but grinding on me will only make me hard. I know you're excited and—"

"I want to have sex with you," I cut Darcy off.

He reared back and stared at me with wide, shocked eyes.

"Neala—"

"Don't, Darcy. Don't you dare ruin this and reject me."

He looked pained. "I don't want to ruin this, trust me. I would love *nothing* more than to explore every inch of you, but I want to respect you, baby. I want your trust."

He was killing me.

"Darcy, please, I'm not a little girl. I'm twenty-five years of age, and I just realised that I've wanted you for as long as I can remember. I've waited long enough to have you; don't make me wait a minute longer."

He was torn between doing what his body wanted and what his mind was telling him, so I decided to make it even harder for him. Literally.

I stood up and reached down to the hem of my borrowed t-shirt and pulled it up my body and over my head, and threw it behind me on the floor. I pushed the trousers down and shimmied my hips from left to right until they gathered in a pool of fabric around my ankles. I stepped out of them and looked up. Darcy's eyes were almost popping out of his head as they roamed over my bare chest.

"Fuck," he hissed.

His look of admiration spurred my moment of bravery onward.

I reached down and slipped my fingers under the band of the boxers I wore and teased him by pushing them down slowly, before pulling them back up. Darcy's breathing had quickened and he sucked his lower lip into his mouth when I smirked and pushed the boxers all the way down, and kicked the fabric away from my feet. I dragged my feet against the floor until my socks slid off, and when the material had left my body I stood before Darcy naked as the day I was born.

"Oh, Christ," Darcy swore.

Was that good or bad?

Fuck, maybe this was a terrible idea.

I opened my mouth to apologise, but Darcy silenced me with the heated look he shot my way. He dropped his eyes to my breasts, then lower and *lower*. I was mortified, and just barely refrained from covering myself with my hands. My breathing increased, and my heart kicked into overdrive when Darcy suddenly got up from the couch and stood before me.

He reached out with his hand and brushed his thumb over my left pebbled nipple and hissed to himself. I licked my lips and looked up at him when he slid his hand up my chest and onto my neck, then cupped my cheek.

"You're beautiful," he breathed.

All worry and doubt fled my body with that single sentence.

"You're perfect, my Neala Girl."

My Neala Girl.

My.

I suddenly had the urge to cry, but I didn't. I was happy, so happy, and I felt more comfortable being naked with Darcy than I ever have fully clothed with anyone else.

I wanted to tell Darcy to take his clothes off, but I couldn't speak, so I reached out and tugged on the hem of his t-shirt. He looked down, then looked back up to me with a grin on his face.

"You have made it impossible for me to be a gentleman and leave you with your virtue intact."

I felt a spike of sassiness shoot through me.

"In that case you'll just have to tear it to shreds."

He growled. "Don't tempt me. I want to be gentle with you."

Gentle?

Not a chance.

"Fine, you be gentle with me, and I'll be rough with you."

I gripped the hem of his t-shirt and pulled the material up his body. I left it at the point where Darcy raised his arms, but couldn't see because the shirt was bunched up in his face. I reached out and ran my hands down his chest and over the six-pack I'd drooled over two days before.

His abs were as hard as I thought they might be.

I dipped my fingers down the tempting V line, but pulled away when Darcy growled and began to remove the shirt over his head. Before he could stop me, I dipped my head to his chest, snaked my tongue out, and circled his left nipple.

"Fuck!" He hissed in time with the soft plop if his shirt hitting the floor.

I placed my hands on his hips and squeezed in warning for him not to touch or stop me. I trailed my tongue from one nipple to the other and licked and sucked until Darcy's breathing picked up to an even faster pace. I bent my knees as I trailed my tongue down from his chest and onto his abs.

"Don't do this to me, please," Darcy begged.

I sank to my knees before him and smiled when he started to recite the Hail Mary and Our Father.

"Jesus himself couldn't get you out of this, Darcy, so take it like a man."

He looked down at me with hooded eyes. "I don't want you to do anything you will regret . . . I don't want you to wake up in the morning and realise you made a mistake and hate me again."

My heart hurt with Darcy's words.

I stood up and placed my hands on his cheeks. "I won't . . . Hey, I won't regret being with you. The only thing I regret is all the lost time we could have had together."

Darcy's eyebrows jumped. "You want us to be . . . *together*."

Should I have said that?

I swallowed. "I don't know. Maybe? I know we're jumping in headfirst here, pun intended, but I need you. I think once I have you it will get this unceasing need for you out of me system and we can start to get to know one another on a romantic level. I mean, if you want to, that is."

Darcy lifted his hand to my face and caressed it gently before he snaked his hand back into my hair and pulled.

"Once I have you, no amount of time together will get me out of your system. You will crave me, Neala Girl."

Oh, fuck.

"I hope you have the skills to back up that big mouth of yours, Hart."

He smirked and released his grip on my hair. "You'll soon find out, Clarke."

I backed up and Darcy grinned. "Go ahead. I'll give you a five-second head start."

Five seconds?

To what? Run?

"Four, three—"

I squealed then turned and took off running out of the living room and down the hallway in the direction of Darcy's bedroom. Suddenly I stopped, the danger of falling dawning on me. There were no lit candles in the hallway and I couldn't see a thing.

"I can't see!" I called out.

I screamed with fright when I felt a hand touch my hip.

"I won't let you fall," he murmured in my ear as he pressed his front to my back.

My insides quaked and I started to sweat with anticipation.

Darcy nudged me forward until I started to walk. I don't know how he could see – everything was black – but he could, because he was guiding my steps. I swallowed when Darcy reached around me and opened the door to his bedroom on my left. Dim light from the candles inside lit the rest of the way, and seeing his bed halted my steps.

"What's wrong?" Darcy asked as he tenderly kissed my neck.

I swallowed. "I'm about to lose my virginity . . . I'm kind of scared."

His lips froze on my neck.

I was momentarily worried I'd said the wrong thing, but he turned me to face him and leaned down and pressed his forehead to mine. "I'm going to take care of you. You know I will . . . don't you?"

I did; I knew he wouldn't purposely hurt me.

"I do . . . It's still a little scary, though. I know the first time hurts, and I'm a wuss when it comes to pain. What if I cry and ruin the entire process?"

Darcy roared with laughter. "Process? Sex isn't a process – it's an act of epic pleasure between two people. You're thinking about this way too much."

I placed my hands on his chest and playfully shoved him before I leaned into him and rested my head against his chest.

"I'm afraid it won't be epic," I admitted.

He tensed. "You think I can't make it great for you?"

Oh, shite.

"I wasn't doubting *your* abilities; I was doubting *mine*. What if I'm crap at it and you would rather die than continue?"

Darcy vibrated with silent laughter, so I shoved him hard.

"I'm deadly serious here!"

He continued to laugh and it ticked me off, so I turned and walked away from him. I crawled onto the end of his bed, and just as I made my way up the mattress Darcy placed his hands on my back and applied pressure. I flattened onto my stomach as his hand slid down my back and over my arse, where he squeezed.

"Darcy!" I gasped.

He chuckled and slid his hands down my thighs all the way to my ankles and back up again. When he came to my hips he gripped me tightly and turned me over. I was now on my back, staring up at the ceiling. I widened my eyes when Darcy placed his hands on my knees and spread my legs apart.

"You have such a pretty pussy, baby . . . and you're so wet," Darcy growled.

Oh. My. God.

My body flooded with mortification, and I slammed my legs closed with a loud clap.

"I *cannot* believe you just said that!" I screeched, and covered my face with my hands.

I didn't want to be embarrassed – I wanted to relish Darcy's words, but I couldn't.

It was just so . . . *dirty*.

He groaned and lightly bit my outer thigh before he said, "Neala Girl, your innocence is killing me."

I kept my hands over my face. "Don't say stuff like that to me and I won't turn into a tomato then. God!"

He cackled. "You're brilliant."

I wanted to sock him one for laughing at me, but I refused to move my hands from my face.

"Are you going to look at me while I taste you for the first time?" Darcy asked, his voice low and husky.

"What are you going to do?" I asked as my body began to shake.

"Move your hands away from your face and I'll show you *exactly* what I mean."

I shuddered, and went against every fibre in my body: I removed my hands from my face and looked down.

I looked down to Darcy and licked my lips when he patted his hands against my knees. I looked at my legs and cringed; they were locked up tighter than Fort Knox. I released the tension in both legs and let Darcy spread them apart. I focused on my breathing when he lay down flat on his stomach and had his face at vagina level.

Bare vagina level.

"Omigod," I mumbled.

Darcy looked up at me and then back to my vagina, where he lightly blew on me.

I hissed. "Darcy."

He hummed. "You're clean shaven," he commented.

I swallowed. "I get waxed."

Waxing was a personal preference for me. I didn't like hair anywhere on my body except on my head.

"I like it," he murmured, then leaned forward and pressed a light kiss against the top of my slit before trailing his tongue down over my tender lips.

My back arched off the bed at the foreign but toe-curling sensation.

"Don't be scared, baby. You will enjoy this, trust me."

I did trust him.

"Are you ready?" he asked.

I nodded, because words were lost to me.

"Eyes on me. *Watch* what I do to you."

I nodded again.

I watched as Darcy hooked his arms under my legs and placed his hands spread out over my hips. I felt the move open my lips and fully spread them apart to reveal the most intimate part of my body. Darcy applied pressure to my hips and held me in place. I didn't know why, because I wasn't going to move even if I wanted to – I was frozen.

I widened my eyes when Darcy pushed my legs open further with his shoulders. He kept his eyes locked on mine as he lowered his head and snaked his tongue out. He placed his tongue on me and licked from my entrance up to my clit.

Oh, fuck.

I gasped and bucked up against Darcy's mouth, but the lower half of my body didn't move, because Darcy had a tight hold of me. I looked to Darcy with hooded eyes when he growled.

"So sweet," he said, before he put his tongue back on me.

This time it wasn't one long lick; it was an assault from his tongue on my clit. I wanted to come up off the bed with the incredible new sensations that racked throughout my body. I'd touched myself before and brought myself great pleasure, but Darcy's tongue was *so* much better than my fingers.

I reached down and buried my hands in his hair and tugged. He hissed against me and nipped at my clit with his teeth in response to my hair pulling.

I screamed at the unexpected sensation of mixed pain and pleasure and pushed my head back into the mattress of the bed. I looked up at the ceiling and focused on it. I tried to think of anything and everything except what Darcy's tongue was doing to me and how it made me want to growl in satisfaction. Any chance of distraction failed, because one thing I couldn't escape from was the feeling of Darcy's mouth on me, and what his mouth was doing to my body.

I licked my lips and whimpered when sharp shocks of pleasure zinged from my clit. I pushed my pelvis up into Darcy's face; he responded by sucking my clit into his mouth and gently shaking his head from left to right. I held my breath for a moment, but when the hot pulses of pleasure became too much I tried to crawl up the bed and away from Darcy's tongue.

"Too much!" I screamed. "Ah, it's too much!"

Darcy ignored my cries and bore down on my clit and licked and sucked at the bundle of nerves until my hips involuntarily bucked against his face and my back arched. I groaned in pleasure as I fisted the bed sheets in my hands. Fire spread from my clit down my thighs and straight up to my lower stomach, where an explosion of delight took hold of me.

My mouth hung open, my breathing halted, and my eyes were squeezed tightly shut.

I felt Darcy move his mouth away from me, and then he jumped off the bed and moved around to his dresser. I heard him open the dresser and then the faint crinkling sound.

I knew it was a condom packet without opening my eyes.

I was so nervous, but my body still hummed with little aftershocks of pleasure, so I was pretty chill as I lay spread-eagled on Darcy's bed. I heard a whooshing sound as fabric hit the floor, then a creak as Darcy climbed back onto the bed.

I opened my eyes when he ran his hand up my thighs and moved between them. He reached forward with his hand and touched his thumb against my still very sensitive clit, and I cried out. He chose that moment to line himself up against me; he thrust forward a few times, and each time the head of his cock rubbed against my clit I bucked and groaned.

"Neala," Darcy whispered.

I opened my eyes, and the moment I made eye contact with Darcy, he thrust forward. I bit my lip with the discomfort. I looked down and even though there was minimal lighting in the room I saw he wasn't fully inside me.

Oh, Christ.

I looked up to Darcy and released my lip, but the moment he pulled the head of his cock out of me and thrust forward again with a little more force, I squeezed my eyes shut as pain exploded inside me.

I whimpered and fisted the bed sheets in my hand.

Darcy stilled. "Open your eyes, beautiful girl."

I opened my eyes and was surprised when tears fell from them, then ran down my temples and into my hairline. Darcy leaned down and kissed over my tear streaks, and then brushed his lips over my eyes.

"You're incredible," he breathed.

I swallowed my sniffles.

"You're big," I replied breathlessly.

Darcy smiled at me for a moment before he leaned down and kissed me. It was during our kiss that he pulled out of me and thrust back inside. He *was* gentle, but it felt like he was cutting into me, because the walls around him stung with the intrusion. I focused on my breathing, and on Darcy's kiss. I allowed myself to get lost in him, and when he pulled out of me and thrust forward once more I didn't feel pain; I felt a little something that was . . . good.

I opened my eyes when Darcy broke our kiss. I looked down at our connected bodies and Darcy's perfectly crafted stomach was the first thing I saw. I looked lower and swallowed.

He was *really* inside of me.

"Oh, my God," I breathed, and made sure not to move a muscle.

Darcy rested on his elbows as he hovered over me.

"Look at me," he said.

I looked at him, and when my eyes made contact with his I started to relax.

"That's it baby, relax. You're okay. Trust me."

I panted, "I do."

I really did.

Darcy licked his lips; then he leaned down and kissed me again. I lifted my hands to his biceps, slid my hands up his arms, up his neck, and buried them in his thick hair. I tugged and knotted my fingers in his brown locks and deepened our kiss.

I relaxed my legs and tensed only a little when Darcy slowly pulled out of me and thrust back in. He went slowly and was very gentle – it helped ease the sensation of him stretching me. With each thrust I started to feel little zings of pleasure, and I felt so much better because of it. The pain was gone – I'd got past the worst of it.

Thank God.

Darcy set a slow and steady pace for a few minutes as he gently thrust in and out of my body until I moaned. I heard him grunt as he ever so slightly thrust into me harder, and picked up his pace.

I broke the kiss Darcy and I shared when he thrust into my body hard, and a shiver of pure satisfaction rushed around my core.

What was that?

"Fuck," I whispered.

Darcy pressed his forehead to mine. "Are you hurting?" he asked. "I'll stop if you are."

Like hell he'd stop.

"The opposite." I groaned and tested the waters by pushing my hips down on Darcy, which caused him to moan in pleasure as he fully slid back inside me.

"Jesus, Neala," he said, and moved his mouth to my cheek, where he bit down.

It didn't hurt at all – if possible, this was turning me on more than I already was.

Darcy moved his mouth to my neck. He kissed, licked, and sucked on me as he thrust harder into my body.

Each thrust caused a slap as our skin smacked together; the sound rang out in the room, followed by our mixed grunts and moans. My body was on fire, and I boldly asked, "Can I ride you?"

Darcy halted his movements, and it caused my insides to contract with disapproval.

"You want to be on top?" he asked.

I nodded.

I screeched when he gripped onto my waist, rolled his body under mine, and pulled me on top of him. I gasped when I sat upright and looked down. I was straddling Darcy, and he was still inside me.

"How the hell did you do that?" I asked in shock.

Darcy didn't reply; instead, he placed his hands on my waist and rolled his hips upwards, causing my eyes to drift shut. I opened my eyes, then placed my hands on his and looked at him for direction.

"Up and down, baby," Darcy encouraged, and hissed when I did as he asked. He bucked his hips upwards when I sank down on him and growled, "Just like that."

I repeated the action of moving up and down until I fell into a slow and steady rhythmic bounce. Each thrust Darcy made as I sank down on him was toe curling. I leaned my head back and arched my back when my inner muscles contracted around him.

He groaned and reached up and palmed my breasts in his hands, tweaking my nipples. I hissed and looked down at him and growled as he smirked up at me.

"You're *so* fucking sexy, baby."

I loved the compliments he gave – each one made me feel more confident than the last.

I bore down on him and contracted my inner muscles around him once more, and watched as his face lit up with pleasure. I loved that I was making him feel good, and I loved that he was making *me* feel this good.

"Neala Girl." He groaned. "I'm not going to last long."

I purred with pleasure that I was the cause of his being about to lose control.

I picked up my pace and rode him faster. He curled his hands around my arms and squeezed me each time I squeezed him with my internal muscles.

"Fuck!" he shouted.

Fuelled on by his shouts I slammed down on him harder and faster, until his body thrust up into me at lightning speed, seeking its release. When he came Darcy's entire body tensed, while his hips bucked up against me in quick spurts.

My entire body was flushed with pleasure as I looked down at Darcy's spent body. I wanted to repeat what we had just done again and again, but I wasn't greedy. I hadn't been expecting to orgasm at all during my first sexual experience, but I had, and that was enough for me. I wouldn't have cared if I never came at all, because it was with Darcy. That made it even more perfect to me.

Darcy was right: it was an *epic* act of pleasure.

"Neala . . . Holy Christ," he rasped after a few moments.

He opened his eyes and gazed up at me like I was a goddess, and it made me feel incredibly beautiful.

"That was amazing; *you* are amazing. Just . . . wow," Darcy said as he licked his lips.

I leaned forward and pressed my lips against his. "It was perfect," I swallowed, then rolled off him, hissing a little when he slid out of me.

I lay next to Darcy's panting body for a few minutes just revelling in what had just happened. I couldn't believe I had had sex. I couldn't believe I had had sex with *Darcy*.

"Oh, my God," I whispered.

Darcy was busy removing the condom from himself. He leaned over and tossed it into the little bin next to his bed; then he turned on his side to face me. He placed his hand on my stomach and bent his elbow to rest his chin in his palm.

"You look stunning," he said, and smiled down at me.

I smiled wide. "I feel amazing."

Darcy glanced down then back up to me. "Any pain?" he asked. I shook my head.

"That's good." He smiled. "There is some blood on the sheets under you, and a little on you and me, but it's completely normal, so don't worry. Okay?"

I nodded and looked down.

I was expecting a lot of blood, but there wasn't much, so I didn't worry about it. I should have felt mortified and wanted to do nothing except run to the bathroom and clean myself up, but I was content and happy.

I just didn't care.

I turned to Darcy, pushed him onto his back, and straddled him. His hands went to my hips, and he grinned. "Again?" he asked.

I nodded.

"You were right." I smiled. "Once with you isn't enough."

I leaned down, covered Darcy's mouth with mine, and got lost in him once more.

CHAPTER EIGHTEEN

I woke up to banging.

Not *that* kind of banging. I mean banging as in something or someone knocking hard on my house – my front door, to be exact. That was impossible, though, because my doorway was blocked with snow.

When everything was silent, I put the noise down to my mind hearing things. But I quashed that idea when I heard my name being called by a familiar voice.

What the hell?

I opened my eyes and made a move to sit up, but the weight on my chest and torso made that difficult.

Weight?

I looked down and blinked my eyes.

Neala.

She was sprawled out over me . . . naked.

Extremely naked.

The events of last night came crashing into my mind, and caused me to widen my eyes. Neala and I had had some wine, made friends, and called a truce on our antics . . . Then we'd had sex.

Amazing sex.

"Fuck," I whispered.

I was so screwed.

I couldn't believe I'd had sex with her. Twice.

I'd wanted to – God, I'd *really* wanted to – but now that I was thinking with the head on my shoulders it didn't seem like such a good idea. It actually seemed like the worst thing that could have ever happened to either of us, because when Neala woke up shit was going to hit the fan.

It had to have been the drinks that caused things to escalate between us so quickly.

There was no way in hell that she would *willingly* want to shag me right after becoming friends. We had hated each other for *fifteen years*, and we were both fools if we thought one night in the sack could make us forget about that.

I pressed my head back into my pillow and closed my eyes.

What the hell was I thinking?

I hadn't meant for sex to happen between us. If anything, *Neala* was the one who'd pressed the idea, but I'd be lying if I said I didn't want her. I hadn't realised until last night that a lot of my hate for her was simply my wanting what I couldn't have.

Well, I'd had her, and it just didn't seem enough. I wanted her again, and again, and again.

I thought of all the times that I'd accidentally caught myself thinking of her in a sexual way, or dreaming of her in a sexual way, then of the times when I could have killed the men who looked in her direction a little too long.

Maybe it really *was* just a case of wanting the forbidden fruit – she was my friend's sister and my archenemy, after all . . . But if that was the case, then why did I enjoy having her in my arms so much?

I looked down to her sleeping form and sighed.

I liked her, and *not* just in a sexual way either.

I liked *her*.

Bollocks.

This was only going to end with my head, and heart, hurting. Neala had probably been drunk after the few gulps of wine she'd had, even though she'd seemed fine, and just wanted sex, whereas I think I'd just wanted sex with *her*.

That was the difference – I didn't want just anyone . . . I wanted *her*.

"Fuck . . . I want her," I mumbled to myself, and lifted my free hand to my face and rubbed my eyes.

Jesus.

When the hell did all my hate suddenly turn into lust and like for Neala?

I was mad at myself.

I felt like my head, my entire body, had pulled a three-sixty and fucked me over.

What was I going to do?

Neala wouldn't feel the same way. I knew she would explode into a fit of rage when she realised what had gone down between us. She would blame me for tricking her into giving me her virginity, and then she would convince herself this was me playing a sick game with her. It would hurt her. It would *really* hurt her that she had had sex with me if she thought those were my intentions.

Even if I explained myself and came clean with an explanation that what had happened between us was real, or real for *me*, she wouldn't hear it. She would make up her own mind and pit it against me. She always did.

I was fucked.

"Darcy?"

I narrowed my eyes and looked down to Neala, but she was still sleeping, so she couldn't have said my name.

Who the fuck was that?

I very carefully removed myself from Neala's hold. I grabbed the pillow from behind my head and put it in her arms so she would still have something to hold on to. She mumbled my name in her sleep, and it caused me to freeze.

Was she dreaming of me?

I shook the thought from my head when I heard the banging noise from outside again, and more than one voice this time. I carefully slipped out of my bed when I was sure Neala wasn't disturbed. I grabbed a pair of boxers from the bottom drawer of my dresser and put them on. I tiptoed my way over to my bedroom door, gently opened it, then stepped out into my hallway, closing it behind me.

"Darcy? Mate, you in there?"

"Of course he's in there, you bloody eejit; they're *trapped*."

I found myself smiling when Sean's and Justin's arguing voices could be heard plain as day. I walked over to my front door and banged on it twice.

"I'm here," I called out.

I heard both my brother and Sean cheer, which made me laugh.

"Told you she wouldn't kill him; pay up," Justin's voice happily stated.

They'd bet on my life?

"It could have gone either way, you prick. Here," Sean grunted in response.

They were *both* pricks.

"You're both something else, you know that?" I shouted.

"Yeah, we know," they both replied in unison, then laughed.

I smiled and shook my head.

I placed my hand on the handle of my door and pressed down. With a little tug the door pulled open and a fair amount of snow spilled into my hallway. I stepped in it and yelped as I jumped backward.

"Fuck, that's cold," I hissed.

I looked up at the same time Justin and Sean looked at me. Sean took one glance at me and narrowed his eyes. He looked back to Justin who grinned at me in amusement.

"What's with you two?" I asked.

Justin scratched the back of his head and fully smiled at me while Sean glared.

"Seriously, *what?*" I pressed.

Justin nodded to my chest; so I looked down to see what the big deal was. When I spotted what had both of the lads acting weird, I tensed and instantly held my hands up as I looked back up to Sean.

"Sean . . . Mate . . ."

Sean shook his head. "She's twenty-five; I can't say anything, but fuck, man . . . She's my little sister."

I looked back down to my chest and at the large red scratches across it that Neala had caused during the second round of sex last night, and decided to get them both seeing my back out of the way, because it hurt ten times more than my chest did. I held my breath and turned around.

"Oh, for fuck's sake!" Sean growled.

I turned back around and grimaced. "If it's any consolation, they sting like fuck."

Sean grunted. "Good. I'm glad it hurts, you bastard."

I looked down and couldn't help but grin.

When I looked back up to Sean he was looking past me. "Where is she?"

I jammed my thumb over my shoulder. "Bedroom."

Both my brother and Sean shook their heads.

"I can't believe this. You both *really* shagged?" Justin asked.

Sean looked like he was about to cry or be sick.

Possibly both.

I groaned, "What happened to saying Merry Christmas?"

"Merry Christmas," they both said, and then Justin repeated, "Did you shag?"

I blushed slightly, then laughed in response, along with a one-shouldered shrug.

"This is the worst Christmas ever," Sean grumbled.

I momentarily felt bad for him – he knew I'd had sex with his little sister. That must be a horrible thing to hear. I was impressed with his composure, though; Neala was everything to Sean, so I wondered how much restraint he was using to stop himself from beating me senseless.

I laughed at Sean and gestured them into the house. "Awkwardness aside, thanks for digging us out. I tried doing it two days ago and the fucking makeshift tunnel I made collapsed on me."

Justin widened his eyes as he glanced to Sean, then back to me. "Fuck. Were you hurt?"

I grunted. "Only me pride, because Neala had to pull me out."

Sean and Justin looked at one another, and after a moment they both burst into laughter.

Dickheads.

"Yeah, yeah. Laugh it up. I was close to blacking out because I couldn't breathe."

That put a sock in the hyenas' laughter.

"Fuck," Justin muttered.

Sean nodded. "Glad you're okay, man, but I'm sort of happy that you almost died. It makes me feel better about you and Neala . . . *you know*."

Yeah, I knew.

I looked up at the sky and smiled. "I never thought I'd be this happy to see the sky. I don't think we would have lasted much longer in there. The power cut out three days ago."

Justin looked at me, his face frozen. "Was there anything for you both to eat?"

I shook my head. "My cooker is electric, so we had to eat beans and stuff, because everything I bought needed to be cooked. I'm out a couple of hundred quid this week already; all me food in the fridge is spoiled, so I have to buy everything fresh."

Justin raked his hand through his hair, while Sean looked down at the shovel that was in his hand and twirled it around.

Odd.

"Was everyone affected like us?" I asked Justin, who looked perplexed. "You said you were snowed in too when I rang the other day."

He gnawed on his lower lip. "Yeah, man, but it wasn't as bad as you and Neala had it. Everyone helped out everyone else in the village, but it was . . . difficult to get up here with the roads being so bad."

I nodded in understanding.

"Yeah, I bet it was bad . . . but it's clear now?"

Sean and Justin nodded. They momentarily reminded me of robots.

"Yeah," Sean said. "The council gritted the roads so they're easier to drive on now."

That was some good news.

I was about to tell my brother and Sean that, but I hesitated when I caught them exchanging glances. I looked down at myself to make sure I wasn't sporting an awkward boner, but when I saw I was wood-free I looked back to the lads.

"What's wrong with you both?"

Sean gnawed on his inner cheek. "Nothing, lad. I'm just wondering how you aren't cold. I'm freezing me arse off here and I'm fully clothed. You're in underpants and you aren't even shivering."

The cold *was* bothering me, but I was just stalling from moving away from the door, because as soon as they stepped inside my house it wasn't just me and Neala anymore.

"His morning mattress dancing probably still has him warm," Justin teased.

I was about to correct him, but I let his comment lie when Sean came at him with his shovel raised.

"I'm messing!" Justin screeched, and fell backward into a huge pile of snow.

I burst out laughing and so did Sean.

"No joking about sex when it involves me little sister, ever."

Justin groaned as he got to his feet and brushed the snow from his clothes. "Noted."

I held up my hands and nodded to Sean so he knew I'd got the memo. I mean, if he came at Justin and threatened him with a shovel for playfully *teasing* about sex with Neala, I'd hate to think what he'd do to me if I pissed him off for actually *having* sex with her.

It wouldn't end well for me – that was for sure.

I looked behind me, and when I saw my bedroom door was still closed I gestured for the lads to come into my house.

"Come in; she's still out," I said.

I walked down the hallway to my sitting room and opened the door.

I smiled when light filled the room instead of darkness.

"I shovelled most of the snow and cleared it away from the glass – I was hoping to scare you if you were in here," Justin said from behind me.

I entered my sitting room and laughed. "Cheers for that, you prick."

The lads froze behind me as they looked through the door.

"You actually *finished* decorating?" Justin asked, more than surprised from the look on his face.

I smiled. "Not me – Neala."

"Sounds like her." Sean commented.

I nodded.

He grimaced then. "So . . . what's happening now with you both?"

My stomach dropped at the question, because I honestly had no idea.

"I guess we'll go back to our old ways and do what we normally do – hate each other."

I didn't want it to be that way, but the Neala I knew wouldn't let go of things so easily. We had had fifteen years of problems, and I just couldn't see Neala forgetting about that after one night together.

Justin furrowed his eyebrows at me while Sean full-on glared.

I swallowed and blew out a breath. "I know it sounds harsh, trust me, I don't want to say it, but when she wakes up and realises what's happened she will go crazy."

Sean stepped forward. "Realises what's happened?"

Oh shite.

I'd worded that terribly.

"She *knows* what's happened, last night . . . We were caught up in the moment. What I mean is that she's gonna regret what we did. I know how she is, and the blame will, as usual, fall at my feet. It's going to ruin what was said before the sex happened. It's too good to be true."

Justin frowned. "What was said?"

I scratched my neck. "We made friends, and called an indefinite truce on our bullshit. We were pretty happy last night, and then we necked down a lot of wine and, bam. Sex."

It was weird now that I thought of it. I had drunk a fair amount of wine, and so had Neala, but we had both been sober. At most I'd probably felt a tiny bit tipsy, but I hadn't even noticed it, so I can say for certain the drinking hadn't made us lose control; we had done that all on our own.

Sean pinched the bridge of his nose. "Sorry, man."

I forced a smile. "Me too."

Justin continued to frown at me. "Do you regret what happened between the pair of you?"

I was torn.

"I don't regret making friends with Neala, but I do regret having sex with her. I mean, not the initial act but the impending aftermath . . . It was just a mistake. I can't believe I thought it would actually be good for us and that it could be a step in a new direction. I was wrong. The best thing for us is just being platonic friends and—"

"And what?"

I froze, Justin froze, and even Sean froze.

The lads took a step away from one another and revealed a beautifully flushed Neala wrapped in my bed sheets. She was a thing of elegance, and just as I was about to smile at her I looked into her eyes, her hurt eyes, and my heart cracked.

"Neala," I breathed, and shook my head.

Neala swallowed. "Finish what you were saying; go on."

I couldn't move or speak.

Neala's eyes began to well up. "Finish it. Tell our brothers how much you regret last night and how much of a mistake we are."

Oh, Christ.

I was frantic. "Neala, please. You don't understand—"

"I understand fucking perfectly! You promised we would be different . . . You *promised* we wouldn't hate each other again."

A nervous sweat broke out across my forehead. "We won't—"

"Liar! *Don't* fucking lie to me!" she screamed as tears streaked down her cheeks.

This was bad.

This was *very* bad.

I wanted to tell her how I really felt, but I clammed up, knowing Sean and Justin were listening intently. I didn't know why, but I froze and couldn't say the words she needed to hear.

When I didn't respond to Neala, she angrily wiped at her face and shot me a look filled with so much hate it knocked me back a couple of steps. I felt sick.

"Please," I managed to get out.

I didn't know what I was saying please for, but I said it anyway, hoping she would have mercy on me.

"Please, what?" she hissed.

I blinked. "Don't hate me."

She looked at me for a long moment and said, "I don't hate you, Darcy . . . I *regret* you. I regret the day I *ever* met you."

I felt like I had had the wind knocked out of me by her words. I was about to reach out and go to her but she turned and stormed down the hallway and back into my bedroom. She slammed the door closed so hard the living room walls shook.

Sean and Justin stood idle by the doorway as they looked at me.

"Darcy . . ." Justin began, but I didn't stick around to hear what he had to say. I followed Neala down the hallway. I stood outside my bedroom and swallowed down the bile that rose up my throat.

I'd only just had her, and in a matter of seconds I'd lost her.

I felt empty.

I felt like nothing.

I placed my forehead on my bedroom door and exhaled.

I regret you.

That was the worst thing she could have said to me. It fucking hurt. I squeezed my eyes shut, and for the first time in my entire life I wished Neala had just said she hated me.

CHAPTER NINETEEN

I was going to be sick.

I stumbled forward into Darcy's bedroom with his bed sheets wrapped around my naked body and slammed the door shut. I grabbed my rumpled clothes from atop the dresser, and out of the corner of my eye I caught something pink in the top of Darcy's slightly open top drawer. I opened the drawer fully and found the pink-wrapped, and moderately damaged, doll box.

I focused on not screaming. He was *still* trying to take the doll from me, after everything – that was his main priority. I steadied myself and bent over just in case I did throw up, but when nothing happened I straightened and began to pant. I used one hand to hold the bed sheet around me, and my free hand to press against my forehead.

This wasn't happening.

Darcy regretted last night?

He regretted the sex we'd shared?

He regretted *me*?

"Neala?"

I choked back a sob, but could do nothing about the tears that freely streamed down my face.

"Leave me alone, Darcy. Please," I said through my tears.

He was as silent as a mouse, because I didn't hear him come into the room after me.

"I didn't mean what I said."

I sat on the side of his bed and reached down for my clothing. I didn't have my knickers – they were in Darcy's kitchen bin – so I grabbed my shoes and pulled my heels on instead. I stood up and uncaringly dropped the bed sheet from around my body. I wasn't embarrassed; if anything I felt disgusted. Darcy had seen every inch of me last night, but he'd said it was a mistake, so it meant nothing to him, which meant changing in front of him would also mean nothing to him. I pulled my dress over my head and fixed it on my body.

"No." I sniffled. "You did mean it; you just didn't mean for me to *hear* what you said."

Darcy moved closer to me – I could *feel* him behind me.

"That's not true, Neala. I said what I did because—"

"I don't care why you said it; I just care *that* you said it. Last night shouldn't have happened, Darcy." I put on my blazer and turned to face him. "You were right. I *did* wake up regretting what we did. It was a mistake."

I lied.

I flat-out lied through my teeth.

I refused to let Darcy know that he had just broken my heart for the second time. I wouldn't give him the satisfaction of knowing he'd pulled one over on me.

"This is the last time I'm allowing you to have the ability to hurt me. I *never* want to see or speak to you ever again. You're a pathetic coward, and if by some chance you even have a heart, it's not working; it's *frozen solid*."

Darcy's face paled and his shoulders slumped.

"Neala . . . I'm so sorry. I feel horrible. Please, I care about you so much. I don't even know why I said what I did. I swear I didn't mean it."

I walked forward, and just as I was about to pass him by I pressed the doll box against his chest. "This should make you feel better; it's want you wanted after all, right? Well, lucky you, you got want you wanted. You win, Darcy. Congratulations."

Neala: 1. Darcy: 2.

I let go of the box and walked out of Darcy's bedroom; then finally, after days of being trapped, I stepped foot out of his house. I made a silent vow to myself that I was *never* going to return.

When I was ready to leave, I left Darcy's house and found my brother was hot on my heels.

"Neala?" Sean said when I clumsily trekked the deep snow towards his truck. It was difficult to get my footing with heels on, but I managed it. I doubt I looked like anything except an idiot, but at least I didn't fall.

"Take me home. Please," I said as my body trembled.

Sean put his arm around me and quickly ushered me around his truck and to the passenger side. He helped me up, then shut the door. The heat in the truck from Sean's journey up to Darcy's house sent shivers up and down my spine. My skin tingled, and the pain that had taken up residence in my head eased slightly.

Sean shouted something to Justin who, standing in Darcy's doorway, nodded. I looked away when Sean came around to the driver's side of his truck and got in. He started the engine and slowly backed up until he could turn the truck around and get us onto the road leading down the mountain.

I think I managed a minute or two before I burst into tears.

"Baby girl." Sean sighed and reached out with his left hand and rubbed my shoulder.

I lifted my hands to my face and shook my head. "I'm o-okay."

Sean removed his hand and changed the gears on his truck, and then focused on driving down the slippery mountain roads.

"Did he hurt you?" Sean asked.

I glanced at him through my fingers and noticed his knuckles were gripped onto the steering wheel so tight that they were turning white.

"Not in the way you think." I sniffled and wiped my eyes.

Sean glanced at me. "In what way did he hurt you?"

I looked down and shrugged. "He said we were a mistake, that we didn't go together. He said he *regretted* me."

The tears came again when I finished speaking and I hated myself for it. I wanted to be strong, I wanted to say 'fuck Darcy,' but my heart hurt so deeply over him.

"Is that all he did?" Sean asked, his voice venomous.

I cleared my throat. "Yeah . . . I mean, when we . . . had sex . . . it hurt and I bled a little, but Darcy said it was normal for me the first time."

Things were silent for a moment until Sean growled low, deep in his throat, "I'm gonna fucking kill him!"

I widened my eyes and looked at him.

He was furious.

"Don't. It was c-consensual."

Darcy had hurt me, but Sean would kill him if he thought he'd forced himself on me, and that was the furthest thing from the truth. Sean looked to me and softened his eyes before he looked back at the road and narrowed them again.

"If he wasn't going to live up to whatever he made you believe, then he should have stayed the fuck away from you. I didn't think you were a virgin. Fuck. A fucking virgin! I'm going to murder the little prick!"

Oh, shite.

"Sean, please," I cried.

My brother muttered curses before he exhaled a large breath. "Why don't you want me to hurt him?"

"Because I care about him!" I snapped, then sank low in my seat, bruised over my admission.

I wished I didn't care.

I wished I hated Darcy again. Things were so much easier when I hated him . . . but I couldn't. I cared about him. I really liked him, and I felt sick that he didn't feel the same way.

Sean looked at me with wide eyes. "You really *care* about Darcy? I mean, I always had an inkling, but it's for real?"

"You th-think I would give myself up to someone who I didn't have a-any feelings for?" I asked, annoyed he would think of me in that light.

Sean shook his head. "No, of course not. I know you're not like that. I just mean . . . Since when do you care about *Darcy*?"

Since last night.

Well, it seemed I had always cared about him on some level; I just hadn't *realised* it until last night.

I wiped my runny nose with some tissues from Sean's glove box. "Things changed between us in his house. We called a truce. I thought we even became friends and things would be good between us . . . but apparently I was wrong, after hearing what he said to you and Justin."

Sean cursed some more. I tuned him out, because the more I listened to him the more upset I got. I looked out the windows at the snow-covered trees and focused on them as we drove.

I felt sick with myself.

I couldn't believe I'd acted like a sex-deprived maniac last night. I'd practically torn Darcy's clothes from his body and begged him to take me. I was beyond mortified, and I was deeply hurt.

Why did he say what he did to Sean and Justin?

Was last night just about him pulling the ultimate prank? Stripping me of my virginity and making me enjoy it in the process?

I was so unsure, and that killed me.

I wanted it to be real, but the chance that it was probably fake gutted me.

"I don't want to talk about this anymore, Sean."

Sean was silent for a moment; then he said, "I'm sorry, Sis."

I looked to him and gave him a small smile. "Don't be sorry; you did nothing wrong."

Sean's face fell, his mouth straightened to a thin line, and his eyes looked sad.

I hated that my situation with Darcy upset him so much.

I looked forward and folded my arms across my chest and enjoyed the silence of the rest of the drive back home . . . and when I say *home*, I mean my parents' house.

"Dinner is in two hours," Sean said as we pulled up. "Go get showered and into something warm – preferably something that covers your arse instead of exposing it," he muttered.

His big-brother ways brought a genuine smile out on my face, so I leaned over and kissed his cheek as he parked his truck in my parents' driveway. "I will . . . Thanks for saving me."

"Always," Sean mumbled, and sighed as I climbed out of the truck.

I folded my arms across my chest as I hopped around the truck and onto the cleared pathway.

"Watch out for black ice. I put salt all over, but I might have missed some spots," Sean called out from behind me.

"Okay," I shouted, and slowed my pace.

The freezing cold breeze had gone right through me by the time I reached my parents' front door. I balled my hand into a fist and banged on the door.

"Cavewoman, press the bell," Sean said from behind me.

I rolled my eyes and pressed the doorbell.

A moment went by before my mother opened the door. She was wearing a Mrs. Claus onesie and she had antlers on her head – it was enough for me not to take her seriously.

"You're free!" my mother shouted.

I raised my eyebrows when Dustin's voice shouted from the living room, "Frrreedddoooommm!"

I looked over my shoulder to Sean, who was grinning. "He watched *Braveheart* with us lads last night."

Of course he did.

I turned back around and gave my mother a closed-lipped smile. "I need a shower." And to be left alone.

My mother placed her hands on my cheeks. "You were crying."

I blinked my eyes. "I don't want to talk about it."

I moved around my mother and walked by the living room and down the hall to the stairs. My parents had never touched my bedroom when I moved out, so it was still the same as when I'd left it at twenty-two. It meant I had clothes here and everything was familiar.

Familiarity was something I needed right now.

As I headed up the stairs I heard my mother ask Sean, "Where are Darcy and Justin?"

"Darcy can't make dinner today; he's busy!" I shouted, and continued to walk up the stairs.

When I was in my old room I broke down, then almost immediately mentally scowled at myself for it.

"Stop it!" I hissed, and shook my head.

I forced my mind to think of simple things, like getting a shower.

Hot water. Shower gel. Shampoo and conditioner.

Heaven.

I stripped myself free of my blazer, dress, and heels – vowing to burn each item as it hit the floor. I walked into the en-suite bathroom and turned on the water. I waited a few moments until steam poured from the showerhead.

I stepped under the hot spray of water and sighed with delight. I did nothing for a few minutes but stand there and revel in the heat as each toasty droplet hit my skin and caused tingles to spread over the surface of my body. When I was relaxed, or as relaxed as I could be, I reached for my shampoo and squeezed a huge amount on my hand. I spread it out over my head with both hands and rubbed it into my scalp until a thick lather of suds appeared. I roughly scrubbed my scalp, then dragged the suds down my hair and gave the middle and ends a good cleanse. I washed my hair out and repeated the step simply because I hadn't washed it once while I was at . . . while I was up the mountains.

I growled at myself for almost slipping up and thinking of the one *thing* that I refused to think of. I switched my mind back to my shower routine and conditioned my hair. When it came time to wash my skin, my hand automatically reached for my favourite shower gel, my vanilla-scented one, but I quickly grabbed the strawberry one instead.

I never wanted to smell the scent of vanilla ever again.

I began to wash my skin, and as I looked down to my chest I froze. After I moment of squinting I spotted a love bite on my left breast. I rubbed the loofah over the bite. I gritted my teeth and rubbed the loofah back and forth over the area until it stung, using the physical pain as a reminder to never let myself be hurt by Darcy again. I looked over my arms and legs and spotted some light bruises and scrapes from last night's events with Darcy. When I thought of him I slapped the shower wall and burst into tears.

I couldn't escape him.

I roughly scrubbed myself with the loofah, trying desperately to remove any and every trace of him from my body. When I was finished my skin was red, raw, and sore. I slid against my shower tiles as I sank down to my behind. I hissed when I sat down; between my thighs was tender and sore.

I cried harder with the reminder of why.

"I hate him," I whispered.

No, you don't.

I placed my face in my hands when my mind whispered the dreaded truth. Hating him was the easiest thing I had ever done. I'd hated him for the last twenty years, but why did one night render that habit now impossible?

Fucking men.

I cried until I couldn't cry anymore, and sat on the floor of my shower until the water ran cold. I turned the shower off and got out, then dried myself with the towel on the towel rack. I went back out into my bedroom and froze when I spotted my mother sitting on my bed.

"Tell me what happened," she said.

I swallowed. "What are you—"

"I asked Sean what was wrong with you and he told me to come talk to you. But when I came in here I heard you crying in the bathroom. What happened between you and Darcy that has upset you so much?" My mother's voice was stern.

I didn't want to talk about it, but I did at the same time, and if I was unloading this on someone, it was going to be my mother.

I blinked my swollen eyes and whispered, "We slept together."

My mother stared at me for a countless number of seconds in silence. I gripped my towel and stared directly back at her in silence. I didn't know what else needed to be said, so I kept my mouth shut.

"You and Darcy?" she asked.

I rolled my tired eyes. "No, me and Frosty the Snowman got it on . . . Of course Darcy, Ma."

My mother swallowed, but said nothing.

It was very unlike her, because, well, she never stopped talking.

"Say something," I pleaded.

My mother looked up at me and with a serious face she asked, "Was he any good?"

What?

Fucking *what*?

"Ma!"

She unexpectedly laughed. "What?"

Really?

"You can't just ask me something like that! Can't you see I'm upset about the . . . *situation?*"

My mother frowned. "I'm sorry, sweetie. I just wanted to make you smile."

"Tell me Darcy isn't coming to dinner – *that* will make me smile," I stated.

She sighed, and that instantly gave me my answer.

"I'm not going to dinner if he will be there, Ma. No way."

I couldn't face him. Not ever.

"Neala, just . . . tell me what happened."

I scrunched my face up in disgust, making my mother chuckle.

"I don't want the dirty details; just tell me what happened before the nastiness occurred."

Nastiness?

I shook my head clear and walked over to my dresser.

"Nothing much happened, Ma," I said as I got underwear and pyjamas from my drawers.

"Put the pyjamas back; you're wearing a onesie to dinner just like me."

She placed the onesie on the end of my bed, and to avoid it I looked up to the ceiling and closed my eyes.

Please help me, Jesus.

"I'm not going to dinner," I repeated.

"Yeah, you are, and don't give me the 'nothing happened' speech. You and Darcy hated one another. So something happened for *sex* to happen."

I knew I'd made a mistake in talking to her the moment she said the word *sex*. She *knew* Darcy; he was like a son to her.

"I don't know, Ma . . . We just got to talking without arguing for once and we went down memory lane and hashed a lot of bullshit out. We apologised, and even called a truce. There was even talk of something possibly happening between us, because we admitted to fancying one another."

My mother nodded and said, "That sounds pretty great to me, but you're very upset, so what's the kicker?"

She never missed a thing.

"I overheard him tell Sean and Justin this morning that the wine we drank caused us to make the mistake of sleeping together." I looked down to my bare feet and frowned. "The thing is, the wine didn't even affect me; my part in it was down to my sober mind . . . I didn't think it was a mistake, and I feel sick that Darcy regrets it . . . regrets *me*." I turned around and looked back up to the ceiling and willed away the tears that were building up in my eyes. "This is bollocks," I snapped. "I hated him a few days ago . . . I don't know how I've landed meself in this position. It sucks."

My mother cleared her throat from behind me. "This will sound cheesy, but there really is a thin line between love and hate."

I growled, "I do *not* love Darcy, Mother."

I knew I didn't love him. If I did, I would surely feel like I was dying without him.

My mother grinned. "Fine: a thin line between *like* and hate, then."

Oh, she was *so* funny.

"Ha. Ha. Ha," I deadpanned.

My mother gave me a sad smile. "Relationships, even brand-new ones, are not easy, sweetheart. You have to constantly work at them, but if they weren't worth the risk of a broken heart, you would never have taken the chance in the first place."

My mother's words hurt my already broken heart.

"What are you saying?" I asked tearfully.

My mother stood and walked over to me.

She kissed my forehead and said, "I'm saying, don't give up on Darcy so easily. You don't want to – otherwise you wouldn't be crying over him so much. Merry Christmas, sweetheart."

I closed my eyes as she left my room and I was alone once more.

I sank to the floor and tried to organise my thoughts, but I couldn't. My mind was a mess.

Don't give up on Darcy.

My mother's voice echoed my thoughts.

I cried softly.

My mother was wrong, because I hadn't given up on Darcy; he had given up on me.

CHAPTER TWENTY

I opened my eyes when a knock sounded on my bedroom door. I wanted to scream out and tell whoever it was to go away, but it was Christmas, and no matter how shitty I was feeling or how down I was, I wouldn't take it out on my family.

"Yes?" I called out.

A throat cleared. "It's me."

Everything stopped.

My breathing.

My heartbeat.

Time.

"Go away," I managed to get out after a long period of silence.

I watched as the knob on my bedroom door turned, and the door slowly opened until all six feet three inches of Darcy stepped into my room wearing black jeans, black boots, messy hair in a sexy styled way . . . and a red Santa jumper?

My mother, I thought.

She always made us wear something 'Christmassy' to dinner on Christmas; it was a tradition we'd had going for years. My onesie was the item she'd chosen for me this year. I remembered her mentioning it to me a few weeks ago. I always tried to get out of wearing the silly outfits, but my mother kept the clothes for me to wear at her house and when I showed up, she made me change or I got no dinner.

I had put it on a few minutes after she left me alone. I looked down at myself and sighed. I was a snow woman; the hood of my hoodie also doubled as a snowman facemask if you pulled it down far enough. It was comfortable, though, so I couldn't really complain.

I forgot about my stupid onesie, though, when Darcy closed my bedroom door and turned to face me.

"Hey, my Neala Girl."

I closed my eyes and shook my head as I lay back on my bed. My heart thudded against my chest, and my stomach churned.

"Don't call me that, Darcy," I whispered.

I heard him take a few steps over to me.

"I'm sorry," he said.

My anger and hurt unleashed itself.

"Don't," I snapped, and jumped to my feet. "Don't come in here because you feel bad, or because my brother made you. I don't want to hear your lies, so get the fuck out and leave me alone! I *told* you I never wanted to see or speak to you ever again. What part of that didn't you understand?"

My skin was burning with rage, and my hands hurt from squeezing them together so tightly when Darcy stood his ground and didn't even flinch at my shouting.

"I'm here of my own accord, not because I was forced to come," he stated. "I'm sorry, okay? I didn't mean any of what I said."

Bull. Shit.

"Yes, you did! You wouldn't have said it if you didn't mean it. I wasn't in the room; I didn't argue with you or make you say anything out of anger. A question was put to you and you answered it . . . honestly."

Darcy lifted his hands to his face and then slid them down behind his neck. "I didn't answer it honestly. I swear on me life it wasn't the truth."

I shook my head and listened to what my mind was telling me. *He was lying.*

"There you go," Darcy snapped at me.

I furrowed my eyebrows together. "What?" I asked.

"You already have your bloody mind made up. You always fucking do this – you don't give me a chance to prove meself to you. You blame everything on me and don't believe a thing I say!" he shouted.

Was that a fucking joke?

"When have you *ever* tried to prove yourself to me?" I screamed.

Darcy dropped his arms from his neck and turned. I kept my eyes narrowed when he turned back to face me.

"I thought I proved meself to you last night," he said, his voice low.

I stared at him blankly, unblinking. "I bared meself to you last night. I put meself and me feelings on the line. I thought you did too; then you showed your true colours this morning."

Darcy blew out a big breath and looked up to the ceiling. "What do I have to do to make you believe I was lying to Sean and Justin?"

I swallowed. "You can't do anything." I turned around and climbed onto my bed. "Just . . . just go away. Please."

I hated how much I wanted to kiss him or touch him in some way, but I forced myself to turn and face my bedroom wall as I lay on my bed. I knew Darcy didn't leave, because I could hear his fast-paced breathing.

My bed dipped moments later and arms came around me as Darcy lay beside me and pulled me into him. My heart jumped and it took every fibre of my being not to turn and wrap myself around him. I was grateful for his comforting touch, though. I didn't realise how much I needed it until he snuggled up against me.

"I *don't* regret you, we *weren't* a mistake, and I *do* want you," he said, squeezing me with each pause in his sentence.

I pinched my eyes shut as my tears flowed freely. Darcy turned me to face him, and I opened my eyes and looked up at his handsome face. I cried harder as I rested my forehead against his.

"I d-don't b-believe you," I whispered.

I couldn't. He was only saying this because of how upset I was; that was the only reason.

"I know you don't, but I've got all the time in the world to prove to you that I am telling the truth," he said, then leaned down and pressed his lips against mine.

My tears fell and mixed in with our kiss.

I cried as I gripped onto his jumper, pulling him into me. Darcy cupped my cheek and tenderly kissed me whilst using his thumb to wipe away my fallen tears. The kiss lasted only a few seconds before we broke apart.

Darcy kissed my forehead and said, "I'm going to prove meself to you. I promise."

I looked down. "Don't make promises you can't keep."

He placed two fingers under my chin and lifted my head up until I was once again looking at him.

"I don't," he said, before he kissed the tip of my nose and climbed off of my bed and walked out of my bedroom, closing the door behind himself.

I lay there, stunned. *What was that?*

Why hadn't I screamed or thrown stuff at him when he kissed me? Why wasn't I angry at him?

I frowned when I realised the answer.

It was because I was sad. The sadness I felt filled me completely and left no room for anything else. I shouldn't have, but I held out a little hope that Darcy would prove himself to me, and even if he didn't I would keep the promise I made to him. I wouldn't go back to my old ways. I wouldn't hate him . . . I'd eventually be his friend if that was all I could be.

"I hate men," I muttered to myself, then laughed.

It wasn't a hard laugh, or even a long laugh, but it was still a laugh, and in light of the shit that had hit the fan over the past few hours I thought of it as progress.

I stood up from my bed and walked over to my full-length mirror. I shook my head at my white pumps, my snow woman onesie, and my curly brown hair that spilled down over my chest. After I had got dried and done my hair earlier I applied some lotion to my reddened skin. I didn't bother with anything else because my face was flushed and rosy from crying so much, and no amount of makeup would have hidden it, so I didn't even try.

I opened my bedroom door and the smell of my mother's Christmas dinner hit me. I was surprised when my stomach didn't churn, but grumbled instead. I licked my lips and tried to remember when I had last had a decent meal. At Darcy's we had eaten only tinned stuff; a bowl of hot cereal would have been a step up. From the smell of my mother's dinner, this was going to be a massive upgrade.

"Neala?" my mother's voice called out. "Dinner is ready in two minutes."

You can do this.

I inhaled and exhaled. "I'm coming."

I closed my bedroom door and descended the stairs. I could hear the jingle of Christmas songs coming from the kitchen. I was about to walk by the living room when I caught sight of the kids sitting on the floor and the adults gathered around them. I figured I'd go in and watch the kids open their presents. I had nothing to give Charli and deserved any backlash I got from her for breaking my promise.

I had sworn I would get her the doll, and I hadn't.

I was officially the worst auntie ever, and possibly the shittiest person ever. I'd failed at keeping my promise, yet again.

"I thought it was dinnertime," I said as I came up behind my mother.

She turned and beamed at me. "The kids want to open some more gifts first."

I looked down to Charli and Dustin.

Both of the kids were already ripping open presents, and I couldn't help but genuinely smile at them. They were both the picture of innocence and happiness as they laughed with one another. I felt like someone was looking at me from across the room, and since I knew it was *him*, I refused to look up.

I just wanted this to be about the kids and not have the focus on Darcy and myself. We'd both ruined countless moments over the years, and I would not let our differences and problems take this one away from the kids. They were mini versions of the pair of us, and if I could stop them from ending up like us, then I bloody well would.

I blinked when a little gasp got my attention.

I looked down as Dustin lifted up the pink, damaged box that I'd wrapped for Charli and looked up to Darcy. I flicked my eyes to Darcy and saw him cringe. I furrowed my eyebrows and looked down at Dustin as he cleared his throat.

"Charli?" he said.

Charli was midway through opening a Barbie dollhouse my parents must have gotten her. I watched as she completely abandoned opening her present as she turned and gave Dustin her full attention. I found myself smiling as I watched the pair of them. They adored one another.

"Yeah?" Charli replied to Dustin.

Dustin's cheeks flushed red as he extended his arm and held out the pink-wrapped box in Charli's direction.

"I got this for you," he said.

I widened my eyes.

What?

Dustin was giving Charli the doll?

What. The. Hell?

Charli gasped, giddily took the box with a chirpy 'thank you' and tore into the pink wrapping paper. When she had fully unwrapped the box, her squeal of delight warmed my heart and everyone else's. We all beamed down at them.

"A *Blaze* Princess!" Charli screamed and hugged the doll box to her chest.

I didn't understand what the hell was happening, but my eyes welled up with tears, because somehow I'd got what I wanted by Charli's getting what *she* wanted.

In the space of a moment I had gone from feeling low as could be to feeling high as a kite. I didn't understand any of it, but I was so grateful that Charli got what she wanted, even if I wasn't the person to give her the doll.

I looked up to Darcy, who was already looking at me. He gave me a small smile and a little shrug of his shoulders as he whispered, "He only told me what he was doing a few minutes ago."

I blinked.

Things could easily have been solved if we had both known what Dustin had originally intended to do. Charli would have gotten her doll, and Dustin would have gotten to be the one to give it to her.

Win, win.

I looked down to the kids and couldn't help but beam when Charli crawled over and threw her arms around Dustin and knocked him onto his back as she hugged him. Everyone laughed while my mother took pictures and Sean recorded the two of them on his phone.

When Charli got off Dustin and looked up at me, a smile stretched across my face. "Look!" She beamed and held the box up for me to see.

I chuckled. "I see. It's brilliant. Just the doll you wanted, right?" Charli nodded and hugged the doll box to her chest. Dustin sat up and took the box from Charli and proceeded to open it for her. It took him a few minutes to get the doll untangled from the wires holding it to the box, but Charli sat patiently waiting on him.

When he got the doll free and handed it to Charli she took the doll in her arms, closed her eyes and smiled as she hugged it to her chest.

"Merry Christmas, everyone!" She cheered, making us all laugh and cheer with her.

Dustin smiled at Charli and saw how happy she was; he then looked up to Darcy and gave him a thumbs-up, which made us all chuckle.

"Charli, why don't you get the purple-wrapped gift under the tree? Neala got it for you," my mother said.

Charli squealed and crawled under the tree to get the gift. Dustin placed his hand on the back of Charli's leg and pulled her from under the tree when she shouted she had the box, but couldn't move. Everyone laughed, apart from me.

I looked to my mother and whispered, "I didn't get her anything."

"Yes, you did." My mother winked.

She actually winked at me.

I hadn't bought Charli anything, so whatever my mother had bought in my name, I hoped it would live up to *Blaze* doll level – otherwise Charli probably wouldn't even notice. But either way I was thankful to say I had something for her.

"Thank you," I mouthed to my mother, who smiled.

We watched Charli open her present and laughed as she screamed so loud that Dustin had to plug his ears with his fingers.

"*Blaze* doll dresses! Omigod!" Charli squealed. "Thanks, Auntie Neala!"

She jumped up to her feet and barrelled into my legs, hugging me as tight as her little arms allowed. My heart leapt with joy as I returned the hug and watched as she went back to the present and began to tear open the box full of doll dresses and accessories.

Her reaction was amazing.

I looked to my mother, who grinned. "Lots of people bought the dolls in the shops, but many didn't bother with the outfits, so I figured I'd get her some from you in case you forgot."

For a moment I thought my mother was snidely implying how forgetful I was, and how often I never came through, but she wasn't: she was treating me like a simple human being, and pitching in to help me out. She was just having my back.

She was so sneaky, but she was brilliant.

I hugged my mother tightly, then looked back down to Charli, who was playing dress-up with her doll. I chuckled when she had Dustin pick out his favourite dress for the doll to wear. The poor lad didn't know which one to pick and kept looking at Charli to get some hint as to which one she wanted him to select.

I coughed and muttered, "Pink."

Dustin heard me and picked out a hot-pink dress, and Charli beamed. "Great choice, Dusty!"

Dustin blew out a breath and looked to me and gave me a big thumbs-up. I winked at him.

A few gifts were exchanged between the adults then. I got perfume, clothes, and some jewellery. Everyone else got similar presents, and when everything was opened we retired to the kitchen to get our food on.

As usual, I hated that there was arranged seating at dinner, because every year Darcy and I were placed close to one another.

In the last few years one of the kids had sat between us just to keep things clean and safe for everyone at the table.

I sat down, and so did Darcy and everyone else.

I glanced around the table; I didn't want to cause a fight, but I also didn't want to not say anything.

"Sean, did you know what Dustin planned to do with the doll?" I asked my brother.

He nodded reluctantly. "Yes, but he made Justin promise not to tell anyone, because he wanted it to be a surprise."

I felt my eye twitch. "You didn't think to clue meself or Darcy in on his plan? You *knew* we wouldn't have told him we knew."

Sean sighed from across the table. "That's Ma's fault, not mine."

I flicked my narrowed eyes from my brother to my mother. "What does he mean by that?" I asked.

My mother had a guilty look about her. "It's been a long time since you and Darcy spent any time together, even if it was just to argue . . . I thought prolonging this doll thing would be good for you both."

A light bulb went off in my head. *That's* why Justin had been forbidden from helping me – our mothers didn't want the war for the doll to end too soon. It was not because they didn't want us to fight at Sean and Jess's engagement party.

I trembled a little as anger rose within me, and tears of betrayal stung in my eyes.

Darcy humourlessly laughed next to me. "We almost *killed* one another for the stupid thing."

My mother froze and said, "Sorry."

Like that was any help.

I looked to Sean, who was gnawing on his lower lip.

"What about you? Are you sorry, Mammy's boy?"

Sean grunted. "Yeah, I am."

Doubtful.

I felt like I was in a sudden state of shock.

Darcy and I had fought tooth and nail for that bloody doll, and now I knew that if I had just let Darcy have it, both Dustin and Charli would have gotten what they wanted. I didn't know where my family got their logic from, because they were all plain bloody stupid.

"It was a surprise, Neala." Justin sighed. "Dustin made me promise not to tell, and since Sean, my ma, and Clare were in the room when he told me why he wanted the doll, he said they didn't count. He made us pinkie swear."

I went through hell over a pinkie swear?

I growled. "A . . . *pinkie* swear?"

"We took an oath too, if that helps," Sean murmured.

I was about to speak again when Charli and Dustin barrelled into the dining room all dressed in their 'dinner clothes,' which consisted of plain t-shirts and trousers. If they got them dirty with food it wouldn't matter, because they'd just change out of them and back into their Christmas clothes for picture time later.

"Auntie Neala?" Charli said as she sat in between Darcy and me.

I looked at her and forced a smile onto my face for her sake. "Yeah, baby?"

Charli tilted her head to the side. "Are you still sad?"

Everyone froze; then after a moment they looked at me. I avoided their gazes.

I swallowed. "What are you talking about, babes? I'm not sad."

Charli clicked her tongue. "Yeah, you are. I heard you crying in your shower earlier when you came home."

I stared at Charli with my mouth open.

I didn't know what to say to her.

"She probably stubbed her toe is all, kid." Darcy chuckled and nudged Charli.

Charli giggled; then she turned to me and asked, "Is it still sore?"

"Yeah," I replied. "It's still pretty sore."

From the corner of my eye I caught Darcy looking at me. He knew I wasn't talking about my toe.

I looked to Charli, who was still snuggling that godforsaken doll while Darcy scooped food onto her small plate.

"What's her name?" I asked.

Charli giggled. "Her name in the film is Reni, but I'm changing it to Neala Girl, like what Uncle Darcy calls you. I love it."

I felt everyone look at me but I refused to show any emotion.

I simply smiled and said, "Pretty name."

Charli hugged her Neala Girl closely to her, and Dustin chuckled from across the table. I looked at him, and found him smiling as he watched Charli. In that moment he reminded me so much of the young Darcy who had fawned over me all the time . . . before the shit had hit the fan, of course.

I could tell from the look on Dustin's face that he loved Charli; he just wouldn't realise the emotion until he was older. They were so much like Darcy and me before we fell out. That knowledge warmed my heart.

I only hoped they wouldn't let something so stupid and petty come between them; their friendship was too precious to lose.

I zoned out for a while, while everyone said grace and then tucked into their food. I wasn't into it at all. I played with the potatoes on my plate and couldn't even look at the meat without my stomach threatening to revolt. I felt like shite and I wanted nothing more than to just go up to bed.

I made it through dinner, though, and after, when everyone retired to the living room, I waited about thirty minutes before I told everyone I wanted to go up to my room to sleep for a while.

I was just about to make my escape when I heard Sean and Justin exchange words outside in the hallway.

"She's really down, man. I feel sick that we pretty much caused it," Justin said, sighing.

Sean grunted and replied, "I know, but we never planned for it to go *this* far."

Planned?

What the hell were they talking about?

I stepped into the hallway, and when Sean and Justin spotted me they both flinched and shook their heads.

"Bollocks." Sean grunted.

Sean and Justin both walked by me into the living room and I quickly followed.

"What did you mean by that, Sean?" I asked him.

Sean walked over to my mother and leaned into her as he whispered in her ear.

My mother smacked his arm when he pulled back.

"What do you mean, you never planned it to go this far?" I asked Sean.

"He meant—"

I held my hand up in the air and cut my mother off – she couldn't tell a lie if she didn't speak.

"What did you mean, Sean?" I asked, my eyes narrowed.

"What's going on?" Darcy chimed in.

I glanced to him. "I overheard Sean and Justin talking about me outside, about me being upset. They said they were the cause of it and that they never meant for it to go this far, and I want to know what the hell they're talking about."

Darcy stood up from the couch and came to my side, and turned to glare at our brothers.

"What the hell is going on?" he asked.

I didn't want him to be in my corner, but whatever Sean had done involved him too.

Sean looked to my mother, my father, and then Justin before he looked back to me.

"It was just meant to be a joke . . . a prank, really. Like the ones you and Darcy pull on each other all the time."

I swallowed down the bile that rose up my throat.

"What. Did. You. Do?" I snarled.

My father sighed. "Just tell them; it's best they know the truth."

I looked from Sean to my father then back to Sean.

What truth?

"Sean?" I pressed.

He lifted his arms and scrubbed his face with his hands.

"We buried you two in," he said, avoiding eye contact. "Us and a few lads from the pub we paid to help."

What?

"Excuse me?" Darcy growled.

Dustin whistled from the hallway. "Uh-oh. Uncle Darcy is mmaadddd."

Sarah, Jess, Jimmy, and Charli walked into the sitting from the kitchen upon hearing raised voices.

Justin nudged Sarah, who moved next to him, and nodded towards the kids. "Take him and Charli up to her room and close the door, will you?"

This was serious if Justin didn't want the kids in the room to hear the exchange.

I kept quiet until Sarah had taken both Dustin and Charli upstairs and I heard Charli's bedroom door click shut.

"Talk. Right now."

Sean sighed and looked to our mother. "This was your idea; you tell her what you had us do."

I began to tremble with fury.

My mother looked at Sean, then to me. "We just wanted to give you and Darcy a little . . . push. It's not every day we can get you together, so we figured having you both in Darcy's house for a few days would do you good."

I blinked. "I don't understand . . . I mean, I do, but you'd *better* be fucking joking. "

My mother looked down to her feet.

"We're not, Neala."

I snapped my head in my father's direction and gaped at him. "*What?*"

My father shook his head. "It was a stupid idea, but both your mother and Darcy's wanted to have one last attempt at trying to make you both get along."

Hold the bloody phone.

They were really responsible for us being buried in Darcy's house for days eating canned food, taking freezing cold baths, having zero fucking heat, and for Darcy almost *dying*?

I exploded. "You can't *force* two people to get along! I am sick to bleeding death of you all trying to control our lives. If we wanted to be together, we would be together. That is up to us, *not* you!"

Everyone flinched as my voice rose.

"She's right," Darcy jumped in. "You're all something bloody else. How dare you force us together like animals!"

I was shaking with anger while he spoke.

"It wasn't meant to be like this. We thought you would both find it funny," Justin protested.

I growled at him. "We've hated being in each other's company for *fifteen years*. Do you understand that? Fifteen bleeding years! What makes you think four days would sort us out?"

Justin raised his eyebrows. "You slept together; hate was obviously not an issue between you in that house."

My heart broke all over again with the reminder, and I was mortified that everyone close to me now knew what Darcy and I had got up to in private.

"*Justin*! Bloody hell, man!" Darcy bellowed as he paced behind me, his eyes burning with rage.

I wiped my eyes before any tears could fall. "Thank you for that reminder, Justin, and thank you for letting everyone know something so personal."

Justin frowned, then grunted when his ma slapped his arm.

"What happened between us wasn't even our choice. You forced us together and knew we would either sleep together or kill each other," Darcy snapped at his mother.

Marie frowned. "We just wanted you both to get along—"

"We know!" Darcy screamed. "We know what you all bloody want, but what about what *we* want? Don't make this out like you were doing this for anyone but yourselves. You all want us together so we can play happy families."

I folded my arms across my chest and looked down as I started to sniffle.

"We're not sheep; you can't just round us up because you want to see us together."

Sean cleared his throat. "I wasn't aiming to get you together; I just wanted you to stop fighting all the time."

I raised my hands to my temples and rubbed.

"How did you do it?" I asked.

My father was the one to answer me. "First, I want to apologise to you both. I didn't like the idea, but I made the decision to go along with it and help out, and that was inexcusable. I'm very sorry," he said.

"Same here," Jimmy, Darcy's father, chimed in. "I'm sorry. I shouldn't have partaken in the scheme, as it was stupid and wrong. I hope you both can forgive me . . . forgive *us*."

"I love how you're all laying the blame at my and Clare's feet!" Darcy's mother snapped.

Sean scoffed, "It was the *pair of you* who came up with the idea. We were just the eejits who carried out the deed."

I was now aware that both our fathers had helped bury us in Darcy's house, but the people I was most furious with were our mothers and brothers. Our fathers would go along with our mothers just to keep the old bats happy, but our brothers wouldn't have gotten much backlash if they'd said no to the idiotic idea. They'd wanted to do it for selfish reasons.

"We apologise to you all every single time we argue in your presence – we rarely even cause scenes anymore – so I don't understand *why* you went to this extent," I said, my voice like ice. "You do understand what you all did, right? You *buried* us inside a house and trapped us for days. Do you have any idea what it was like? It was scary, dark, freezing, and uncomfortable. We both fought the majority of the time there. I had to endure insults day and night from a parrot . . . a fucking *parrot!*"

Darcy placed his hand over his mouth, and I snarled in his direction.

"I'm not laughing," he said quickly, and looked away from me. *Bastard!*

I looked back to my father, who suddenly looked depressed. "Go on," I snapped. "Tell us how you did it."

He sighed. "After Darcy left the pub the night of the engagement party, I knew you were already on your way to his house. I mentioned it to your mother and told her I was going after you because I was worried you would get hurt and freeze your arse off going up the mountain. Your mother, and Darcy's, came up with the idea that once you got inside the house, because we knew you would get in, we'd block all the exits, thus keeping you both together to . . . settle your differences."

My father shook his head.

"Myself, Jimmy, Sean, and Justin and a few others from the pub headed up the mountain after you, but we kept our distance in case you caught on to us. After an hour or so we reached Darcy's house and we could hear you both arguing inside. Sean went to the back door and said it was over the parrot, so we figured it was nothing serious."

Nothing serious. Ha!

That fucking bird traumatised me.

"Go on. Don't stop now," Darcy growled.

Justin took over. "We got shovels from your shed and got to work – you should put a lock on that, by the way. The heavy snowfall made things easy. I was expecting Neala to storm out at some point and catch us, but she didn't. We were very careful about how much noise we made and just piled the snow up until it covered everything. I really thought one of you would have heard us, but you didn't. When we were finished we *did* have second thoughts, but we thought we'd just let it play out and see what would happen."

I was insanely mad, but them – they were fucking crazy. I could not believe this group of idiots thought, even for a second, that what they had done was a good idea.

"You're a bunch of eejits; I hope you realise that."

Everyone hung their heads.

They knew.

"I hope you also realise that I almost suffocated trying to dig our way out through the fucking snow," Darcy snapped.

Everyone but our brothers gasped.

"Yeah," I chimed in. "The snow in the tunnel he made collapsed on him and I had to pull him out. You almost *killed* Darcy."

I was telling the truth, but I added a touch of drama to my voice to really get my point across – and from the look on everyone's face, it worked.

"I'm so sorry," Darcy's mother cried.

Legit cried. Real tears.

I had never seen Marie cry before, so I did a lot of staring. I even felt bad. Just for a minute, though, until I reminded myself what the group of eejits had orchestrated.

"I honestly can't believe you trapped us in a house by burying the exits; is that even legal?"

My father huffed. "Pretty sure it's not."

Interesting.

"What? You're going to have us arrested?" Sean asked me, his tone sarcastic.

I curled my lip in disgust. "It's no more than you bloody deserve."

Sean didn't reply; he only looked down. Everyone seemed to favour looking at their feet.

"What about the blackout? Did you cause that too?" Darcy growled.

Everyone shook their heads.

"That wasn't our fault. The village power only came back on yesterday. The mountain houses and lodges should have power by Thursday – the council is working on it," Justin explained.

Burying us in together was bad enough; I might have smashed something just then if they'd messed with the power too.

"From this moment on I never want to hear anyone mention my and Darcy's names in a sentence together in a way that is suggestive to us being a couple or *ever* being a couple. I don't want anyone trying to play matchmaker, and above all, don't trap us anywhere together *ever again*. Got it?"

"Got it," everyone replied in unison.

I nodded, then glanced to Darcy before looking back to everyone else.

"And for the last time, there will *never* be a Neala and Darcy relationship. He doesn't want me . . . and I don't want him."

With that said I turned and walked out of the room, up the stairs and into my bedroom. My heart was pounding against my chest and my stomach churned.

I hated myself.

I hated liars and I hated lying.

Yet I had just told the biggest lie of all.

I was no better than the rest of my so-called family.

It seemed being a liar came naturally me.

To all of us.

CHAPTER TWENTY-ONE

Another, Darcy?" the owner of O'Leary's Pub asked me in his thick Northern accent.

I looked up at Bob and nodded my head even though it was starting to spin. He sighed, rested his elbows on the countertop in front of me, and stared at me.

"What's the matter, kid?" he asked me.

I liked a girl a hell of a lot and I missed her like fucking crazy.

"I fucked shite up with a moth I was seeing and I'm a bit gutted about it," I said, and shook my head. "She's a good girl and I was a prick to her."

"You cheat on her?" Bob asked as he leaned back, picked up a beer glass, and wiped it out with a cloth.

I frowned at him. "No, I shagged her, then told her I regretted it when I really didn't."

I didn't want to mention that I hadn't directly said those words to her, that I'd said it to Justin and Sean instead, but Bob would have picked up that it was Neala I was talking about. Bob was a nice man, but he loved a bit of gossip, and this juice would be all over the village by the New Year if I let too much information slip.

"So tell her you didn't mean what you said," he said with a shrug.

If only things were that simple.

I grunted. "I did, but she doesn't believe me."

"Rightly so." Bob nodded. "You hurt the lass and she is wary of trusting you again. That's understandable."

"Yeah," I agreed glumly. "The thing is, I told her I'd prove meself to her and show her I do like her and want her for more than a dirty romp between the sheets, but she's having none of it. I haven't seen or spoken to her in a few days."

Bob whistled. "Sounds like you really bruised the lass's heart."

I lowered my head to the countertop and groaned. "Yes, I'm aware of that. Thank you."

Bob chuckled. "Sorry, laddie. Didn't mean to stick the dagger in deeper."

I sighed and lifted my head. "It's grand. I deserve it."

Bob tilted his head to the side as he watched me. "You really like this lass?" he asked.

I nodded. "More than I've ever liked anyone," I admitted.

Bob raised an eyebrow. "Even Laura Stoke?"

Who?

Oh, yeah. Laura.

Fuck.

She didn't even compare to Neala. No woman did or ever would.

She'd ruined me for anyone else.

"Even Laura Stoke." I nodded to Bob.

He smiled. "Prove it."

What?

"I don't under—"

"Darcy Hart. Long time no see, which is bad for you *and* me."

I turned from Bob's watchful gaze to Laura's heated one.

L.A. CASEY

I forced a smile. "Hey, Laura . . . How are you?"

"I'm good, honey." Laura smiled seductively. "You?"

"Not too bad," I lied.

"Did you have a good Christmas?" she asked.

I'd had an amazing Christmas Eve, but a shitty Christmas Day.

"Yeah. Spent it with family . . . You?"

"Same," Laura said, leaning into me. She frowned at me when I pulled back. "What's wrong?" she asked.

I blinked. "Nothing. Why?"

She gave me a knowing smile. "You're down about something – I can tell."

How?

"I'm fine . . . really."

Laura chuckled, "Okay then."

She continued to smile at me until I cracked.

"It's . . . a girl," I mumbled, feeling embarrassed for talking to her about another woman. "I recently just realised how much I like her, but I said something very hurtful to her and messed everything up."

Laura frowned, and then reached over and rubbed my shoulder. "I'm sure Neala will forgive you, Darcy. I can see how down you are about whatever happened. I'm sure she will see it too."

Doubtful.

"Nah," I muttered. "She doesn't believe me when I say I'm sorry or that I didn't mean what I said – Wait a second, how did you know it was Neala?" I asked, my eyes wide with shock.

Laura dropped her hand from my shoulder and laughed. "Come on, Darcy. I'd have to be blind to miss the connection between you two. You've had it since we were kids; it just showed itself in the form of hate and anger."

I stared at Laura, at a loss for words. How did she know Neala and I had a connection when *we* hadn't even known?

240

She continued to speak. "I'm glad you both finally figured it out, though – better now than when you're both old and grey."

I was so confused. She'd willingly slept with me all these years when she thought Neala and I had a connection?

Did she really hate Neala *that* much to keep me from her?

"I don't know about anything anymore . . . I'm just confused, and I don't know what to do with meself. It's bollocks."

Laura chuckled and patted my arm. "I'm sure you'll figure it out. Good luck, Darcy." She leaned in and kissed my cheek. "Bye," she whispered before she stood up and walked away.

Just like that, our involvement was over, and I wished I'd never spent a moment with her in the first place. I felt like a dick for thinking it, but my life would have been so much different had I never acted on my crush with Laura Stoke.

I was glad she wasn't bitter about my having feelings for someone else. If I couldn't have Neala, I wanted no woman.

I looked straight ahead and picked up the fresh pint of beer in front of me. I looked to my right as Bob walked back toward me and grinned.

"So you *do* really like this girl," he said.

I wanted to laugh, but I just blew air out through my nose and said, "Yeah, man."

Bob smiled at me. "Then do everything you can to get her." He moved away to take care of some other punter who wanted to order a drink.

I was left alone with my thoughts, but not for long.

"I *told* you he'd be here. Pay up, bitch," Sean's voice cheered.

The annoyed growl of my brother followed. "Here, dickhead."

"Stop making money off me misery, you pricks," I said before downing half of my pint.

Sean sat on the empty stool on my left while Justin sat on the empty one on my right.

"Did I just see you turn down Laura Stoke?" Sean asked me.

I shrugged. "Yeah, for good. She's cool with it, though."

Sean whistled. "You've got it bad, kid."

Tell me about it.

Both of the lads clapped their hands on my shoulders.

"How you doing, chief?" Justin asked me.

I grunted. "How does it look like I'm doing?" I asked.

"Like shite," Sean replied.

Ding ding ding. We have a winner.

"That about sums me up," I said. I took another gulp of my pint and shook my head when I swayed a little.

Both of the lads sighed.

"If it helps," Sean began, "she hasn't talked to any of us either. Except the kids, of course."

My stomach lurched.

She was all alone right now when she shouldn't be.

I felt like even more of a massive dick.

What our families had done to us was shitty enough, but her having to deal with what I'd said just doubled the shittiness.

"Other than the obvious problem, is she okay? Is she eating and taking care of herself?" I asked out of worry.

I'd hate myself even more if I'd made her sad enough to become sick. Granted, I'd barely eaten since Christmas, but fuck me, I couldn't care less about myself.

"Yeah, she's eating and showering and doing all of the normal stuff . . . She's just sad, man."

I swallowed and looked down. "I know. I wish I'd never said what I did."

"Do you mean that, or do you mean you wish she'd never heard you?" Sean asked.

I looked at him and replied honestly, "I wish I'd never said it. I lied to keep from looking like a pussy-whipped bitch in front of the pair of you so you both wouldn't see that I'd be gutted if she regretted me. I made my worry a reality by lying. I fucked everything up and I've no one to blame but meself."

"Don't be so hard on yourself, bro," Justin said, and nudged me. "It'll work itself out, you'll see."

"It won't fix itself," I said, shaking my head. "I wrecked this, so I have to fix it . . . I owe it to her."

Sean patted my shoulder in support while Justin flagged Bob down and ordered a round of drinks for us. Bob quickly got the order to us, took away my now-empty pint glass, and frowned as I started on the fresh one he'd laid before me.

Justin looked at Bob, then to me.

"How many has he had?" he asked.

"This is number five," Bob replied.

I rolled my eyes when Justin hissed.

"Do you want to get drunk off your face? Drowning your sorrows won't get you back your Neala Girl, little brother."

He didn't get to call her that; only I did.

I snarled, "What do you know? You have a wife and a kid. You don't know what I'm feeling."

Justin laughed, and it only fuelled my rising temper.

"You think things have always been smooth sailing with Sarah? I started going out with her when I was twenty-five, and we're still together *and* happily married because we work to keep what we have. No one is gifted with a healthy relationship, so stop feeling fucking sorry for yourself. You fucked up with Neala; go fix it if she means that much to you."

I knew Justin was right, but I shoved him simply because I was looking for a fight. I wanted to feel something other than the sick feeling that was constantly in my gut.

Justin jumped up from his bar stool and I took it as an invitation to exchange blows. I threw the first punch and it caught Justin square across the jaw. It knocked him backward against his stool and then onto the floor.

"Ah, fuck!" Sean snapped from behind me, and smacked the back of my head with such force my brain rattled. "You wanna fight, you come at me. It's *my* little sister you fucked over, remember?"

I saw red and speared Sean down to the ground.

I pulled back and unleashed a series of punches on his face, but not one landed, because he had his head guarded, so I switched, getting a few hits in on his chest.

"It's fine, honestly. Don't be worried. A minute or two and it'll be fine. Sit back down," Bob's loud voice broke through my clouded one. No doubt he was talking to the other punters in the pub.

A ringing noise blocked everything out and my vision spotted.

It took me a second to realise I'd been punched in the head.

Sean, the bastard, had broken through and punched me.

I was just about to return the favour when I felt arms come around my neck from behind and pull me off Sean. I reached back and hit Justin, who had a hold of me, but he didn't let up until I stopped throwing punches. My head was spinning and my stomach threatened to spill at any second.

"Are you done?" Justin snapped in my ear.

"I'd have killed you both if I could see straight!" I snapped, then coughed when Justin's arm tightened around my neck.

Sean laughed from the floor. "I don't think so, little Hart. I *let* you get some hits in to help relieve some stress. You feel better?"

I blinked my eyes and when my vision focused I could see Sean, but it looked like he was swaying while sitting down.

Unexpectedly, I laughed. "Yeah, I feel better."

Justin's hold on me loosened, and then both he and Sean got to their feet and they helped me up to mine. They both shoved me and playfully slapped my head.

"Okay, everyone. Show's over," Bob announced.

The people who had bothered to look our way turned and continued on with their conversations like we hadn't just been fighting a minute ago.

"I can't believe he put you on your arse with one hit." Sean poked fun at Justin as we straightened our stools and sat back down on them.

Justin rubbed his jaw. "Me last fight with him was five years ago. He's perfected throwing a decent punch since then, it seems."

I snorted as I laid my head on the countertop.

Justin smacked my back with his hand. "I've never seen you like this over a girl."

"She's not just some girl, man," I stated. "It's *Neala*."

Sean nudged me. "Your Neala Girl?"

Yeah.

My Neala Girl.

"Yeah, she's mine," I said, and sat up straight. "I need to make this right . . . but I don't know how."

Both of the lads patted my shoulders.

"We'll help you, bro," Justin said.

I smiled inwardly.

I sighed. "How?"

We all sat and thought about it for a few minutes; then Sean snapped his fingers. "You have to get her on her own – you won't get her full attention in a room full of people."

I rolled my eyes. "She won't leave her apartment. How the hell can I get her on her own when she won't speak to me?" I asked.

That sent us into another few minutes of silence as we thought.

"I've got it," Justin said. "We can trick her to come out—"

"Do you remember what happened the last time you deceived her?" I cut Justin off with a growl.

Justin frowned. "That wasn't just me, man . . . And we all said sorry about that."

I shook my head and looked at my half-full pint of beer; I didn't even want to drink it anymore. I had come here to drown my sorrows, but no matter how much I drank I still couldn't escape the way I felt. I pushed the pint away.

"It's New Year's Eve . . . What if we get her to come to the party here tonight?" Sean suggested.

I looked to him and deadpanned, "If she won't come out of her apartment, then she won't come here."

Sean grinned and smirked. "You leave that to me. I'll get her here; you just make sure you head home and that you're all cleaned up and ready to lay everything on the line for her. You got that?"

I raised my eyebrow and looked to Justin, who shrugged. I looked back to Sean and decided what the hell? Who better to help me win Neala over than her own brother?

"I got it," I said with a firm nod.

I just prayed that whatever Sean had planned would work, because one way or the other I was starting the New Year with my Neala Girl in my life *as* my girl.

I wouldn't settle for anything less than her heart.

CHAPTER TWENTY-TWO

Neala?"

Uh.

"Neala. I *know* you're in there; open the door. Please."

Go away.

"Neala!" my mother's voice shouted. "Please, open the door."

I shot up from my bedroom when my mother's voice rose to one of panic. Her voice sounded strange, and quite faint, but it was unmistakably her. I envisioned something horribly wrong with her, so without a second's thought I ran from my bedroom, tore down the hallway, and pulled my front door wide open.

"Ma?" I said, my tone laced with worry.

I blinked. My brother stood before me, not my mother.

I was confused.

"Where's Ma? I heard her," I said.

Sean gnawed on his lower lip and then lifted up his arm and pressed on the screen of his iPhone.

"Neala?" my mother's voice played from the phone.

I furrowed my eyebrows in confusion, then looked to Sean, who shrugged and pocketed his phone.

"I knew you wouldn't open the door to anyone but our distressed mother," he said.

The bastard *tricked* me. Again.

I snarled at him and tried to slam my door shut in his face, but he threw his body between the door and the doorframe, making it impossible for me to close the door.

"Get. Out!" I snapped.

Sean grunted in pain. "No, we need to talk."

The hell we do.

"I don't care for a single word you have to say, you piece of shite!" I bellowed, then lifted my hand and proceeded to slap Sean's head.

He yelped. "Neala, stop it! That hurts! Ow!"

Feel pain, you fucker.

"No! You deserve everything you get, you lousy excuse for a brother," I said, then fell backward onto my arse when Sean burst through the door and fell face forward onto the floor next to me.

Ha-ha-fucking-ha!

"That hurt," Sean murmured.

I glared at him. "I'm glad."

"You're the dark lord of evil." He groaned.

I grinned. "And someday I'll rule the Earth."

Sean groused as he rolled over onto his back. We were silent as he lay next to me and stared up at the ceiling. I was looking upward too, but only because I didn't want to turn my head and see his stupid face.

"This is breaking and entering, you know?" I grunted.

Sean snorted. "You're me *sister*."

"So? I don't want you here, so it *still* counts as breaking and entering," I said as I sat upright, griping as a slight pain radiated up and down my arse from the impact of hitting the floor when I fell.

I got to my feet, placed both hands on my behind, and rubbed the pain away. I looked down at my brother and rolled my eyes.

"You're almost thirty-two, and yet you still act like you're fifteen," I said with a shake of my head.

Sean looked up at me and smirked. "I bet you'll be having a repeat of this conversation with me in fifty years."

I snorted. "Doubtful. I plan to disown you long before then."

Sean clumsily got to his feet, and when he straightened up he flung an arm around my shoulder and hugged me to his side. He kissed me on the crown of my head and said, "You couldn't disown me – you love me too much."

True.

My eye twitched. "It's a shame how I could never disown you, but you had no problem doing it to me for *four days*."

Sean raised his eyebrow. "Four?" he questioned.

I huffed, "I'm meshing Friday night and Tuesday morning as one whole day, so yes, hours-wise it adds up to four days."

Sean nodded, then hugged me again. "I'm sorry, Neala, *truly* sorry. It was a stupid idea, utter rubbish really. Please forgive me. I'll never trick you into anything ever again. I promise."

I stepped away from my brother and closed my front door before I turned back to him.

"What do you call playing Ma's voice on your phone in order to get me to open up the door then?" I asked.

Sean opened his mouth, closed it, then opened it again. "Starting from right *now* I won't trick you anymore. Promise."

I snorted and shook my head at him.

"Come on, Neala. It's New Year's Eve; you can't start a brand-new year not speaking to your family."

Says who?

"Watch me."

Sean frowned. "We miss you, Sis. Ma cries every day because she feels so horrible about everything that's happened."

That hurt. "Are you using Ma crying as a guilt trip on me?"

Sean shook his head. "No, I'm just telling you how hard she is taking you ignoring her. She didn't mean to hurt you; none of us did . . . even Darcy."

I widened my eyes. "You're on *his* side?"

He was my brother! How could he be on *his* side?

"Hell, no," Sean stated. "I'm backing you all day, every day. I'm just saying the kid isn't taking the aftermath of your falling-out very well."

Part of me wanted to ask if Darcy was okay, and the other half wanted to go to him and *make sure* he was okay, but I forced down the feelings of longing and shrugged. "Yeah, well, I'm not exactly the picture of happiness here either, Sean."

I walked around him and went into my sitting room, where I sat down on my lounge chair and covered myself with the blanket that hung over the back of it. Sean followed me and sat across from me with his elbows resting on his knees as he stared at me.

"Do you not think ignoring us for six days is punishment enough? We see each other every day – we're all invested in one another's lives, and for you to block us out hurts like hell. I constantly think about you and wonder if you're okay or not."

I looked over to my living room window and sighed as I watched the snowfall.

"You hurt me. I just needed to be away from you all for a while."

I looked back to Sean as he sat back and scrubbed his face with his hands. "Do you not believe we're sorry?"

"I do," I replied. "I believe you're very sorry. I'm just still pissed about the whole thing, Sean."

Sean rested his chin on his right hand and frowned. "I don't blame you, but blocking us out isn't the answer."

I grinned. "You got in here, didn't you? Blocking you out doesn't seem to be working."

Sean winked. "Damn right."

We sat in silence for a few minutes until he said, "Are you coming to the New Year's Eve party in O'Leary's Pub tonight?"

I didn't reply right away, because I wasn't sure of my answer.

I knew my family, and Darcy's, were sorry for what they had done to us, and even though I was still angry at them I couldn't help but miss them. I hadn't seen my parents in six days, which is the longest I'd ever willingly gone without seeing them, so I saw no reason to delay seeing them any longer. Besides, Sean was right: I didn't want to start the New Year on bad terms with everyone.

Besides, as much as I hated to admit it, I wanted to see Darcy. It was selfish of me, but I wanted to see if he was as torn up as I felt.

"Yeah, I'll go," I replied to Sean, who looked shocked at my answer. "Were you expecting a fight?" I asked.

Sean blinked at me, then nodded. "Well . . . yes. I wasn't expecting you to come without some resistance."

I shrugged. "I'm fed up with staying inside this apartment, and with the way I'm feeling, a pub sounds like the perfect place for me to go."

Sean didn't say anything; he just watched me.

"What time is it?" I asked.

"Half six in the evening."

I nodded. Sleeping in till all hours was a pattern I'd fallen into over the past week.

"I'll go and get showered and changed. You can take me to your house for a while so I can see Charli and Jess, and then we'll go to the pub."

Sean scratched his head. "Sounds good to me."

I got up and headed out of the sitting room and down to my bathroom. I was going to this party tonight just to make peace with my family. Once that was done I was parking my arse at the bar.

A few drinks might erase Darcy and all the bullshit that came with him from my mind, but that was just wishful thinking.

~

"Ma is down the back in the booths with everyone," Sean said to me as I entered the pub with him and Jess.

Charli was at home in bed; a babysitter was looking after her while her parents rang in the New Year together.

I nodded to Sean and followed them through the pub like a puppy following its master. I felt so out of place in my own local pub with a crowd of faces I had grown up seeing. I sighed to myself as I walked.

Maybe coming here was a bad idea.

I shook my head clear and continued to walk behind Sean and Jess. I glanced around as I walked, and when I spotted a familiar person over at the bar and saw what she was doing I almost fell over my own two feet.

Laura Stoke was kissing a man that was, in no shape or form, Darcy.

I knew the man, though. I stared a little longer and widened my eyes when I realised the lad Laura was tongue-raping was Dan Jenkins, the lad I'd had a date with and bailed on nearly two weeks ago.

Glad to see he was taking my rejection so well.

More than anything, though, I was just relieved Dan wasn't Darcy. I mean, if it *had* been Darcy she was kissing I probably would have killed him, so luckily for his sake it was Dan. I was a little too caught up in watching Laura and her new kissing buddy – I walked into someone's back.

"You okay?" Jess laughed as she turned around and steadied me.

I blinked. "Sorry, I was distracted."

"By what?" she asked.

I nodded over to the bar where Laura and her buddy sat.

Jess scanned the area I nodded to, and when her eyes landed on Laura she grinned. "Huh. Sean wasn't joking. Darcy really *did* give her the elbow."

What?

"He what?" I asked, shocked.

Jess smiled. "Earlier today Laura came up to Darcy all sexy and shite, but Darcy was having none of it. Bob told your ma it was because he was so down from hurting a girl he really liked and couldn't think of any other girl but her."

No way.

"Really?" I asked.

Jess nodded her head. "Honest to God truth."

Oh, wow.

Darcy had ended his fuckery business with Laura because of *me*?

"She seemed to bounce back quick," I muttered.

Jess laughed. "Of course she did. She'll be on the prowl for some new meat, since Darcy isn't available anymore."

I raised my eyebrows. "He *is* available."

"Not emotionally." Jess winked, turned, and continued to walk in the direction of the booths where my family sat.

Darcy wasn't available emotionally?

What the hell did that even mean?

Did that mean he would still shag people physically, but emotionally he would be shut down like a slutty zombie?

Why couldn't people just be straight when they were speaking?

I hated all this confusion.

I brushed some invisible dirt off my dress and followed Jess over to the booth. I wanted to laugh the moment I stepped out in front of it, because every person seated in our section turned his or her head and looked at me at the same time.

It's wasn't just my family at the booth; Darcy's family was there too, of course.

"Evening," I said curtly.

Justin was the first one to stand up and greet me.

"You look gorgeous," he said as he leaned down and wrapped his arms around me. "I've missed you, kid."

I smiled and hugged Justin back. "I missed you too, Wise One."

Justin chuckled and released me.

I hugged Sarah and his parents and assured them I was fine when they asked how I was. When my father stood up I gave him a wink so he knew we were cool. I saw his shoulders loosen up as relief filled him.

"I'm sorry and I love you," he said.

I hugged my father and told him I loved him too.

My mother burst into tears when it was her turn to say hello, and I couldn't help but laugh as she pulled me into a bone-crushing hug. She buried her face in my neck and sobbed like I had just come back from the dead.

"It's only been a few days, woman!" I said making everyone laugh.

My mother continued to cry as she hugged me.

"Ma," I said, leaning my mouth down to her ear. "I know you're sorry and I forgive you. Don't worry about it."

I was still pretty annoyed, but dragging it out wouldn't do anybody any good, so in that moment I put it behind me and looked forward to the New Year.

My mother released me, then went to my father for another little cry because she was happy everything was back to normal. Well, sort of.

"Is he here?" I asked Justin.

I both hoped he was and dreaded seeing him if he was.

Justin leaned in and said, "He's around here somewhere."

I nodded.

I knew I'd have to speak to Darcy eventually; I just hoped it wouldn't go badly, because I honestly couldn't handle any more bullshit between us. I made small talk with everyone in the booth and chitchatted with them for an hour or so. It had been late when we arrived and the pub was packed, but now that it was close to midnight, the place was overflowing with people.

"Neala!" Sean called out.

I looked at him, then stood up from my seat and walked over to where he stood at the edge of the seating area. I had to squeeze by a few people to get to him.

"What?" I asked him.

He sighed. "You need to speak to Darcy."

I blinked at Sean. "You do realise what he did to me, right? I thought you would be on *my* side."

"I *am* on your side." Sean frowned. "But I'm on his side, too. I know what he did to you, but he explained himself to me and I believe him, Neala. Give him a chance to explain and you'll see he's telling the truth. The poor prat has never been a good liar."

"Where is he?" I asked, curiously.

I knew he was in the pub somewhere. It was one of the reasons I had come to the party. I wanted to see him, but at the same time I didn't because I didn't know what to say to him.

Sean looked around then looked back to me. "I don't know. He was meant to message me when he wanted me to bring you—"

"Bring me where?" I asked, then narrowed my eyes. "You'd better not have arranged for me to come here, Sean."

Sean didn't say a word.

Oh, my God.

I couldn't believe it.

"You said you'd never trick me again. You bloody *promised*, Sean!" I shouted and stepped away from my brother.

Sean sighed. "I'm not tricking you. I *was* going to try to persuade you to come here tonight to clear the air between you and Darcy, but you came here of your own accord. The only place I'm bringing you is outside for some fresh air. Having you here is no evil scheme. This time, I'm letting everything pan out on its own."

I looked around once more for Darcy. "Did he know I'd be here?"

He nodded. "Yes, he did . . . He misses you, Neala. He just wants to talk, but if you really don't want to, I'll take you home. No questions asked."

I looked at my brother and swallowed. "Do you really believe him?" I asked.

"Do I believe that he misses you?" Sean asked, his eyebrows raised.

"Yeah."

"Without a fucking doubt," Sean stated. "The lad is a wreck after what happened between you two. He was in here trying to drink himself silly earlier just to escape from his own head for a little while. He ended things with Laura Stoke, too. I witnessed it with me own eyes. He doesn't want anyone but you."

I blinked my eyes at my brother, unsure what to feel or believe.

"I can see you're hesitant, so let's go outside and get some air. We can come back in or go home when you sort your head out."

I looked around the room once more and nodded. "You're right, I need some air, but I wanna go on me own. It's already ten to twelve – go find Jess and be with her for the countdown."

Sean shook his head. "What about you?"

I smiled. "I'll be fine. I just need a few minutes to meself. Okay?"

"Okay," Sean said slowly, "but if you decide to go home, come back in here and I'll drive you – I'm not drinking tonight. Okay?"

"Okay."

He opened his arms and I stepped into them. "I love you, Neala."

"I love you, too," I said and gave my brother a tight squeeze before I turned and walked through the crowd of drunken locals.

I took a deep breath as I stepped outside.

I folded my arms across my chest and rubbed my hands over my upper arms to generate some heat. It hadn't snowed since this morning; there was a slight breeze, though, and it was a bloody cold one.

I snorted to myself.

Why had I come out here?

Why hadn't I just gone to the ladies' bathroom like every other female did when they wanted some alone time?

"Neala?"

I froze when his voice sounded from behind me.

"How did you know I was out here?" I asked.

Please don't say Sean told you.

"I saw you walk outside after your talk with your brother . . . I wasn't sure if you were going to attempt to hike home or not. You haven't got a very good record of trekking through the snow in high heels, so I came out here to see if you needed any assistance," Darcy said, and I could hear the smile in his voice.

I found myself smiling too.

"I'm not leaving . . . I just came out here to think about a few things."

Darcy walked up beside me. "Do I happen to be one of those things?"

I kept my gaze straight ahead.

"Yeah," I replied.

We were silent for a few moments before Darcy sighed and turned to me.

"I'm sorry for hurting you. I have no excuse for the hurtful things I said. I've been sick with myself for days knowing that I've upset you so much."

I swallowed as I turned to face Darcy. I frowned when I took in his appearance. He was dressed in his trademark black jeans, black boots and a blue button shirt, and his hair was messy in that sexy way I loved . . . but he didn't look like Darcy. He looked like a shell of his former self.

"Have you been eating?" I asked.

He looked like he'd lost some weight.

"Well . . . no," Darcy admitted. "I wasn't joking when I said I feel sick about what I said about the night we shared."

I frowned. "Darcy, I don't want you to get sick over me."

He shook his head. "None of this is because of you; it's because of me, because of the stupid things I said."

I was taken aback by how hard he was on himself. He was definitely taking our falling-out seriously.

"I know you said you didn't mean what you said, but if that's true then why did you say it in the first place?" I asked, and continued to rub my arms.

Darcy swallowed. "I truly thought you would wake up and freak out. I woke up before you, and when I realised how much I liked having you in my arms and how much I liked you, I got scared." He stepped closer to me. "I was so sure you would blame me for us sleeping together and that you would hate me again. When we made up and just had a laugh together thinking of all the silly things we did in the past it made me happy, and I was afraid it wasn't the same for you."

Holy. God.

"I had no idea you felt that way," I whispered.

"How could you? I never mentioned it to you out of fear you didn't like me back, so I decided to lie about our night together to our brothers so I wouldn't look affected . . . That plan failed horribly because both of them saw me at my lowest point earlier today. They're sporting the bruises to prove it."

I gasped. "You fought Justin *and* Sean?"

Darcy shrugged one shoulder. "Just for a minute. I needed to hit something and they were willing targets."

Wow.

I didn't know what to think.

On one hand I was worried – I didn't want to set myself up for more hurt – but on the other hand I was so incredibly happy Darcy felt the way he did.

He said he liked me out loud.

"If I said okay, that I believe you and I'm willing to forgive you . . . what would you do?" I asked.

Darcy reached out and took my hand in his.

"I'd ask you out on a date."

My stomach burst into butterflies.

"A real date?" I asked, smiling.

Darcy nodded, his eyes hopeful. "Yeah, a *real* date. I'd then ask you out on another date when that date was over, then *another* when that date was over, and then another when *that* date was—"

I cut Darcy off with my laughter, and it lit up his whole face with a beaming smile.

"It sounds like you want to get to know me," I teased.

Darcy reached up and brushed my hair out of my eyes. "I already know you. I just want to get to know you all over again."

I blinked as my heart thudded against my chest.

"I believe you," I whispered, "and I forgive you."

Darcy gazed down at me with smiling eyes.

"Neala," he murmured, "will you go out on a date with me?"

I pretended to think about it and Darcy growled, making my insides jump.

"I'd *love* to go on a date with you," I said, biting on my lower lip.

Darcy smiled and lowered his face to mine as people began to shout inside the pub.

"Do I have to wait until after our first date before I can kiss you?" he whispered, his eyes locked on my lips.

I began to tremble.

"Hmmm," I mused. "I'm not a kiss-on-the-first-date kind of girl."

The cheers of people counting down from ten inside the pub was deafening.

Darcy grinned at me. "Will you make an exception?" he asked.

"Six!"

"Five!"

"Four!"

"Three!"

"Two!"

"Just this once," I whispered.

Darcy brought his mouth to mine as fireworks and bangers went off all around the village. Everyone was screaming and laughing inside the pub as they rang in the New Year.

Darcy broke our short kiss and rubbed his nose against mine. "Happy New Year, my Neala Girl."

A warm feeling of joy spread throughout my body as I hugged Darcy's body to mine.

"Happy New Year," I replied, and smiled up at him.

He gazed down at me with so much emotion that it made me chuckle.

"What's so funny?" he asked, grinning.

"I was just thinking that you're a new Darcy."

Darcy winked. "A happier Darcy now that I have you."

"Well, what do you know," I teased. "Your heart isn't *frozen* after all."

Darcy scrunched up his face and brought his hands down to my sides and tickled me. I burst into laughter and gripped onto his body until he laughed loudly and stopped his attack. He kissed the crown of my head and hugged me.

I closed my eyes and sighed.

When I opened my eyes I smiled.

I was happy, and Darcy, my *boyfriend*, was happy, but God himself only knew how happy our families would be. Fireworks would go off again once they found out Darcy and I were taking things slow, but giving *us* a go. The fuckers had just better keep their meddling noses out of our relationship.

I'd be doing some burying of my own this time around if they didn't.

THE END.

ACKNOWLEDGMENTS

I would never have been able to finish *Frozen* and get it together for the public to read without my crew of helpers.

My little sister, Edel: thank you so much for sitting down and outlining *Frozen* with me, and for believing in Neala and Darcy as much as I do. I love you!

My mini-me: you're the sweetest little minion God could have ever blessed me with. I love you to Neptune and back!

My family: thank you for the incredible support you give me.

Jill Sava: the world's greatest PA! Thank you for everything you do for me. I'd be lost without you. Literally lost!

Yessi Smith and Mary Johnson: I don't even know what to say other than I absolutely adore you both.

My agent, Mark Gottlieb: thank you for believing in me and my work, Mark. I appreciate everything you do for me.

Tiffany Yates Martin: thank you for your flawless editing, and your help with shaping *Frozen* into the book it is today. I couldn't have done it without you.

Jennifer McIntyre: Thank you so much for copyediting *Frozen* and polishing off a story that I love.

Sammia and all the crew at Montlake Romance, for taking a chance on *Frozen* – thank you so much.

And last, but never least, my readers. Without all of you I wouldn't be able to call writing, my passion, a job. You have made my dreams come true and I can't thank you enough for it. I hope you enjoyed reading Neala and Darcy's story as much as I did writing it. ☺

ABOUT THE AUTHOR

 L.A. Casey is a *New York Times* and *USA Today* bestselling author who juggles her time between her mini-me and writing. She was born, raised, and currently resides in Dublin, Ireland. She enjoys chatting with her readers, who love her humour and Irish accent as much as they love her books. You can visit her website at www.lacaseyauthor.com.